Santa Cruz Noir

EDITED BY SUSIE BRIGHT

BROOKLYN, NEW YORK, USA
BALLYDEHOB, CO. CORK, IRELAND

This collection comprises works of fiction. All names, characters, places, and incidents are the product of the authors' imaginations. Any resemblance to real events or persons, living or dead, is entirely coincidental.

Published by Akashic Books

Series concept by Tim McLoughlin and Johnny Temple
Santa Cruz map by Sohrab Habibion

ISBN: 978-1-61775-622-1
Library of Congress Control Number: 2017956553

First printing

Akashic Books
Brooklyn, New York, USA
Ballydehob, Co. Cork, Ireland
Twitter: @AkashicBooks
Facebook: AkashicBooks
E-mail: info@akashicbooks.com
Website: www.akashicbooks.com

ALSO IN THE AKASHIC NOIR SERIES

ATLANTA NOIR, edited by TAYARI JONES
BALTIMORE NOIR, edited by LAURA LIPPMAN
BARCELONA NOIR (SPAIN), edited by ADRIANA V. LÓPEZ & CARMEN OSPINA
BEIRUT NOIR (LEBANON), edited by IMAN HUMAYDAN
BELFAST NOIR (NORTHERN IRELAND), edited by ADRIAN McKINTY & STUART NEVILLE
BOSTON NOIR, edited by DENNIS LEHANE
BOSTON NOIR 2: THE CLASSICS, edited by DENNIS LEHANE, JAIME CLARKE & MARY COTTON
BRONX NOIR, edited by S.J. ROZAN
BROOKLYN NOIR, edited by TIM McLOUGHLIN
BROOKLYN NOIR 2: THE CLASSICS, edited by TIM McLOUGHLIN
BROOKLYN NOIR 3: NOTHING BUT THE TRUTH, edited by TIM McLOUGHLIN & THOMAS ADCOCK
BRUSSELS NOIR (BELGIUM), edited by MICHEL DUFRANNE
BUENOS AIRES NOIR (ARGENTINA), edited by ERNESTO MALLO
BUFFALO NOIR, edited by ED PARK & BRIGID HUGHES
CAPE COD NOIR, edited by DAVID L. ULIN
CHICAGO NOIR, edited by NEAL POLLACK
CHICAGO NOIR: THE CLASSICS, edited by JOE MENO
COPENHAGEN NOIR (DENMARK), edited by BO TAO MICHAËLIS
DALLAS NOIR, edited by DAVID HALE SMITH
D.C. NOIR, edited by GEORGE PELECANOS
D.C. NOIR 2: THE CLASSICS, edited by GEORGE PELECANOS
DELHI NOIR (INDIA), edited by HIRSH SAWHNEY
DETROIT NOIR, edited by E.J. OLSEN & JOHN C. HOCKING
DUBLIN NOIR (IRELAND), edited by KEN BRUEN
HAITI NOIR, edited by EDWIDGE DANTICAT
HAITI NOIR 2: THE CLASSICS, edited by EDWIDGE DANTICAT
HAVANA NOIR (CUBA), edited by ACHY OBEJAS
HELSINKI NOIR (FINLAND), edited by JAMES THOMPSON
INDIAN COUNTRY NOIR, edited by SARAH CORTEZ & LIZ MARTÍNEZ
ISTANBUL NOIR (TURKEY), edited by MUSTAFA ZIYALAN & AMY SPANGLER
KANSAS CITY NOIR, edited by STEVE PAUL
KINGSTON NOIR (JAMAICA), edited by COLIN CHANNER
LAGOS NOIR (NIGERIA), edited by CHRIS ABANI
LAS VEGAS NOIR, edited by JARRET KEENE & TODD JAMES PIERCE
LONDON NOIR (ENGLAND), edited by CATHI UNSWORTH
LONE STAR NOIR, edited by BOBBY BYRD & JOHNNY BYRD
LONG ISLAND NOIR, edited by KAYLIE JONES
LOS ANGELES NOIR, edited by DENISE HAMILTON
LOS ANGELES NOIR 2: THE CLASSICS, edited by DENISE HAMILTON
MANHATTAN NOIR, edited by LAWRENCE BLOCK
MANHATTAN NOIR 2: THE CLASSICS, edited by LAWRENCE BLOCK
MANILA NOIR (PHILIPPINES), edited by JESSICA HAGEDORN
MARSEILLE NOIR (FRANCE), edited by CÉDRIC FABRE
MEMPHIS NOIR, edited by LAUREEN P. CANTWELL & LEONARD GILL
MEXICO CITY NOIR (MEXICO), edited by PACO I. TAIBO II
MIAMI NOIR, edited by LES STANDIFORD
MISSISSIPPI NOIR, edited by TOM FRANKLIN
MONTANA NOIR, edited by JAMES GRADY & KEIR GRAFF
MONTREAL NOIR (CANADA), edited by JOHN McFETRIDGE & JACQUES FILIPPI
MOSCOW NOIR (RUSSIA), edited by NATALIA SMIRNOVA & JULIA GOUMEN
MUMBAI NOIR (INDIA), edited by ALTAF TYREWALA
NEW HAVEN NOIR, edited by AMY BLOOM
NEW JERSEY NOIR, edited by JOYCE CAROL OATES

NEW ORLEANS NOIR, edited by **JULIE SMITH**
NEW ORLEANS NOIR: THE CLASSICS, edited by **JULIE SMITH**
OAKLAND NOIR, edited by **JERRY THOMPSON & EDDIE MULLER**
ORANGE COUNTY NOIR, edited by **GARY PHILLIPS**
PARIS NOIR (FRANCE), edited by **AURÉLIEN MASSON**
PHILADELPHIA NOIR, edited by **CARLIN ROMANO**
PHOENIX NOIR, edited by **PATRICK MILLIKIN**
PITTSBURGH NOIR, edited by **KATHLEEN GEORGE**
PORTLAND NOIR, edited by **KEVIN SAMPSELL**
PRAGUE NOIR (CZECH REPUBLIC), edited by **PAVEL MANDYS**
PRISON NOIR, edited by **JOYCE CAROL OATES**
PROVIDENCE NOIR, edited by **ANN HOOD**
QUEENS NOIR, edited by **ROBERT KNIGHTLY**
RICHMOND NOIR, edited by **ANDREW BLOSSOM, BRIAN CASTLEBERRY & TOM DE HAVEN**
RIO NOIR (BRAZIL), edited by **TONY BELLOTTO**
ROME NOIR (ITALY), edited by **CHIARA STANGALINO & MAXIM JAKUBOWSKI**
SAN DIEGO NOIR, edited by **MARYELIZABETH HART**
SAN FRANCISCO NOIR, edited by **PETER MARAVELIS**
SAN FRANCISCO NOIR 2: THE CLASSICS, edited by **PETER MARAVELIS**
SAN JUAN NOIR (PUERTO RICO), edited by **MAYRA SANTOS-FEBRES**
SÃO PAULO NOIR (BRAZIL), edited by **TONY BELLOTTO**
SEATTLE NOIR, edited by **CURT COLBERT**
SINGAPORE NOIR, edited by **CHERYL LU-LIEN TAN**
STATEN ISLAND NOIR, edited by **PATRICIA SMITH**
ST. LOUIS NOIR, edited by **SCOTT PHILLIPS**
STOCKHOLM NOIR (SWEDEN), edited by **NATHAN LARSON & CARL-MICHAEL EDENBORG**
ST. PETERSBURG NOIR (RUSSIA), edited by **NATALIA SMIRNOVA & JULIA GOUMEN**
TEHRAN NOIR (IRAN), edited by **SALAR ABDOH**
TEL AVIV NOIR (ISRAEL), edited by **ETGAR KERET & ASSAF GAVRON**
TORONTO NOIR (CANADA), edited by **JANINE ARMIN & NATHANIEL G. MOORE**
TRINIDAD NOIR (TRINIDAD & TOBAGO), edited by **LISA ALLEN-AGOSTINI & JEANNE MASON**
TRINIDAD NOIR: THE CLASSICS (TRINIDAD & TOBAGO), edited by **EARL LOVELACE & ROBERT ANTONI**
TWIN CITIES NOIR, edited by **JULIE SCHAPER & STEVEN HORWITZ**
USA NOIR, edited by **JOHNNY TEMPLE**
VENICE NOIR (ITALY), edited by **MAXIM JAKUBOWSKI**
WALL STREET NOIR, edited by **PETER SPIEGELMAN**
ZAGREB NOIR (CROATIA), edited by **IVAN SRŠEN**

FORTHCOMING

ACCRA NOIR (GHANA), edited by **NANA-AMA DANQUAH**
ADDIS ABABA NOIR (ETHIOPIA), edited by **MAAZA MENGISTE**
AMSTERDAM NOIR (HOLLAND), edited by **RENÉ APPEL & JOSH PACHTER**
BAGHDAD NOIR (IRAQ), edited by **SAMUEL SHIMON**
BERLIN NOIR (GERMANY), edited by **THOMAS WÖERTCHE**
BOGOTÁ NOIR (COLOMBIA), edited by **ANDREA MONTEJO**
COLUMBUS NOIR, edited by **ANDREW WELSH-HUGGINS**
HONG KONG NOIR, edited by **JASON Y. NG & SUSAN BLUMBERG-KASON**
HOUSTON NOIR, edited by **GWENDOLYN ZEPEDA**
JERUSALEM NOIR, edited by **DROR MISHANI**
MARRAKECH NOIR (MOROCCO), edited by **YASSIN ADNAN**
MILWAUKEE NOIR, edited by **TIM HENNESSY**
NAIROBI NOIR (KENYA), edited by **PETER KIMANI**
SANTA FE NOIR, edited by **ARIEL GORE**
SYDNEY NOIR (AUSTRALIA), edited by **JOHN DALE**
VANCOUVER NOIR (CANADA), edited by **SAM WIEBE**

Bear Creek Road

9

Mount Hermon

17

North Coast

UCSC

Wilder Ranch State Park

Pacific Ocean

1

Soquel Hills

Grant Park

Seabright

Pacific Avenue

Capitola

Mission Street

Cowell's

Yacht Harbor

The Circles

Steamer Lane

Pleasure Point

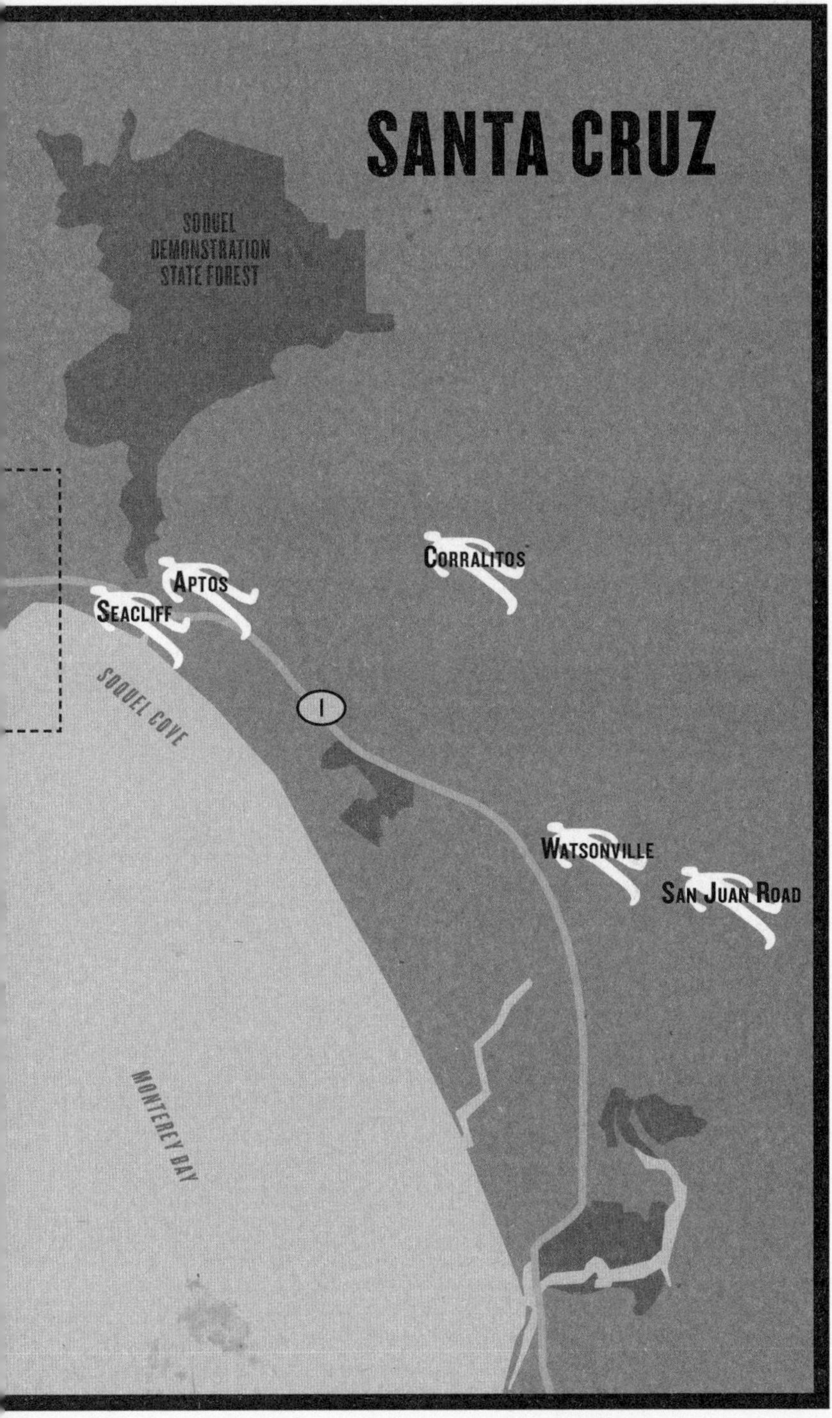

SANTA CRUZ

SOQUEL
DEMONSTRATION
STATE FOREST

CORRALITOS

APTOS

SEACLIFF

SOQUEL COVE

1

WATSONVILLE

SAN JUAN ROAD

MONTEREY BAY

TABLE OF CONTENTS

PART III: GOOD NEIGHBORS

PART IV: KILLER SOUTH

This anthology is dedicated to my companion editor, Willow Moon Pennell, who was here first.

Santa Cruz Noir *is also dedicated to the memory of Logos Books & Records, 1969–2017.*

INTRODUCTION

Beauty and the Break

Every town has its noir-ville. It's easy to find in Santa Cruz.

We live in what's called "paradise," where you can wake up in a pool of blood with the first pink rays of the sunrise peeking out over our mountain range. The dewy mist lifts from the bay. Don't hate us because we're beautiful—we were made that way, like Venus rising off the foam with a brick in her hand. We can't help it if you fall for it every time.

We live in a place where the screaming never stops. No, not the publicly psychotic. Our crown jewel, the reason a million-plus pleasure-seekers visit every year, is the Santa Cruz Beach Boardwalk, a roller coaster–screamin', cotton-candy amusement park. Our most famous ride, the Giant Dipper, will plunge you seventy feet down its wooden tracks at fifty-five miles per hour. We hear your cries all the way down the riverfront. Hell yes, you had a good time!

My companion editor, Willow Pennell, is second-generation Santa Cruz. She reminded me that the 1980s Santa Cruz film *Lost Boys* is still screened on our Main Beach every summer.

"How does it hold up now?" I asked.

"It doesn't matter." Willow is firm. "Every shot, from the Boardwalk to the leather jackets on predatory vampire boys—that was my teen experience. I, too, had a hippie name and sparkly Indian skirt like 'Star.' The combination of hippie and punk. The cliques, the Pogonip. And don't forget: *Lost Boys* is the only cinema of the pre-1989-earthquake Pacific Garden Mall."

Pacific Avenue, our "downtown," was nearly flattened in a late-twentieth-century earthquake—the one time we really crumbled on the outside.

Since the 1960s, most people who've landed in Santa Cruz arrived because they fell in love, got high, found an under-the-table gig, walked through our cute little doors of consciousness, and couldn't find the way out. We are historic bootleggers, and we don't let anyone go too easily. It's a pleasant place to bottom out.

Our origins are colonial and grisly, like all the Americas. Father Junipero Serra enslaved and buried the Ohlone Indians who lived here precontact. Mexico was kicked out next, by the Anglo settlers—but that's always been a bit of a joke. *Spanglish* is our native tongue.

We're haunted by an ancestral race war, but we intermarried the fuck out of each other. Our fertile land, the ag and range bounty, saved us from disaster again and again. In recent years, our equilibrium has been shot through a Silicon Valley cannon, the billionaire-boom over the hill.

We've been on the precipice of class war since the beginning. But perhaps all the good bud and coastal blue has made us soft. Everything stinks and yet . . . *surf's up.*

What makes Santa Cruz different from other California seaside towns? We have serious bragging rights. The Hawaiian princes brought surfing to the mainland, when they first paddled out our San Lorenzo River mouth in 1885. Their *aloha* is one of the best things that ever happened to us.

The psychedelic experience may not have been invented here, but it was perfected. We prize our sensual roots. We were once the home of a Wrigley Chewing Gum factory, and the

Doublemint smell still permeates the old factory site at the city limits. It's one of those little reminders—we were first a working-class joint, before the university arrived in 1967 with its dream to become the American Oxford.

Monarch butterflies migrate here en masse every year, coating the coastal eucalyptus, a mass of orange and black beating wings. Our bay faces south, not west. That is not Hawaii you see on the horizon; it's the Monterey Peninsula.

Yes, we were once dubbed the Serial Murder Capital of the World by the press, at our trippy-dippy apex in the 1970s. Willow reminds me: "Serial murderers seemed to like the pretty coeds around here. Despite the chipper holiday persona, our town always felt dangerous."

Downtown and the university are well-known to visitors—our North Coast, Westside, and Eastside (divided by the San Lorenzo River) are just around the bend. To the south, Santa Cruz County turns far more rural—but never let it be said, bucolic.

The first person I dialed when I got the *Santa Cruz Noir* gig was my favorite editor, Ariel Gore. She spoke with darkest authority. She defined "noir" in a short list I kept in my pocket for a year:

Often . . . the narrator has her own agenda.
The darker twist.
Moral ambiguity.
More cynicism. More fatalism.
The femme fatale. Even if she's mother nature herself.

Ariel stoked my film noir nostalgia. "Yes," she wrote me, "it came out of the WWII-era realization that people were not, in fact, basically good, but rather easily overcome by their base impulses—or that they tried to be good, but were swamped by outside forces. They were drawn into bad things, and couldn't figure how to get out. After all, people betrayed their own neighbors and lovers to the Nazis . . . that's the worldview we inherited—which is actually quite timely now."

This afternoon, one of my merry weekend visitors walked in the back door, complete with a happy sunburn and Foster's Freeze Softee in hand. "If I lived in a place like this," she said, "I'd wake up with a smile every day."

Oh, we do, thank you for that. There's no beauty like a merciless beauty—and like every crepuscular predator, she thrives at dawn and dusk. You're just the innocent we've been waiting for, with your big paper cone of sugar-shark cotton, whipped out of pure nothing. We have just the ride for you, the longest tunnel ever. Santa Cruz is everything you ever dreamed, and everything you ever screamed, in one long drop you'll never forget.

Susie Bright
Santa Cruz, CA
March 2018

PART I

Murder Capital of the World

BUCK LOW

BY TOMMY MOORE

North Coast

The Mexicans say that the devil sleeps under the mouth of the San Lorenzo River. On moonless nights, he rides a black horse up the bank and through the streets of the Flats. If he catches you then he'll tie you over his saddle and, before the sun rises, take you with him, beneath the river. I've spent nights waiting for their devil in the street, but of course I've never seen him.

I often end up here, by a fire in the dunes. Hitting a good vein in these hands is tricky. There is just the faint tickle of coke behind the watery brown chiva.

"Let's take your car up the coast, leave Santa Cruz for the night, like a little vacation," I'd told her. My fingers find their way along the scalloped edge of my ear, tracing the bite she left—remembering Katie's mouth. The waves crash onto the shore below, the whitewash hisses up the sand. We brought blankets, beer, mushrooms, food, a tarp. We built a fire. Tonight, the moon is almost full. Then, it was just a sliver and the stars were bright.

I met Katie downtown. Jerry Garcia had just died and she didn't know what to do. The first times, she wouldn't come alone, she'd bring a girlfriend. They would use my place to shower, smoke some weed, and then wash the dishes, vacuum, take out the trash. It felt like a very honest and pure exchange. "Katie, come by yourself next time," I told her.

She started sleeping on the couch. I liked that, watching her dream, blissed out and far away. Eventually, she got into my bed. I took my time with her.

On the beach that night, the mushrooms hit her hard. We were both laughing at nothing and she settled down next to me by the fire. I put her on top of me. I liked her like that. I kissed her. She became very still. She froze sometimes. I didn't mind. I kissed her again, unbuttoned and pulled down her jeans, and then slid her up my chest and onto my face. The warmth between her legs. I had all of it. I felt a shift in her again as I laid her down. When I came, she pushed me off. Her pupils were huge, spooked. I put my arms around her, held her tight. She struggled. I hugged her tighter. "I've got to go, let's go," she said.

"Calm down," I said. "It's just the mushrooms. Sit down with me by the fire. We'll smoke some weed." She struggled. I hugged her tighter, her head on my chest. "It's okay. It's okay. Relax," I whispered as I stroked her little head. Her whimpers turned to panic, then screams.

I nuzzled her head into my neck and that's when she bit my ear. I hit her but she just bit down harder, so I hit her again and when she let go, I grabbed her by the hair and pulled her to the ground. She was blubbering, drooling blood. It was my blood and I could feel it warm, running down my neck. I kneeled on her chest and held my hand over her mouth until she was still and the only sound was my beating heart and the raw ocean wind and waves upon the shore.

Had it really been a year? We could have had so much more time together but she didn't give me the chance to plan, to curate a final moment for us, to draw it out, nice and slow.

The night fades into a soft purple. The fire has burned out and the ashes are scattering in the wind. There is the faint, sweet must of earthy matter decomposing in a dark channel within the ranging estuary behind the dunes. I love watching the sun rise up from behind the mountains.

In the bright morning, I follow the tracks I left on the beach in the night, stepping into each faint footprint. A wad of torn flannel is entangled in a matted patch of dry kelp. I pick it up, shake off the sand, stretch it taut, loosening the crusted salt from the fabric. Why did she have to bite my ear?

Between swaths of mussels, there are tide pools in the pocked surface of the rocky point at the northern limit of the crescent cove. I walk out to the widest pool, near the edge, just above the waves. Surrounded by sea anemones, there are hermit crabs between patches of eel grass. They are trudging along, dragging their shells, leaving little trails across the sandy bottom. I reach in, catch one, and hold it upside down, just beneath the surface of the water, until its alien head pokes out. The little crab lifts its soft body, tries to right itself, and pinches at my finger. The sea anemones seem to be waving at me. Their tentacles quiver in excitement. I drop the crab and the anemone puckers the meal into its gut.

The sun is hot on my neck. I've been crouched over the pool for hours. Feeding crabs to the anemones has become automatic, almost meditative. I ram the last hermit crab deep into an anemone's distended blossom, overflowing with empty shells. It chokes on the meat and spews forth whole, half-digested crabs. The tide is rising and a wave washes over the pool, soaking my jeans. Another wave crashes over the rocky spit, I hold on and as the ocean recedes, I make a run for the edge, jump to the shore, and walk onto the dry sand.

The sun feels good. I pull off my wet pants and drape them on a flat rock to dry. I'm very hygienic. With Hep C, HIV,

AIDS, one has to keep it clean. I have distilled water in a bottle and a little container of bleach, just in case, but I rarely share needles or spoons. With my jacket over my head to cut the breeze, I cook a bit of tar for now, no coke, and then for a little while, I let the windblown sand collect in my ears, my hair. I wish she was here, buttery and naked under the sun.

There are people at the far end of the beach walking their dogs. Maybe they'll see me, the naked guy, and fuck off? I guess not. It's a long walk and I don't want to hitch in the dark. I put on my pants and leave. The path to the headland, up through the ravine, is steep and I'm careful not to slip on the loose, chalky scree. Between tilled fields, the path becomes a dirt road. Crows hop around something dead in a fresh row, stabbing at a chocolate clog of blood and fur.

If I sit here long enough with my thumb out, someone will stop. While I dump the sand from my shoes, a truck rattles by. Boxes of cabbage are on the open bed. As I lope over the highway, the wind scatters upon the harvested fields, rustling the faint smell of sulfur from the hollow brussels sprout stalks. More cars pass, no one stops. I pull down my stocking cap.

Finally, a pickup pulls over. The driver pushes open the passenger door. I get in. It's good to always have a knife, especially when you hitchhike. I can feel it in my front pocket when I sit down and I shift forward a bit in the seat so it's easier to grab. The Mexican behind the wheel looks harmless. His hands and face are dusted in fine, cut grass.

"Thank you."

"*De nada.*"

"Katie was a lovely creature but she shouldn't have bitten my ear."

He shrugs.

I lift up my cap and show him.

He nods and says something about a kitchen. Out my window, corduroyed farm rows flicker by. The torn strip of flannel has made its way into my palm and is soft on my lips. I catch him glancing at me.

"You've probably seen her picture in the paper, maybe downtown near the bus station."

"*No sé.*"

"You're correct. I don't know. They asked me about her, the police. So many people pass through this town. Transients, on their way north, south. People come, people go, it's hard to figure where they'll end up."

"*Sí.*"

"Yes. Not me, though. I'm from here. What about you? Mexico? Where you from?"

"Watsonville."

"The original Santa Cruz Town Charter of 1866 forbade the ownership of property by Jews, Negroes, Mexicans, and subjects of the Ottoman Empire. You have a bunch of kids? Collect welfare? I'm sure you have a bunch of kids. Right?"

"*Sí*. Watsonville."

I pat the cooler between us. "*Cerveza?*" and I pull out two beers. "Now, it's just nukes. The city don't allow nukes. A fucking shame." I open both cans and hand him a beer.

He takes a small sip and then puts it between his legs. Five miles per hour under the speed limit. On his own, he would never ever drink a beer on the road. He's been here awhile. He's careful. I suck mine down and open another. I want to cut his throat but we're in town now, on Mission.

"Drop me here."

He pulls over. I get out.

"You be good, " I say and then slam the door.

Walking through downtown, I notice the fresh crop of

girls from the university shopping, enjoying their freedom. They all have perfect pussies.

"Hey, you, Katie's friend!"

I turn to see a kid who seems to be somewhere between deadhead and squatter punk. "Can I help you?"

"She was only seventeen, man."

"I haven't seen her. I talked to the cops already."

"Well, talk to me."

"Look, kid, I'm sure she's fine. She took a few things, her backpack, a sleeping bag. She's probably up north doing the same shit; maybe she got some work trimming weed."

"She wouldn't just split. We spent eight months in my van going to shows. I know her. I know her mom and dad. She always called them to check in."

"What can I say? She seemed happy, and then one day I came home and she was gone." I step off the curb into the street. "Hey, kid, I miss her too. You know where I live?"

"Yeah," he says.

"Come by in a bit. She left a few things that the cops didn't take. You can have them."

I can't help but check the message board as I pass by the bus station. There are some new *Missing* posters: *Katie Rose*. Boyfriend probably put them up. That photo of her, a class picture. So cute. So clean. I'll keep trying but I'll never find another one like her. If I could have it my way, I'd fuck her every afternoon, kill her at night, and she'd be there, waking up next to me, smiling, in the morning.

As I walk along the bike path on the levee, the San Lorenzo River is green and still. Two distinguished cholos emerge from the stand of willows along the riprap.

"Yo, Carlos. I need a gram—"

"Keep walking, blondie. It's hot."

I'm sure they're not looking for me, but just in case I take the back way into Beach Flats, through the community garden. The cops have the basketball court taped off. Eight of my neighbors are sitting on the ground, handcuffed. I go around the block and cut through my yard. On the back door, someone tagged, *FUCK YOU*. How dare they? Fucking beaners. No class. And they left their spray can on the ground next to their paper bag still wet with *activo*. Huffers, no less. Brain-dead lumps of shit.

I can't buff this today so I take the can and paint the *F* into a *B* and then turn the *Y* into an *L* and I'll just double the *U*.

BUCK LOW. That's a bit better.

The faded sheets covering my windows give the living room a pleasant soft pink glow. I dig a roach out of the ashtray, get comfortable on the couch, and nibble on some pretzels. Little boyfriend will come by. He can't resist the opportunity to hold something of hers. He probably loves her. I cook up a shot of chiva and coke. It's good. I wish I had some speed. I shoot some more coke and then some chiva which evens me out a bit.

There he is, I hear him on the steps. I slide the works under the couch and wait for him to knock.

"Come in," I say as I open the door.

"This is my friend Owl," Katie's friend says.

"That's fine," I say. This has become a bit more difficult than I anticipated, but I'm almost unable to contain my joy. "Come inside. Please, make yourselves comfortable."

I lock the dead bolt, latch the chain, walk past them, and sit on the couch. Owl takes a seat on the La-Z-Boy. Boyfriend stays standing in the middle of the room.

"You like my place?" I say.

"So, where's her stuff?"

"This is my grandparents' house. The neighborhood has changed a lot since I was a boy." I pull out some weed from beneath the couch cushion and start rolling a joint on the coffee table. "It was mostly hippies, artists, in the sixties and seventies, and then in the 1980s the Mexicans came and took over."

"Really, that's great."

"Her heart was so pure, just a perfect angel," I say. I light the joint take a hit and pass it to Owl. "I miss her."

"No thanks," Boyfriend says.

"Hey, don't be rude," I say. "I'm trying to be hospitable."

"Stop fucking with me and just give me her shit."

Owl is hitting the joint.

"Fine," I say, and get off the couch and open the door to the bedroom. "In the box, under the bed."

"Stay in the living room. And Owl, watch my back."

"Hey, man, chill out. *Mi casa es su casa.*"

I can see the kid through the doorway as he pulls the box out from under the bed. I back up a few steps until I'm right behind Owl, who is still puffing on the joint. I take the knife out of my pocket, open it up, and then grab Owl by his dreads and slit his throat. He makes a sound somewhere between a wheeze and a whistle. The blood gurgles, runs down his chest, and he gets up, leaps for the door, fumbles at the knob, and falls to the ground. The boyfriend is in the bedroom doorway, stunned, holding onto Katie's patchwork Hubbard dress. I pounce and drive the knife deep into his gut. With my hand over his mouth, I stab him over and over again.

I black-bag both of them, tape up the seams, and lay them side by side. Then I cut the black oversized trash bags and wrap up the La-Z-Boy. It was my father's chair and I'm a bit reluctant to get rid of it but it's covered in Owl's blood. I'll dump everything up north, near Pittsburg or Alameda, in the backwater of the San Francisco Bay.

I keep my grandfather's old panel van parked in my garage. Inside, I've got my kit: quickset concrete, extra-large duffel bags, exercise weights, black contractor trash bags, duct tape, a hacksaw, bleach, gloves. I load the bodies in first and then the carpets and cover everything with a furniture blanket before putting the chair on top. *Cal's Plumbing "The Local Pro"* is still proudly painted across both sides of the van. When the logo shows some wear, I touch it up, keep it looking fresh. I apprenticed under my uncle. It's a family business and a good trade.

I get high and lock up the house while the van idles in the garage, and pull out and drive north onto Highway 1. The moon is waning but still full and bright, so after Davenport I turn off the headlights and drive by the moonlight.

Katie is close by. Passing the beach where she's buried, I almost pull over so we can spend some time together before I set off on the road for a while. But leaving my van parked on the side of the highway with these two assholes in the back is a bad idea. I keep driving north, switch on the headlights, and light up a joint. I should be in San Francisco by dawn.

One night, long ago, just out of high school, I wandered through Golden Gate Park with a tire iron beneath my parka. A few people were around. I checked out a couple of kids my age passing joints, bottles of beer. I followed two bums until they cut through a hedge to a secret hollow in a thick patch of bush. I stalked a lone dog walker past the windmill to Ocean Beach. Unable to get up the nerve, I turned around and walked back toward the Haight until I came across the buffalo paddock. They were just standing there, cowlike and tame. So I climbed over and cornered the smallest one. It was just a baby, really. I clubbed it in the back of its thick skull. It wobbled, ran, I chased it down and whacked it again—and again, until it fell.

On its side, in the grass, the little creature's boney chest rose and fell with deep, slow breaths. Unconscious, she seemed at peace, and I reached out, running my hand through her wooly fur. Then I put my ear to her side and her great heart was still thumping in its cage. I laid down beside her, spooned up against her back, nuzzled my face into the long, fine hair along the nape of her neck. In the languid warmth of the dying beast, I found a wonderful peace.

At sunrise, I pull off the highway at Pacifica and into a service station. As I pump gas and the surf rolls into Rockaway Beach, I know the tide has changed the estuary's course. The sand has shifted. Katie has become unburied.

I hang up the nozzle, screw on the gas cap, go inside the mini-mart, and buy two bundles of firewood. I open the back of the van and toss the bundles on top of the bodies of Owl and Boyfriend. I notice that the blood has pooled beneath the furniture blankets and is now seeping under the door and over my rusted chrome bumper. I need to get rid of the mess in the back as planned, clean up the van. I should stay away from Santa Cruz for a bit, head north, lay low.

But I can't just leave her back there.

A workman's truck pulls up on the other side of the gas pump. A man in coveralls gets out with an oversized coffee mug and walks into the mini-mart. I wipe down the bumper with some paper towels and scan the parking lot before I throw all my bloody towels into the trash.

The man exits the mini-mart, coffee steaming in the cold morning sunlight. I get in the van, start it up. I can see her there, on the beach. Her blond hair is tangled in the wind-swept dune grass and her face is open to the bright sky. I put the van into gear, wave at the guy, and pull away from the station. He smiles and nods. In the side mirror, I watch him lean against his truck, put his mug down on the hood, and holler to the gas station attendant as I turn left onto the highway and head back south.

WHATEVER HAPPENED TO SKINNY JANE?

BY ARIEL GORE

Pacific Avenue

The acid was just coming on. Bob Innes, the lead singer of Fleece the Rich, took the Catalyst Club stage—and there was his girlfriend, rushing on to join him like panic with faint tracers. She wore this see-through Indian dress with a stuffed pillowcase underneath, like she's pregnant, right?

And in the middle of the show, when they're singing,"*I awoke in a sweat from the Amerikan dream / Our rage against the war machine,*" the girlfriend just started SCREAMING—I mean, bloody-murder-shrieking—and she's performing a spontaneous miscarriage with all these bloodred fabrics from the pillowcase spilling out.

I think it's part of the show—hell, it's the Catalyst on Halloween—but Bob Innes and everyone else just looked like they're trying to keep going.

"*Their trickle-down fuckonomics obscene / Their 'freedom' is a pyramid scheme.*"

The girlfriend's still shrieking and then she started pulling handfuls of real blood from herself and what looked like small body parts and I remember thinking: *Shit, I wish I had a girl like that.*

I didn't even think of myself as gay or straight back then, but I knew I was attracted to the fucked-up.

The room spun tangerine. Shrieks became hysterical laughter and "Names Have Been Changed to Protect the Guilty" and yes, I wanted a girl like Innes's girl.

And, you know, sometimes I think I conjure people right up.

Does that sound crazy?

It's the next day and I'm down at the Clock Tower 'cause Food Not Bombs is serving lunch without a permit and I'm not hungry or anything, but I just dropped another tab and I'm in the mood to start some shit with the police. Before I even get a chance, here comes this skinny girl in a skirt and no fuckin' shirt on and she's all limbs and yellow hair and tiny pink tits and she's hungry—she's practically starving, right?

So, *fuck the police*—I've got my steel-toed boots on and I'm gonna to get this skinny girl some food so I'm dodging SCPD billy clubs and I'm made of steel and the Food Not Bombs guy with his goatee is serving his grub fast, and it's all sirens and pigs trying to shut it down, and I get this girl some lentils and I'm kind of sheltering her with my body as she spoons stew into her mouth, and when she's done, I say, "What's your name, sweetie?"

And she says, "Jane."

I mean, who's named Jane, right? You can't make this shit up. So I say, "Pleased to meet you, Jane, I'm Apex." And obviously she's new in town or I'd know her already and she smiles real sweet like something you could crush and I think, *I gotta have this girl.*

I say, "I don't know if you've already got a place to stay, Jane, but I've got a tent at San Lorenzo Park—" And right then I look up and the Food Not Bombs guy is shaking his head and smirking like that's the oldest line in the book, like next thing, I'm gonna say, *What's your sign?* and start reading to her from *Real Astrology*.

I wink at the Food Not Bombs guy, but also kind of scowl. I mean, motherfucker can back up off my action. I look back at Jane and she's got the face of a hummingbird but I play it off like I don't see that and I take her fluttering hand and that's the day I moved skinny Jane into my tent and everything smelled damp like sea salt and eucalyptus.

Now, I won't lie: all the other dropouts and runaways in San Lorenzo Park say my girl Jane was psycho right from the get-go, like they could tell by lookin' at her skinny, smiling face.

But I said, *Don't judge, man*, and *Who cares, anyway?* I mean, her parents had her locked up at Agnew's for kissing girls and slitting her own wrists, but you'd probably try and kill yourself too if you were stuck in that god-awful pale-blue suburban tract house with your straight-ass parents for all eternity. Did you know Agnew's was once called the Great Asylum for the Insane and fell down in the 1906 quake and all the lunatics ran out when the building crumbled?—never got caught.

We were never going to get caught neither. I liked the way Jane needed me to hold her at night, the way she asked me to pin her arms to her sides real gentle-like, but tight.

She had nightmares.

She whispered stories about serial killers to soothe herself back to sleep. She whispered, "You ever hear of the Coed Killer, Apex?"

And truth is, I hadn't.

I had Jane's arms pinned to her sides and she's whispering to me about this 1970s serial killer, and she lets her voice get kind of raspy when she whispers. She says, "He hated his mother, that was the thing, and his mom worked at the university and he had an IQ of, like, 145, and he was a giant too, maybe six foot nine, and heavy. His mother was completely narcissistic and abusive, so this giant grew up to be this homicidal psycho—he killed his grandmother when he was a teenager, and when his grandpa got home, he killed him too, and he served maybe five years in the Atascadero State Hospital, but they released him back to his mom up in the Santa Cruz Mountains in 1969."

I tried holding her just a little bit tighter, but Jane wanted to keep talking.

"He started killing girls he picked up hitchhiking. He buried one girl's head in his mother's garden like it was this twisted joke because he said his mom always wanted people to look up to her." Jane's breath kind of settled as she talked, like other people's terror calmed her own.

"He hung out in this cop bar on Ocean Street called The Jury Room and he befriended all the detectives so he could keep a step ahead—and not ONE of them suspected him. They just filled him in on the case, night after night. Finally, he killed his mother and her best friend—maybe her lover—and he ripped out her vocal cords and blasted them in the garbage disposal, and then he felt better! Cops never would've caught him, but he was done. Over it. He turned himself in. Confessed to everything." Jane took a deep breath and sighed in my arms. "Apex?"

"Yes, Jane?"

"You're gonna think I'm fucked up."

My heart raced. "No, baby."

"Sometimes I have this fantasy that I get strangled and somebody severs my head and buries, buries me looking up . . ."

I held her arms so tight. She finally trailed off and fell asleep.

We lived like that in my old tent in the bushes for almost three weeks. But the rains were coming on, and the cops were getting crazy on everybody, not just us—coming through at sunrise like they owned the place and kicking everybody awake. I'd already sold all the LSD I came to town with, except for my personal stash, and the outlook seemed pretty bleak. So when my girl Jane came running across the grass one morning, skinny limbs flying in every direction, scaring the ducks in the pond and yelling that she got us a room at the St. George Hotel, I wasn't about to ask her how she pulled that one off.

I mean, for all I knew she had her suburban parents wire her money straight from their Costco lasagna dinner in Cupertino. I just packed up my tent and followed her skinny ass across the river and onto the Pacific Garden Mall.

I'm telling you, the old St. George was the best. Seedy and fancy at the same time, art deco and cracked plaster, creaking floors and red carpet. I was high, I admit it, but I knew that old-fashioned elevator was a portal to another realm the minute I stepped inside of it and pulled the metal grate door closed and the machine heaved us up, just rope and iron.

Jane said right then, "All the *ifs* are gonna become *is*," and I wanted to kiss my girl so hard right then, but I didn't.

Our room had black-and-white tile floors and a blue lightbulb hanging from the ceiling. *Who let Joni Mitchell in here?* Me and skinny Jane had a place to get us through mudslide season.

"Or until the culmination," Jane whispered.

I didn't know what the hell she was talking about. We could've been happy there.

Jane pulled the blinds closed against the morning gray and killed all the lights except the blue one. The place glowed dark like it was moonlit and Jane's eyes gleamed. Her face looked so thin.

She said, "Now we can listen to it," and she unzipped her backpack and pulled out an old cassette tape and a boom box and said, "This one is gonna blow your mind."

"Should we smoke a bowl?"

"Don't you have any acid?"

So I reached into my wallet and we each put a tab on our tongue and we stretched out on our thrift-store blankets and my Jane pressed *Play* with her big toe and grabbed my neck.

She said, "Listen."

And it's Edmund Kemper on tape, the Coed Killer himself, confessing his whole life. All calm. He said: "*It started with surrogates at that, uh, nonhuman level. Physical objects: my possessions, other people's, destruction of things that are cared about. And then to destruction of things that are living, on a lower level: small animals, uh, insects, animals, and then finally people.*"

I opened my eyes and everything, every single thing, was indigo.

"He just started with objects that were cared about," Jane whispered.

I wondered if we'd ever have anything we cared about. I imagined painting birds on canvas and blue glass goblets we could cherish and smash and that's when I noticed the walls of our room were becoming less solid, melting like wax, maybe, melting like confines.

Kemper's voice reverberated against the unsolid walls. He said: "*If it'd been in a city, I'd have been a mass murderer at age fifteen. I would've killed until they gunned me down. I wouldn't have been able to reason my way out of it. I was scared to death and I was violent. I felt my back hit that wall. I was the rabbit that always ran, that always backed away; always burned his bridges."*

My girl Jane says, "You ever burn your bridges, Apex?"

The acid came on. I get up on all fours and close my eyes and concentrate until I turn myself into a rabbit and I'm running—like scampering down the Pacific Garden Mall—and Jane says, "Apex! Let's hitchhike."

Her words pop my rabbit spell and I open my eyes and say, "Hitchhike where, baby?" 'Cause we didn't have any damn place to go, but I look around our room just then and the walls have completely vanished.

Kemper is saying: "*I was losing a grasp on something that was too violent to keep inside forever. As I'm sitting there with a severed head in my hand, talking to it, or looking at it, and I'm about to go crazy, literally . . . I told myself, 'No, it isn't. You're saying that, and that makes it not insane.'"*

Kemper's voice is all there is. I'm my own rabbit again and I'm running, but I've been decapitated, a headless rabbit, and I'm trying to catch my breath. Then I'm human again, just us under the blue light at the St. George.

My girl Jane was nineteen right then and I was eighteen. I was thinking, *No way*, right? But then Jane said, "Let's find our serial killer, Apex," and who the hell could say no to that?

"Culmination," Jane said. Her eyes were sapphires. Had her eyes always been sapphires? In those gems I saw our two minds become one—the *ifs* all became *is*. The fucking Apex right there.

Kemper's voice kept rolling: "*I didn't go hog wild and totally limp. What I'm saying is I found myself doing things in an attempt to make things fit together inside."*

And just then—I got it. That was my problem too—needing to make things fit together inside.

We stood close, right on Mission Street. All the lights on.

The first car that pulled over was this Audi with a Michael Dukakis bumper sticker. The guy driving looks creepy as all get-out with his horn-rimmed glasses and I look at Jane and I can tell she's excited. We both get in the back and he turns around as he starts the car and says, "You girls really shouldn't be hitchhiking out here, you know? Are you students?"

For a second I think he means *he's* the weirdo we shouldn't hitchhike with and my heart races, but Jane rolls her eyes and shakes her head. 'Cause she knows.

The guy turns out to be some do-gooder biology professor and Jane's looking at the door handle, wondering if we can make a break for it, roll on out while this guy is driving, but it's useless.

He isn't gonna be happy until we are all tucked in next to our mommies and our Barbie dream houses. So Jane says, "We're sisters, we're from Canada, and we're meeting our aunt on Water Street and we missed the bus, okay?" She directs him to some better-than-Denny's place which seems to satisfy his sense of propriety and we scramble out of the backseat and head over to The Jury Room to regroup.

Now, you gotta love a bar that looks like the goddamn Foursquare Church from outside. More than that, you gotta love a bartender who barely glances at your fake ID that features some blond bitch you never knew who once lived in your tent in San Lorenzo Park.

The place smells like smoke and Roy Orbison croons on the jukebox. We sit on the red vinyl barstools and order a couple of Coors, 'cause up on the chalkboard it says they're as cold as your ex's heart.

I say, "How about let's try the road up to Felton." It's Highway 9 and it narrows fast and deep into the redwoods and I can already see the serial killers cruising up and down those curves waiting for two little girls with their thumbs out, and Jane nods. Her skin flickers red in the bar light.

Outside, the asphalt's wet, but it isn't raining.

First car that stops is some old sedan and the woman driving it cranes her neck toward us and says, "Where're you headed?"

And I say, "Felton?"

I glance at my girl Jane, like, *Can we trust a woman to murder us?* Jane gets my question telepathically and she nods, so we climb into the back and it smells of patchouli. The woman starts talking, chattery-chat, and there's graham cracker crumbs between the seats and I'm just shaking my head because where's a goddamn serial killer when your girl wants one?

Little Miss Chatty-Chat, mother of graham-cracker eaters, says, "Where in Felton?"

My girl Jane looks like she's gonna cry and I'm really about to lose it. I say, "Any goddamn place."

The woman driver startles, offended, and pulls over at the first stop sign in town. "You girls be careful out there."

I can feel all the blood moving in my veins and Jane takes my arm, like everything's gonna be all right. We cross the street as the sedan rolls away and we stick out our thumbs again and skinny Jane winks at me and she says, "Third time's a charm."

Maybe she's right. We're waiting out there a long time. Hardly any cars. It's getting cold and I whisper to my girl Jane, "Are you cold?"

She smiles at me sad, sad blue smile light, and that's when

the VW van rolls up and the front door flies open and I climb up into the front seat and Jane takes the back. The driver has long, greasy hair, and he says, "You wanna do some coke?"

Hell yeah.

He gets out this cracked old mirror and cuts three lines on it. Powder feels like power. I snort it and pocket the razor.

You ever sever a whole fuckin' head with a razor?

It's not easy. All the skin and tendon and throat and bone. I gotta be honest with you: I blame Jane.

Kemper said: "*I am an American and I killed Americans, I am a human being and I killed human beings, and I did it in my society.*"

That cassette tape of hers really did a number. Even as I tightened my grip around her skinny little neck, she still begged me to squeeze harder. She was begging me with her sapphires, wasn't she? I was just trying to give her what she wanted. For all the *ifs* to become *is*? I'm a runaway. I killed a runaway. Do you get that? I'm a dropout who killed another dropout. And even as I severed her psycho little head, all blood and tendons, I was thinking, *I'm taking care of my girl, right?*

It's not like I don't have a conscience. I know a person's eventually supposed to turn their ass in and make some calm confession. But that's why I'm telling you right here at The Jury Room, where everything smells like smoke and Roy Orbison is still crooning. I had to get this whole thing off my chest before I blow this fuckin' town. And while I'm at it, I'll tell you the weird part.

I went back to San Lorenzo Park. I couldn't very well stay on at the St. George. For the first few nights I was paranoid, like the cops at sunrise were coming just for me. But they kicked everyone out like they always had, and I didn't care—

but, you know, not one of the kids in the park asked me what happened to my girl Jane.

Like, how can a person fuckin' vanish and nobody's gonna come looking for her?

I lace up my boots and walk up to the Clock Tower and the Food Not Bombs guy is getting ready to set up his grub and I ask him, I say, "Don't you wonder what ever happened to skinny Jane?"

Guy scratches his goatee and looks at me quizzical-like, and he says, "Apex, you're the only person I ever met named Jane." He smiles and shakes his head. "I remember when you showed up here emaciated and topless and bragging about the ten sheets of acid you stole from your psychiatrist before you busted out of Agnew." He shakes his head again. "I was worried about you back then. You seemed really vulnerable."

I could just taste the faintest bile in my mouth.

Sometimes I still think about that. I put a tab of acid on my tongue and I run my hands over my pink little tits and I wonder if skinny Jane was ever separate from me or if she was just the part of myself I wanted badly and knew had to die—like Bob Innes's girlfriend's baby back at the Catalyst.

I remember a lot more about where Jane came from than where I did. I try to remember my life before I got here, and the furthest back I can recall is when I was on a bus riding Highway 17 up into the mountains where the oak trees give way to second-growth redwoods. I remember cresting the Summit, my passenger window cracked, and the wisp of ocean air and smell of eucalyptus.

But then I let the questions go.

What does it matter, really?

I killed my girl Jane.

I'll never know if we started out as two, 'cause truth be

told, nobody ever came looking for either one of us.

I buried her head in San Lorenzo Park, right next to the duck pond and blue playground slide.

I buried her looking up.

MONARCHS AND MAIDENS

BY MARGARET ELYSIA GARCIA

Capitola

That little girl stood right in my way.

"You're lucky to be here," she said.

I was carrying the last of the boxes from the U-Haul trailer to my new furnished cottage. It was one of those mother-in-law units—sharing a long driveway with a main house up the road.

"These were built to be maid's quarters, you know," the girl continued. She looked to be about ten, with straight dirty-blond hair and small brown eyes. I was taking an instant dislike to her. She was the kind of child privy to too many adult conversations and too many items on her Christmas list. She already knew she belonged to a class far above me, and likely most of the other tenants she encountered in Capitola.

I smiled to acknowledge she was talking, but I said nothing back. She didn't offer to help.

"Really. This unit is never empty for very long. We used to use it as a guest room, but we've remodeled rooms in the main house. You could've wound up in the trailer park," she said.

I was to be here for six months, working on a grant project out of UC Santa Cruz. I wanted to tell the girl I owned a house someplace else. Someplace just as nice as Capitola, if not better. I was taking this job to be helpful and useful to the world—and because primo academic jobs were hard to come by. It was an honor. A feather in my cap. Why did I feel the need to explain this to a ten-year-old?

"Sometimes my parents allow the tenant access to the pool too. I can put in a good word for you." She sat in an oversized wicker chair by the door. Her legs dangled over the edge. She kicked at the marble umbrella stand with two long black umbrellas in them.

I hadn't even noticed how odd the furnishings were. It felt like the whole cottage was Hawaii-themed from the 1970s—perhaps an effort to make Capitola-by-the-Sea feel warmer and cozier than the fog would allow for.

I smiled at the girl and stood in front of her to offer my hand and help her up. She didn't take it. "Well, that looks like that's my last box," I said. "Going to go return the U-Haul now. You can come by some other time."

"I don't need to go anywhere."

"But you do. I've rented this place from your parents. It is mine for the time being. I need you to go."

"But I always hang out in here."

"Not today, I'm afraid."

"You're going to need me," she said. She stood up and walked around me, eyeing me up and down. I felt defensive about—well, everything—my dress with its pilling around the arms, my shoes from five years ago. Everything. The girl opened the door and looked back. "Suit yourself. Though it is very—*very* ill-advised. My parents can tell you more about it." She walked toward the main house.

I exhaled, locked the door behind me, and headed out to return the trailer.

As I merged onto Highway 1, I could feel the fog settling in. Perhaps the Hawaiian décor would help a seasonal depression that was sure to take hold given the constant damp I'd felt in just a few days of being here. It was September and I felt like I couldn't get warm.

I found the Capitola cottage while having a bite to eat at the local strip mall book café. There were poetry anthologies out front and a giant brass elephant head on the wall. Both things made me calm. Their bulletin board said a cottage was available and that the owners only took graduate students or visiting professors. I fit in somewhere in between. I took their ad to mean they would be serious, older, and, for some reason, childless. They would, no doubt, invite me to tea. We'd exchange poetry.

Sharon, the wife, had bobbed blond hair and a country-club smile. The husband, Bradley, seemed a little out of it, but innocuous—sandy brown hair, overly groomed face. I admired a Victorian chair they had in the foyer when I came for the interview. Its upholstery was faded yellow, with bright leaves in the print. Holes and a few brown stains. The arms were solid oak and the legs had an inlay of cast-iron fleur-de-lis. I liked the chair immediately. It signaled that they'd be appreciative of antiquities but not too fussy about having everything absolutely manicured.

"This chair?" Bradley said. "It has a fascinating history. The innkeepers who used to own this property back in the early 1900s. Well, the wife shot herself in the face in *this* chair. You can still see the stains. Isn't it marvelous? What a story!" He pointed out frays in the fabric and told me he just didn't have the heart to restore it. He was sure you could still smell the gunpowder if you breathed in deep. He never looked at my face to gauge my reaction. Part of me appreciated him for that.

Then they led me out to the cottage they were renting

for nearly four hundred dollars under the current market for houses in the Santa Cruz County area. The girl wasn't with them.

U-Haul had the usual queue. I couldn't wait to drive back to the cottage to set up my desk. I'd made sure to leave space in the living room to house the library I'd need for the six months.

The girl was sitting on my couch when I opened the door. "You took too long," she said.

"You've broken-and-entered my cottage. Are your parents home?"

"You seem stressed out. You shouldn't get stressed out. Although I suppose that's what your kind does?"

"My *kind?*"

"Why, yes. The lower middle-class is always stressed out," she said.

I dropped my eyes. I couldn't look at her. "I need time alone to set up my office," I said.

"It's too bad you probably can't afford a new laptop. This space could do without the clutter of older technology. But, *chacun* à *son gout*, as my mother says." She stood up and I escorted her out and locked the windows and dead-bolted the door this time.

"When people around here want to chill out, they go to Natural Bridges Park," she said over her shoulder. "You should, too. Relax."

I unboxed my books and set up my old iMac on the old secretary's desk I brought with me. I had a laptop too. A MacBook Air. Sure, it was a few years old—that just proves they last. I was muttering to myself again. I took out my old iPod and speaker out of a box and put on something old too. There was nothing on that iPod newer than 2006. I mean, my phone has newer things, but this particular device didn't.

Little girl wasn't even there and I was still justifying. I picked up my phone and dialed Sharon's cell phone. I left her a message. Could she meet me somewhere so we could have coffee and chat? There were a few things I wanted to go over.

The phone rang. Sharon said to meet her at the book café.

"Oh. I'm so sorry," she said the moment she arrived. "Madison is hanging out over there? She did kind of like to use it as a life-sized dollhouse. I'm so sorry. We'll speak to her."

"Thank you," I said, and took a sip of the hot chai I'd ordered. "I think it's great that she takes an interest in people, but I'm here to do research and promote this new program and that's going to really fill my time."

"I so understand. I do apologize for her. Madison doesn't have many friends."

Yes. Yes, I might have known that. "Where does she go to school?"

"Oh, we homeschool now. It's really better this way—especially since the accident." Sharon barely registered my raised eyebrow; she was practiced. "Madison did have a really good friend. They used to love gardening together. Well, one day Ashley and Maddy were climbing trees to catch butterflies. And Ashley missed a branch and stepped on one that was too small for her. Maddy was always telling her she was too fat to climb the trees. It broke and she fell out of the tree. Dead. Maddy said she couldn't catch her. It happened too fast."

"I'm so sorry." What else could I say? Jesus. It's not what I thought going out to coffee would be about. "Madison does seem very adult for her age."

"Yes, I know she does."

I chickened out going further. There was no way of not sounding like an asshole. I drove back to the cottage to finish setting up my desk. Madison was on the doorstep. At least she wasn't inside.

"Your mother tells me you are homeschooled," I said.

"Yes. For now," the girl replied. "I've had a few tutors—the last one lived here, in fact. The other is around here somewhere. Anyhow. Yes. It suits me much better."

"So is that why you keep hanging around my cottage? Because you used to come here for lessons?" I tried to keep my face from giving me away.

"My parents are busy. I manage our property for them since I'm home more often. I pay the gardener and the maid. I order the groceries. We have to make sure you're a good fit for this place."

"I signed my agreement with your father and mother," I said.

Maybe I was hoping she'd see reason. I kept forgetting she was ten. This time I just closed the door and dead-bolted it behind me. I thought I could hear her mouth-breathing outside the door. I turned on music to drown her out and finished setting up my new temporary home.

In the early evening, before it went dark, I decided I'd take a walk into the village.

I saw Bradley pulling up the drive as I walked down our little hill of driveway. He waved good-naturedly and rolled down the window. *Did I need a lift?* I politely declined. There was no sign of Madison or the mother.

I walked clear down to the beach. It was a sweet two-street downtown filled with old-time-y quaint buildings. Present history clearly started at a specific time in architecture, by design. As darkness fell, my hair tangled in the salt air, I felt an uneasy veneer of displacement. I'd read that Capitola was once an Indian village—the Soquel people—driven out, of course, by those who sought to "better the land." They were on my mind as I walked back up the hillside. That, and the knowledge that no matter what I did with my life now, I would never be able to afford to buy a house anywhere in my native California; I would always feel driven out.

When I got back, there was a small tray on the porch with a lacquered black box on it and a note. A monarch butterfly painted on the top. I put water on for tea, placed the tray on the coffee table, and read the note: *Don't agree to be a tutor. It isn't safe here.*

I looked over the message with the fortune-cookie-sized advice several times. I didn't know the handwriting. It didn't look like Bradley's or Sharon's when I checked their signatures on the lease agreement for comparison. I opened the black box and it contained a small crucifix necklace with a butterfly where the body of Christ would be.

I drank my tea and showered before bed. I put on my new necklace.

I was sitting in my kimono on the couch, staring at the same page of a book for what seemed like hours, when there was a knock on the door. It was Bradley. Maybe he found out about the Madison stuff and was here to apologize too.

"Hi, Bradley. What brings you out here?"

"Madison told us over dinner," he said, "how impressed she was with you and your book collection and what you're working on for the university. We know you're probably busy, but we also know that college budgets are tight. We were wondering if you'd be interested in tutoring Madison in exchange for lobbing off a few more hundred from the rent. Think about it and let us know?"

In truth, it would bring down my rent considerably. Bradley's offer meant my rent would actually be reasonable for six hundred square feet. I thought about the note I received. It was probably from Madison herself. I had a feeling I'd be seeing her all the time anyhow. Might as well get paid for it.

I said yes.

"Excellent," Bradley said. "You can start tomorrow. Just an hour a day would keep her on track with her studies."

I saw Bradley out. There was a small tray with another box and note on the ground by the planter.

"Secret admirer, huh?" said Bradley, as he whistled off across the driveway toward his house.

I opened the second box. It held a tiny petrified cocoon that had been made into a perfect lapel pin. I opened the note, my heart racing.

Protect yourself. And don't look too closely in the backyard.

I went inside and found a flashlight. I immediately went to the backyard. I saw nothing out of the ordinary, but there were large mounds of dirt in the rosebushes that looked as if something had been buried there. I went back inside and locked up the house. I locked up the rooms and slept on the couch. It was buttressed by a wall and seemed like the safest place. I hardly slept at all.

The next day I got up early and drove to the university provost's office to check on paperwork and orientation. In the afternoon I headed home and Madison was waiting on the front step.

"Hello, my new tutor."

"Yes, I suppose I am. You'll have to tell me where you are in your studies so we can plan a course of study."

"I need to know everything. For instance, who is sending

you notes and boxes?" Right next to Madison's Mary-Jane'd foot was yet another box and note.

"Tell you what, Madison—why don't we start in an hour? I have to eat some lunch and attend to a few things first. I will meet you up at your place." Again I whipped inside the house and dead-bolted the door behind me.

I opened the box. In it was a silver charm bracelet. Each charm was a butterfly but one was a tombstone. My name and birth date was inscribed on the largest charm. With a question mark at the other side for a death date.

You aren't going to make it here.

I got out my laptop and began hunting for other places to live. Perhaps someone knew someone at the college who could put me up a couple of days. There was a knock. Of course, Madison had come back already. But it was Sharon. She had mail in her hand for me. A letter from the college. It was one of those glassine envelopes with something pink inside.

"Did your job get cut? That seems to happen all the time these days." Sharon half-smiled.

Indeed. I figured I might as well open it up in front of her.

Something had happened with the funding. The job was on hiatus but the department head was sure they'd find funding from another source.

"Seems like it's a great windfall for us. We can use you full time!" Sharon acted like she'd won a prize at the Boardwalk. "Let's get a drink up at my house, shall we? When are they going to treat academics with the respect they deserve?"

"I told Madison I'd tutor her in an hour."

"And you *will*, but first a drink! Then I'll show you the library where she takes her lessons."

Sharon led me by the hand up to the main house. I was

stunned that my prestigious job was gone so fast, so fleetingly. A nice glass of wine was needed. *At least Sharon is understanding*, I thought.

"Let's drink in the wine cellar. We had it custom-made and built into the hillside. It's like a little café in there!"

I followed in Sharon's footsteps. She punched a code in the side of the cellar door and a metal door opened. There were rows and rows of bottles inside. A little French café table and two chairs in the middle. She offered me the nicest one and found a pinot noir she thought would suit the occasion.

I drank two glasses on an empty stomach. And then a third. I felt sleepy. I felt Sharon's fingers on my face brushing my hair back behind my ear. "It's so unfair what you've been through!" she said. I felt her kiss on my neck. Then I felt nothing at all.

I woke up groggy and in my own bed. I couldn't remember a thing after that kiss. There was no sign of anyone around me. I made coffee. I called Sharon's number but there was no answer so I left a message: "Uh, it's me. I don't think this is going to work out. Money isn't everything." I opened the front door thinking perhaps Madison was out there, but she wasn't.

I took Maddy's advice from the other day. I drove out to Natural Bridges State Park to check out where the monarch butterflies migrate to hang in the trees by the thousands. A group of schoolchildren was leaving as I entered the trail. They'd all just been down there, so why couldn't I do the same?

If you're like me and don't have the best vision, you don't notice the butterflies, at first. But as you go closer to the trees, you realize they are moving. Thousands of monarchs beat their wings about the eucalyptus and pine so that trees appear to dance. They move back and forth like a kelp forest in a tide zone. Orange and black and white, so thick that the tree colors are hidden. The farther you go on the trail, the thicker the colony. By the end of the path there seem to be nothing left but the beating of a million orange wings.

It had a dizzying effect. I stumbled and found a park bench to sit on. My breath was quick—like the life of a butterfly itself. Had Madison known the effect it would have on me? Had she suggested this place for a reason? I wanted to be kind now—to bridge whatever it was that had set me to hate her. But I couldn't help it.

And then I saw a girl around Maddy's same age, staring up at me from an opposite bench. She had a neck brace on.

"I'm Ashley," she said, "the dead girl who fell from the tree. Perhaps you heard of me? You're one of the tutors, aren't you?"

"I guess I am," I said.

Ashley pulled a phone from her pocket and called a number. "Found her. I can wait till you arrive," she said.

"You're not dead?" I asked. I reached out to see if she was a ghost.

"Well, of course I am. But I have a job now."

Two figures appeared at the top of the trail. It was Sharon and Bradley in their Land's End trench coats. They smiled and waved.

"You need to remember to ask permission, young lady," Sharon said, marching up to my side. "We can't have you just wandering off like that. Give Bradley your keys."

I did as I was told and dug into my pocket to get them. At the same time, I pulled out the cocoon pin and the butterfly necklace.

"What is that?" Sharon shrieked. Her whole body pulled away from me, like she was retreating into the air itself. Bradley stepped forward to shield her, but with the amulets in my hand, he too screamed and flapped away.

Ashley cackled hysterically.

"What's going on?" I asked her. "What's happening to them?"

"Nothing they don't deserve," she said. "But you've broken the spell. Thank you." She sat down on the bench again. Her neck sank brokenly against her shoulder. Her eyes closed and she slumped over—and died.

I put the necklace around my neck and the pin on my dress. Sharon and Bradley squawked like chickens in a pen, helpless. They couldn't get any closer and they couldn't run away.

Wherever the jewelry touched on my skin it felt warm. I clasped the charm bracelet on my wrist and noticed that the butterflies seemed to be moving. Wings flying around my wrists. Sharon and Bradley were naked.

"Aargh—after all we've done to help teachers like you! We're the only ones who really care anymore!" Sharon screamed.

"We rented for under market value! You should have been grateful!" Bradley seconded his wife.

I heard a wind come up from the eucalyptus—one of the strongest I'd ever heard, deafening. It was the monarchs' wings. They were swarming, and all at once they descended upon the couple—a whole grove of butterflies—onto Sharon and Bradley's pink flesh. I backed away and left the butterflies to it. None of them touched me.

Madison was waiting for me at my car. "Thanks," she said. "CPS was totally useless, you know. You were far better."

"I'm not even sure what I did," I said.

"You weren't really willing to be bought."

"Oh yeah," I said.

"You don't have to move out, you know . . . and I kind of need a guardian now. At least on paper."

Madison had a point. The housing market still sucked.

"Okay," I said. "Just promise me not to lurk around the cottage so much?"

"I'll try not to lurk at all."

"We'll see how it goes," I said. The fog had rolled all the way in. I drove us home. My jewelry had cooled off. It felt just right on my skin.

54028 LOVE CREEK ROAD

BY JESSICA BREHENY

Bear Creek Road

I walk from my classroom at San Jose City College to the faculty lot, my coat draped over my elbow, tote bags full of papers that need grading slung on each shoulder, my hands gripping my dinner leftovers and an invitation to a union picnic. I don't have a hand free to pull up the worn waistband of my skirt, which keeps falling down lower and lower on my hips. Dim amber lights illuminate the fog that trolled in while I was teaching my evening class. My white car is a smudge in a far corner of the lot, now, at 9:45 p.m., nearly empty.

I cut diagonally toward my car and hear the voice of my student Frank Gonzalo yell, "Miss! Doctor—Profess—Miss Janet—" His arms pump back and forth as he walks toward me.

Frank has missed the last two weeks of class, and his essay is late. He's a tall man in his forties with a doughy face. He is wearing a shiny short-sleeved shirt printed with flames and skulls, and he smells of Bleu de Chanel. He brandishes a rolled-up piece of paper.

"My essay!" he says. He is out of breath. "Here, I'll help you to your car." He takes my leftover dinner and one of my bags and hands me his paper.

I pull up my sagging skirt as we walk. I have been teaching since 8 a.m., starting with two morning classes at Cabrillo College with its Monterey Bay views, then an afternoon class at West Valley College in Saratoga where every student drives a Benz—and, finally, ending my day at San Jose City College, flanked on one side by the freeway and on the other, an emergency room. I am hoping to get home to Ben Lomond with an hour or so of time to myself to shower and read before going to bed.

"You've missed a lot of classes," I say. After his last paper, I'd hoped he wasn't coming back.

"It's my stomach. I have a note from the doctor. He says I have an ulcer. I have to keep, you know . . ." he lowers his voice to a whisper, "going to the bathroom."

A motorcycle screeches past on Moorpark, the four-laner that divides the college from Highway 280.

"You can't miss any more classes, okay? Or I have to drop you." I fish my keys from the bottom of a bag of papers and open my car.

"I need to pass," he says. "It's—" again he whispers, "my probation officer. She wants me in school."

His first essay was about his probation officer who, he wrote, was "always in all of my business." She even stopped by his house sometimes unannounced. He ended his paper by saying he was in school to be an inspiration for his nieces and nephews and to earn a good living to "support his lady."

"You need to come to class to pass."

An airplane bellows overhead, descending toward the airport. Frank hovers so close I think for a moment that he might be planning to get into my car. He is very tall. I am eye level with a skull on his shirt, a flame burning in its mouth.

"No, no, you see, you don't understand." He gestures to his belly. "I'm not feeling very well. But I need to pass. And my group, you know, they still require a lot from me."

Frank's "group" is one of the major gangs—he hasn't told

me which one. His "group" was the topic of his second essay, a wandering mess describing his position of leadership. He is busy with a full-time job as a bouncer at a club downtown, and he said he was trying to get out of his gang but he still had to give them money and help run meetings. He made being in a gang sound boring, like serving on the board of a neighborhood association, except that in his conclusion he said he'd "hurt a lot of people."

I tuck my bags into the back of the car, next to stacks of papers from my other classes. Frank's cologne lingers.

"I need to go. It's late."

"Don't drop me," he says. "Read my paper. I was more descriptive, like you said we should be."

I settle into the driver's seat and close the door. He says something I don't hear. He smiles and waves as I pull away.

To avoid the late-night construction on Highway 17, I take the hairpin turns of Bear Creek Road home to Ben Lomond. I'm tailgated most of the way by a car so close behind me that all I can see are its brights. I can't make out the turnouts on the unlit road. Just after the Summit, the tailgater turns off, and I'm left alone in the darkness to muddle my way home. I pass a pile of car parts in a driveway. To my right are steep drops. It would be so easy to miscalculate a curve and drive right off.

When I get home, I turn on the space heater in my one-room rental and change out of the clothes I've been wearing since dawn. It's only October but starting to get cold already. I look through my half-fridge for something to eat. Last night's dinner and this morning's breakfast dishes are piled in the sink; a dirty pan sits on the hotplate with a crust of pasta starch and rancid oil shimmering under the overhead light.

My landlord's house is dark. He's gone away on a vision quest with his shaman and won't be back until Thanksgiving. I'm by myself on his six-acre property, up a long gravel driveway above Love Creek. The nearest neighbors are a mother and daughter who breed Burmese cats. The lights of their cabin are visible in the distance through the forest. I have never stayed for any length of time in a place this isolated before. The aloneness has taken on a heavy quality.

I make toast while I sort through the papers from the five classes I taught today. I unroll Frank's paper, conscientiously stapled on the right-hand corner, his name typed on the first page, and a centered title, "My Life." The assignment asked students to write about a single decision that changed their lives—not their entire lives—but he begins, "I was born in San Jose. The son of two parents a single mother and a father which was absent mostly." I am about to check on my toast when I see the word "bleeding" near the bottom of the first page.

> *The guy was part of another group and he was talking about stuff and in some faces of some individuals whom he shouldn't be. He got stabbed bad he was critical bleeding internal in his organs one guys kicked him hard in the stomach with its big boot now pray to god for mercy because stabbed him.*

I read the sentences again. They are set in a paragraph about the "group." The next paragraph is about going to church and how God can "transform everything unto something better." Smoke wafts from the toast that is now burning in the toaster oven. I unplug it and look again at the paper. On the last page, he writes in his conclusion, "I had done a lot of things in my life. I'm am changing who I am and what I'm going to be."

I look again at "pray to god for mercy because stabbed him." He has left out the personal pronoun that should precede the word, "stabbed," but obviously, someone was stabbed by someone. I make another piece of toast and get into bed.

The quiet in my house is so loud, I put earplugs in to muffle it. My bed is cold as dirt. I turn and face the wall and think, *Because stabbed him.* I see a young man, maybe twenty-five, the age of my daughter Zia, bleeding, too hurt to even beg for his life, being kicked. And Frank—maybe this stabber—standing there, watching. I will need to report the paper to someone in the morning. The campus police, perhaps the dean.

My alarm goes off at six. I'm exhausted and can't imagine teaching "citation" in my morning English 1A at Cabrillo. The more tired I am in class, the more my students tend to slip away from me, into their phones, or wherever it is they go in the space they stare at, when I call their names. It will be another day where I won't be able to hold their attention. I still owe them grades on papers they turned in two weeks ago.

Over coffee, I check my campus e-mail accounts. Two students who've been absent in my West Valley "Intro to Lit" write to tell me they were absent. An e-mail at Cabrillo alerts employees that e-mail will be down for maintenance. The dean at San Jose City College writes about an upcoming division meeting I can't attend. The SJCC union sends another reminder about the union picnic. And I have an e-mail from Frank: *Don't tell anyone what I wrote, okay. It is confidential. I just want to be descriptive.* And then, under that: *54028 Love Creek Road.* My address.

For a moment, I don't register what the e-mail means. A

spring of nausea bubbles up from my stomach and percolates into the tips of my fingers. Frank knows where I live. Frank is telling me he knows where I live.

I stand up and walk to the other side of the room, as far away from the computer as possible. I want to run outside, away from 54028 Love Creek Road, and I want to check the locks on the door and windows and stay inside 54028 Love Creek Road. I don't do either. I am having trouble breathing.

I turn on my phone to call the campus police but stop after the area code, my index finger hovering over the number. Frank knows where I live, and if he got in trouble, he could come to my house. And even if the police took his description of the stabbing seriously and arrested him, he could always send someone else.

I pace around the house. It's too small for my belongings, and I don't have time during the semesters to clean. Each week of the sixteen-week semester it gets messier. Now, eight weeks into the fall term, dishes sit on the floor under my futon with dried pasta noodles, the recycling bag overflows with yogurt containers and diet soda cans, a flow of dirty clothes erupts out of the open drawers of the small dresser I picked up at the Abbot's thrift shop in Felton. I stare at a pile of clothes on the floor. I imagine a bleeding man being kicked over and over again by a heavy boot.

My ex-husband Ben is a lawyer, and our daughter Zia is in law school. I want to call them both to ask advice. But I can't get them involved. The paper might be evidence of a crime, and they would want to report it to the police.

I'll just pass Frank. That's it. He doesn't want anything else from me. I'll tell him his descriptions are good in his paper and leave it at that. It's none of my business what he's done. It's between him and his conscience. Besides, he never actually says he stabbed anyone, just "because stabbed him." Without a subject in the sentence, anyone could have done the stabbing. I imagine the grammar lesson I could give with Frank's sentence—*I stabbed him / You stabbed him / They stabbed him / Frank stabbed him.*

I reply to his e-mail: *I got your note. I understand.* I add, *No problem,* in an effort to sound casual.

Frank is absent the next class. I spend the three hours of class time working on run-on sentences, fragments, and paragraph organization, while eyeing the classroom door for any sign of him. Jorge, a dance major with thick, beautifully shaped eyebrows, asks if you can begin a sentence with "and."

"Sometimes," I say unhelpfully.

Jorge writes down my answer. He is a diligent student.

Yesenia, who is studying to become an occupational therapist, asks if you can begin a sentence with "because."

"Of course." I catch the curt impatience in my voice, but I'm too nervous to speak gently. "You begin sentences with 'if,' don't you?"

Yesenia looks down at her desk. "I was just wondering. My other English teacher said you can't."

"I'm sorry; let me show you how to do it," I say. And then I try to demonstrate how to begin a sentence with "because," but my purple whiteboard pen gets fainter and fainter and disappears entirely at the end of: "Because the cat was hungr—"

"Sorry," I repeat, "I'll e-mail you a handout about all this."

My students look back at me, blank and disbelieving.

At the end of class, I collect a new batch of papers and add it to the file folder bulging with last week's papers.

On the way home, my steering wheel starts making a moaning sound, punctuated by a sharp squeal on tight turns.

The steering gets less and less responsive as I make my way past the stoplight by the Ben Lomond Market and onto Love Creek Road. My headlights catch the red memorial toy box at the mudslide where those little boys died in the 1980s and were never found. As I pass the memorial, I see that someone has arranged a group of dolls in a semicircle as though they are holding a little class. I leave the paved part of Love Creek behind and rumble along the narrow stream canyon, my steering column bleating and my car bottoming out on the dirt road.

The house smells of old milk. I put half a burrito I saved from lunch in the microwave and check e-mail. In the four hours since I last looked, I've received forty-three new messages, mostly about campus events and items—a flash drive, a stack of papers, a jacket—left behind by faculty in classrooms. I have the usual absent-student-excuse e-mails, and then I see a subject line, *Probation Check—Important.*

It's Frank's probation officer, a woman named Lindsey Johnson, doing a "routine evaluation." She asks me to answer a few questions:

- *Has* Mr. *Gonzalo missed any classes? If so, how many? (Please provide dates.)*
- *How would you characterize* Mr. *Gonzalo's behavior as a student in your class?*
- *Finally, do you have any concerns about* Mr. *Gonzalo that you would like to share?*

I am overcome, for a moment, by a sense of relief, as though I had been in a dark room but found, finally, a rectangle of light around an unlocked door. I'll unburden myself to Lindsey Johnson, a sensible-sounding person—a professional—who will know exactly what to do about Frank's paper, about the pressure he's putting on me to pass him, about his intimidating e-mail.

But then I remember Frank's gang. I can't tell Ms. Johnson the truth.

I click out of her e-mail and scan my inbox. I have an e-mail from Frank. *Dear Miss Janet, I need to talk to your office hours ASAP that is about some new issues.*

The smell of my microwaved burrito turns sickeningly sweet. I throw it away and stare into the garbage. My mind scurries through a pile of thoughts—a man being stabbed, Frank e-mailing me, Frank coming to my office hours, what it would feel like to be stabbed in the stomach. I think the word "spleen" and feel like throwing up. I wonder if it would hurt, or would it just feel wrong and . . . final?

Too agitated to go to bed, I start cleaning the house. Things keep slipping more and more out of my control. If I could just get organized, I'd be able to think clearly. I do the dishes. I try to take out the garbage, but the bag rips when I remove it from the bin, leaving a pile of to-go containers and toilet paper rolls and coffee grounds on the kitchen floor. I can't find another bag to collect the spilled garbage, so I shovel it into small plastic grocery bags which drip as I carry them to the bin outside. I mop up the drips with my last few paper towels and a handful of bunched-up toilet paper and give up on cleaning. I sit down to grade papers.

I wake up with my neck in knots. I'd drifted off sometime in the early morning with the lights on. Essays are scattered around my chair. A few are graded. I hear songbirds outside and a squirrel chirruping some argument. Through the window, cobwebs of fog are dissipating around the redwood branches. The sun is already up.

I check my phone. It's 8:48, and I've missed my Cabrillo class. I call the division office and tell Ana Ling, the division assistant, that my car broke down on the way to campus. I hate lying to Ana, and her friendly voice over the phone makes me want to cry. For the first time this semester, I wish I were in my class teaching that day's lesson on proper use of citations.

I take a long shower and make coffee before turning on my computer. In my e-mail is another message from Frank. This one says: *Please call when you can earliest convenience.* He includes his phone number.

I call. He answers with an out-of-breath, "Hello."

"Hi, Frank." I try to sound friendly and casual. "What's going on?"

A low bass thumps in the background. A dog yaps. "Be quiet," he calls out to—I assume—the dog, which keeps barking. "It's just . . . so, I need some help," he says. "You know how hard I'm trying to better myself, you know, for my family, and for being an example and everything, and, you know, getting out of the group and getting on with my life. I want to be a citizen, productive—so what I'm saying is, my probation officer, Ms. Johnson, she's always on my ass—my butt, if you can excuse my language—and I need you to just tell her I haven't missed any classes because of all of my medical emergencies—she doesn't buy it even though I have doctors' notes."

I stare at the papers on the floor. "So you want me to lie to your probation officer?"

"Well, it's not really lying because I *have* been in class when I'm not having a medical emergency. It's just my stomach, I need to go to the bathroom with that, and I can't come to school. But she doesn't believe me. She thinks I'm off doing something else. And I have to account for my time with her because of the level of supervisory situation I'm under with the probation office . . . Are you on campus right now? I can meet you to talk about this furthermore."

I tell him about my car.

"Oh, yeah, I know, I saw you had that old Honda—Accord, 1992? I figured it wouldn't last much longer. You need a new car? I can find you one, I know a guy."

"No, I don't need a new car. It's just the steering."

"Okay, you know, I have a buddy over on your side of the hill in Live Oak. He has a lot of cars he fixes up." The dog erupts again into a scream of barks. "Baby," he calls out to someone, "can you get her to shut up? Okay, sorry about that. So, I just need you to tell her the truth, tell her I've been a good student. Just don't tell her I was absent."

I leave my car with my mechanic in Felton and walk to the White Raven café. I feel dizzy and cold. My neck aches from sleeping in my chair and my fingers tingle. I wrap my sweater tightly around my chest. This is the first time all semester I've had time on my hands—time to kill. I laugh, because it really is a funny phrase.

I get a text from Frank: "Please remember what we discussed in this morning. And please keep my paper contents conference." I assume he means "confidential."

I pass a group of teenage girls huddling over a phone in front of Redwood Pizza. They're wearing knotted hemp jewelry. One looks up and smiles. I see how I must look to her, so old, with my long gray hair wisping around my head, my baggy clothes. She has no idea that she'll be old one day too, if she's lucky. Like everyone else over fifty, I have been lucky.

I order a bagel and tea at the café. When I return to my table, I have a voice mail from Frank.

"*Hi, Professor Janet—*" I can hear the dog again in the background. It sounds like a poodle or a Maltese. "*I was wondering if you could forward me the e-mail you send to Johnson so I can make sure she tells the truth about it. Sometimes she lies about—Hey, can you shut that dog up?*" His voice is sharp and piercing.

I hear a woman mumble something softly, then a painful yelp.

"*Yeah, sorry about that, so Johnson sometimes lies about me to her supervisors about what I'm doing, and I don't want to get in any more trouble.*" The barking turns into a whining with a pitiful rhythm to it, like the dog is trying to sound out words.

The White Raven is playing Peruvian pipe music, and the place smells like incense and French roast. The contrast between the world I'm sitting in and the one I just heard through my phone makes both seem unreal.

I take out my laptop and compose an e-mail to Lindsey Johnson:

Dear Ms. Johnson:

Frank Gonzalo is a student in my English 280 (Basic Writing Development) class. He is in good standing. Below are answers to your questions.

- *Has Mr. Gonzalo missed any classes?*

No, Mr. Gonzalo has perfect attendance.

- *How would you characterize Mr. Gonzalo's behavior as a student in your class?*

Mr. Gonzalo is a good student.

- *Finally, do you have any concerns about Mr. Gonzalo*

that you would like to share?
I have no concerns about Mr. *Gonzalo.*

I send the e-mail, then copy and paste it into a separate message to Frank. I don't want to risk forwarding it and having him accidentally reply to Lindsey Johnson. I check my sent mail to make sure both went out. Relief. This is not my problem. Frank's story is not my story. I have my own life to deal with.

I call my mechanic for an update. The repair will cost $360. I'm down this semester to seven classes from my usual eight, and my credit card balance has crept above $4,000, close to my limit. I start calculating the rest of the month. I get paid again in six days, and I should still have a couple of hundred left in credit after I pay for my car. And there's a little cushion left in checking if I pay my PG&E late.

I eat my bagel and order a salad. For the first time today, I'm famished. Before I leave the café, I get a cookie.

On the way home from my afternoon class, I check the mailbox at the base of our driveway. There's an overdue notice for my Visa, though I'm sure I paid it online. There is also a white envelope with my address lettered in gold. Inside is a Safeway gift card for $200 and a note that says, "Thank you for you're help. Sincerely, Frank."

I can't take a gift in exchange for lying to Frank's probation officer. I remember my diminishing checking account balance and think about what I could buy at Safeway with $200—some good cheese, wine, salmon. It dawns on me how humiliating it is to be bribed by a gang member with food.

I'm supposed to catch up on grading, but I waste time reading the *Huffington Post*'s "Wellness" section, which has two articles on lifestyle choices that reduce stress. Dogs and exercise, and exercising with dogs, are supposed to be helpful. I think about the squeal of the dog crying in the background during Frank's last voice mail. I click out of the article.

Before I settle in to grade, I check e-mail. Lindsey Johnson has written to thank me for the information I sent her about Frank and to ask to set up a phone appointment for "a few follow-up questions."

I make a quick decision to delete the e-mail. I did what I needed to do. I sent the e-mail Frank wanted me to send. I didn't tell anyone about his paper. I don't need to do anything else. Before I can change my mind, I go into my deleted mail and delete Lindsey Johnson's e-mail one final time. I then delete her original e-mail, my reply, and all of the e-mails from Frank.

Monday is Halloween. I wake up long before dawn. I sip coffee and browse the news, which is peppered with local ghost stories. There is one about Love Creek Road, but it's just a reminder of the mudslide tragedy, not a ghost story.

In the *San Jose Mercury News* "Crime & Courts" section is the headline, "Gang Leader Arrested for Probation Violation, Weapons."

> *Local gang leader Frank Gonzalo was arrested on November 6 at his home in the Blossom Hill neighborhood of San Jose. Deputies searched Mr. Gonzalo's home after his probation officer reported a number of violations. Mr. Gonzalo was found to possess drug-manufacturing paraphernalia and illegal weapons, including two Daewoo Telecom K7s and a sawed-off shotgun. He was charged and released on bail pending a preliminary hearing.*

Frank's mugshot looms over the article. His hair looks greasy. His round face wears a slight smile.

I close the computer and turn on my phone. I have a text Zia sent to me and Ben. She made it to the top percentile in her torts exam. I text back, "Congratulations," then pace around my house. I could call Frank to tell him I saw the article, offer sympathy, let him know I tried my best to help him with his probation officer. Or I could contact Lindsey Johnson and confess my lie. But I decide it's better to act like nothing has happened. Lindsey Johnson can't help me with Frank. No one can.

I watch the sky lighten outside. I figure Frank thinks I did everything I could to protect him from Lindsey's suspicions. He has no way of knowing that I ignored her request to ask me more questions.

My classes are sparsely attended. Some of my students show up in full Halloween costumes, a few wear fuzzy ears, funny hats, face paint. Colleagues at all three schools joke and gossip by the mailboxes, but I avoid them.

A few of my evening students at SJCC are excited to talk about an essay I had them read about why so many people believe in ghosts. The conversation digresses when Yesenia, wearing fuchsia wings and twirling a glittery wand, tells the class about an episode of *Ghost Hunters* where they record a voice saying, "They killed us all."

"It's not a belief," Yesenia says. "It's a real event."

Jorge, whose first essay attempted to prove the existence of God, tells Elena that ghosts aren't in the Bible and are against God.

George, a cigar and science-fiction enthusiast, whispers, "They killed us all," and laughs.

One of my students, Neda, a young Baha'i woman from Iran, says, "It's why there is freedom of religion. Yesenia can believe in ghosts if she wishes."

"Yes," I say, "I believe that's true."

Tatiana, who has slept through most of the class, lifts up her black-hooded head and asks if I've given back the papers yet.

"No," I say. "Sorry."

She rolls her mascara'd eyes. "When will we get our papers back?"

"Soon," I say.

The moon is a dim shard over the parking lot. A faculty member dressed as Willy Wonka walks past me and waves with his top hat before getting into his car and driving away. Mine is the last car in the lot. I hurry toward it, and another car pulls in and drives slowly toward me.

"Miss! Miss Janet!" It's Frank calling from an open window. I can see his thick hand waving.

I pretend I don't notice him and toss my books, my papers, and myself into the car. My tires squeal as I pull out of my parking spot and then make a sharp turn onto Moorpark. I take the freeway entrance so fast I feel the car pull to the left. I slow down and look in the rearview mirror. All I see is the usual anonymous flow of white lights behind me.

My GPS insists I take Bear Creek Road, so I exit Highway 17 and begin the winding journey up the mountain. A tailgater appears behind my car with its high beams blinding me. *Frank's following me*, I think. But I remind myself that I am usually tailgated on Bear Creek. The driver will probably turn off any minute.

The tailgating continues. I speed up. The driver behind

me speeds up. I see a small road up ahead, pull out onto it. The tailgater speeds past me. I start on my way once more.

In a few minutes, I'm being tailgated again. The driver slows down and brakes, then careens forward toward me, off again, then forward. I look straight ahead to ignore the brights that keep rushing my bumper. The driver stays behind me till Boulder Creek when I pull over at the New Leaf Market parking lot and let the car pass.

I make my way down Highway 9 through Boulder Creek. Joe's Bar and the brewery are open, but no one is lingering out in front.

As I pass the shuttered Brookdale Lodge, a black car pulls out behind me. It stays close, honks, backs off, gets close again, flashes its lights. I accelerate and swerve on a curve, nearly hitting a car in the narrow oncoming lane.

I speed faster. My steering wheel makes a whimpering sound on the curves, the sound of Frank's yelping dog.

I turn left onto Love Creek Road. The car stays behind me. I skid past the toy box at the slide. The dolls are scattered in the road. I drive over them. One gets caught up in the wheel and bleats sickeningly.

My phone buzzes again, startles me, and my foot slips off the accelerator. I am losing control, but I'm afraid to slow down.

I'll drive to my nearest neighbors, the Burmese cat breeders. I often see their lights on late. If that car keeps following, I'll yell for them to call the police.

Love Creek forks uphill to the right where the pavement ends. My phone buzzes, and I reach for it. A text from Frank. I see the word "probation," and my car fishtails. The back wheels leave the road. The car pauses before falling, then tumbles upside down and onto its side. It happens slowly and—somehow—carefully.

My headlights shine into the oak brush. There is blood in my hair. I'm covered in student papers that were in the passenger seat. I unbuckle my seat belt and try to sit up. Something is holding me down. I grab the steering wheel and try to pull myself up toward the passenger-side door above me, but I don't have any strength.

A shadow moves outside. It stops. I say, "Help." My voice is barely audible.

The shadow gets closer. I hear a man say something, and then I realize the radio has turned on. Calm, low voices are murmuring on NPR, though another station is coming in too, with music and static over the voices. My phone buzzes. I tell my hand to reach for it. My hand doesn't move.

I hear, "Miss! Miss!" The shadow? Or is it just the radio?

I want to see who is standing there on the other side of my cracked windshield. I can't see anything. The headlights are out. My phone buzzes and buzzes like a trapped insect skimming a windowpane.

"Miss? Miss?"

POSSESSED

BY NAOMI HIRAHARA

Mount Hermon

It was cabin time: sharing and praying. Karen Abe was sitting on the floor when one of the girls got up from the circle and stared out from the wire netting of their open-air windows.

"I think something's going on in Twenty-One," she said.

A chill went up Karen's spine. Lisa Tanizaki was in Cabin Twenty-One. They were best friends—or at least that's what other people at Paradise Park Camp would say. They lived three blocks away from each other in the San Fernando Valley, and had always gone to New Hope Church. Every summer they went to a Japanese American Christian camp here in the Santa Cruz Mountains.

Karen was assigned Cabin Twenty with Rachel Kubota from their same school, plus four girls from Monterey Park, whom she referred to as the Lukewarms—and their cabin leader, Wendy Kanegoe, a sophomore at Cal State LA.

Wendy tried to call the Lukewarm back to the circle and focus. But then she also rose and looked outside. The rest of them followed, Karen at the rear, leaving their Living Bibles and the tan-covered four-scripture law tracks on the ratty carpet.

Every light was on in cabin Twenty-One. It glowed yellow with a tinge of algae green. Outside, flashlights from spectators blazed dots in the darkness. Karen inhaled the grapefruit burn of Douglas fir and smoke from the nearby campfire.

"Some girl's getting exorcized," a chubby boy in shorts called out from the dirt pathway. He was new to camp. Karen had heard that he had just accepted Christ at group worship last night.

The Lukewarms squealed and gathered tightly as if that would keep them safe.

The boy waited a few minutes as if he expected them to join him. When no one did, he disappeared across the way to see what was happening.

"The Catholics call it exorcism, but Christians don't," Rachel said. Rachel's father was the minister of New Hope. Lisa's grandparents had been in the same World War II camp as Rachel's.

"If you're born again, you can't be demon-possessed," Wendy assured them. "The Devil has no hold on you." Wendy, always the good cabin leader, was steady and calm.

"But you can be oppressed," Rachel said.

"What does that mean?" a Lukewarm asked.

"That a demon can attach to you," Karen said. "They can't take over, but they can still bother you. They can enter through a weak spot."

Rachel squinted her eyes as if she was reassessing Karen's level of spirituality.

Before Karen could say anything more, the chubby boy in shorts was back standing in front of their cabin. She began to realize that he had a crush on someone in the cabin.

"It's Lisa Tanizaki," the boy called out. "They want Karen Abe to come to Cabin Twenty-One."

"Why?" Karen tightened her fists. The boy said her name as if he knew her. He didn't know her.

"You're her best friend, right? They think you can help."

The Lukewarms made room for Karen to get through the door.

"I'll go with you," Wendy said, pressing lightly on her elbow.

"And I'll take care of things here," Rachel volunteered.

What a kiss-ass, Karen thought.

Wendy wrapped Karen's hand around the crook of her arm and together they walked down the stairs of the cabin, the screen door flapping behind them.

As they crossed the dirt walkway, something crackled and then landed on her white long-sleeve T-shirt. "Shit! What is that?" Karen felt here throat closing up. She hated bugs, especially spiders and cockroaches. But this one was worse because she didn't know what it was.

The boy pointed his flashlight at Karen's T-shirt. It was about an inch long with six legs and white stripes on its back. "Oh, it's a Mount Hermon june beetle. I think they're endangered."

Of course this nerd would know about bugs. "God, get it off me!"

The boy started slapping at her body, even grazing her breasts in their A-cup bra. Karen pushed him away.

"It's okay." Wendy put herself between the two campers. "They don't bite."

They examined Karen's T-shirt with Wendy's soft flashlight. No bug.

"What is wrong with you?" Karen frowned at the new boy. His bare legs were caked with a layer of pink.

"It's just calamine lotion. Got into some poison oak today."

You better not've given me your poison oak, Karen thought to herself. She silently swore at him, noticing Wendy giving her a sideways glance.

The three of them continued walking through the crowd

of high school campers, most of them in college sweatshirts, their faces frozen. Someone murmured that the local hospital had been called and an ambulance was on its way.

They were greeted at the door of Cabin Twenty by its cabin leader, a skinny young woman with her hair tied back in a ponytail. Karen recognized her as Wendy's good friend Tammy. The two leaders awkwardly embraced, their stiff, thin bodies knocking together.

Karen continued through the porch to the bunkbeds. The room smelled of barf, and Karen stifled a retch.

There were grown-ups surrounding the far bunkbeds. Camp admins, all men in polo shirts embroidered with the camp Christian cross ablaze above a redwood tree, were absorbed in their walkie-talkies. As they quickly huddled for an impromptu meeting, the view to the bottom bunk opened. From a distance, Lisa Tanizaki looked like sleeping beauty in her baby-blue UCLA T-shirt.

But as Karen got closer, she saw there were streaks of vomit on Lisa's cheek. Her eyes were half-open, as if she was watching everything transpire in front of her.

"No, young lady, you'll have to stay in the other room," a walkie-talkie man stopped Karen. She looked down and saw a dark circle on the rug.

"I'm her friend. Karen Abe. I was told to come here."

"We'll get you when we need you," he said, practically pushing her back out onto the enclosed porch.

"Lisa was acting weird, like she was high," a voice said from a corner of the porch.

In the dark, Karen spied someone else from New Hope: Jacob Conner. He was *hapa*, half and half. In certain contexts he looked more white, in others, Japanese. Here he seemed otherworldly. An elf. An angel.

"What are you doing here?"

Jacob paused before answering. "Lisa forgot her jacket in the hall after worship. I was here to bring it back."

That's a lame excuse. Weren't you here to spy on her, make sure she kept her mouth shut?

Cabin Twenty-One leader Tammy's back was turned toward them, but Karen could still overhear her talking to Wendy: "Her body got all stiff like a board. She was grinding her teeth."

"Sounds like *The Exorcist* to me," the poison-oak boy said to Jacob and Karen. "You know, there are Satan worshippers up here in these mountains."

The back of Karen's neck tingled like when a tine of a fork accidentally hit the middle of a cavity.

"Shut up, Carl," said Jacob. He was acting tough, but Karen saw right through it.

"No, really. I even saw something when I was hiking around Mount Hermon."

Karen's body lurched. So this stupid boy Carl was in Mount Hermon today too; did he see anything?

Carl couldn't shut up: "I went to this clearing and there was a pentagram carved into the rock floor. And stones piled up at each point of the star."

"That doesn't mean anything," Jacob scoffed, as if he were trying to convince himself.

"And this dark mark in the middle of it. I think it was blood."

He's so full of shit. Karen turned her back and gestured for Jacob to do the same.

Rachel walked up onto the porch in a Stanford beanie. "Is Lisa still alive?"

What a question to ask, thought Karen. "Of course, she's alive. An ambulance is coming for her."

"Since I've known Lisa the longest, I thought you might want my input," Rachel said, as if she was making some kind of public announcement.

What a bitch, Karen thought. Just because their grandparents were interned together, that didn't mean anything.

The two camp leaders turned to listen. "Whatever information you may have, Rachel, please share," Wendy said.

"If you ask me, Lisa hasn't been herself. At our last youth praise meeting, Lisa usually helps lead worship, but she said that she couldn't do it. She sat in the back of the church. I mean, just sat there. She didn't sing or anything."

Karen remembered that night. She was, in fact, relieved that Lisa wasn't up there in front, hogging the spotlight. Jacob had sat right next to Karen in the third row of the padded pews, for the very first time. The side of his thigh grazed hers. Karen was so self-conscious, she only mouthed the lyrics to the praise songs.

"Maybe Lisa was just feeling sick?" Wendy said.

"But then she dropped out of the worship team for camp too. Something was definitely going on with her." Rachel took a deep breath. "Maybe Karen would know. Because the two of them took a walk to Mount Hermon during our afternoon free time today."

Jacob's head jerked up. "You spent time with her today, Karen?" His voice sounded strange. On edge.

"How did Lisa seem?" Wendy asked.

"The same. Like always." Karen tried to keep her voice light and normal.

"I mean, I hate to ask something like this, but was she taking any kind of drug?" Tammy stuffed her hands in her front sweatshirt pouch.

"Absolutely not," said Rachel.

As if she would know, thought Karen.

Tammy kept her gaze on Karen. "Because it would really help Lisa now."

"No, no drugs," said Karen. "As far as I know."

"Maybe a problem at home?"

"No," Miss Know-It-All Rachel said.

"I don't know her that well," Tammy said, "but she's been super quiet. She asked me to pray for her tonight, but she wouldn't tell me for what. We even got cooking oil from the kitchen to anoint her. And that's when all the trouble happened."

Tammy took her hands out of her pockets and started to cry. Wendy put an arm around her. The campers hung their heads. They didn't know what to do with a college person's tears.

Karen took a deep breath. She didn't know how the words reached her lips, but they dripped out like fresh honey: "You know, I think we saw that pentagram up there. Lisa was checking it out. She was really fascinated by it." She now had the attention of everyone on the porch.

"You mean you think that Lisa is demon-possessed?" the chubby boy said, almost ecstatic.

"It's just that Lisa really started acting weird after she saw that pentagram. That's all I'm saying."

An ambulance siren pierced the hum of the insects outside. It stopped and restarted. Help had arrived.

Lisa hadn't been herself, all right. Karen knew it. But she took full advantage of it.

In fact, in the caravan from the Valley to Santa Cruz, Lisa volunteered to ride in a van with one of the parents and the camp supplies. Why would she do that? Karen got a backseat with Jacob and his best friend in the second car. It was pure heaven. She got to be with Jacob for six uninterrupted hours and that was all that mattered.

Jacob's friend held his pillow to his chest and immediately fell asleep. Most of the drive, Jacob and Karen took turns trying to throw Doritos in the boy's open mouth. It was hilarious.

After hours on the road, Karen felt that the old Karen was fading away. Wasn't that even in the Bible? *New wine in new wineskins*. Her old wineskin—the less popular one, less smart, less pretty—was blowing away. New Karen had everything going on.

When they arrived at camp, Karen was relieved to see that she wouldn't be sharing a cabin with Lisa. More distance, more independence. More time alone with Jacob, maybe.

Lisa cornered her in the dining room. Karen was still holding her breakfast tray. "Go for a walk with me during free time." It was a command, not a request.

That was the last thing Karen wanted to do, but Lisa had blindsided her so early in the morning. All Karen could do was nod her head yes.

On their walk, Lisa took the lead, like always. She was smaller than Karen, more nimble. She jumped up and down from rocks with ease. *A damn billy goat*.

Finally, when they reached a clearing, Lisa stopped dead in her tracks and turned around. "I need to tell you something."

Karen felt unsteady. Ordinarily she would relish hearing some stain, some sin in Lisa's life, whether it was true or not. To hear it directly from Lisa herself, though. There was no pleasure in that.

"I was raped by Jacob Connor."

Karen's first inclination was to laugh. What a stupid practical joke. But then Lisa didn't laugh back.

"When?" She was barely able to speak.

"After the car wash fundraiser. A month ago."

Somehow that didn't surprise Karen. She noticed how chummy-chummy they'd been. Goofing around and spraying water on each other. Karen was burning with jealousy and left the fundraiser early. "Who knows about this?" she asked.

Lisa started crying. She never cried. There were two dark smudges on her forehead like the ones on the Japanese empress doll in Karen's grandmother's house.

"Just you, now. And Jesus."

This is the biggest sack of horseshit ever.

"I spoke to Jesus. Really, I did. During this morning's quiet time." A breeze moved up the mountain, whipping Lisa's black silk hair over her face. "He told me that I need to talk to my parents; that He would take care of me through all of this."

"What are you going to tell them?"

"Everything. I have to."

"You're not going to mention Jacob, right?"

"He did it to me. He raped me."

"But you'll ruin his life."

"I don't give a fuck about that. He raped me."

Lisa never swore either. And to hear the F-word from her mouth in the quietness of Mount Hermon jarred Karen. "C'mon, he didn't *rape*-rape you. How can you be so awful?"

"Yes, he did. I didn't want to do it. I had never done it before. I told him to stop."

Karen couldn't stand it. She couldn't imagine that Jacob had such insatiable passion for Lisa. "You're the one who kept throwing yourself at him that day. I saw you at the car wash fundraiser. I remember. You were in your cutoffs. You weren't even wearing any underwear."

"What, are you saying that it was my fault?"

"I'm not sure. I would've known."

It was Lisa's turn to look incredulous. "And why's that? Because of your crush on Jacob? Everyone knows you like him, Karen. I wanted to tell you first because I didn't want you to hear this from someone else. You know, he even makes fun of you liking him."

Karen's anger flip-flopped into shame. No, that couldn't be true. Beautiful Jacob with his lean swimmer's body, his long hair tinged light brown from sun. Jacob, who Karen imagined kissing every single night.

"You are such a bitch!" Karen saw the pile of stones in the clearing, calling her to action like David facing Goliath. She scooped one up and threw it as hard as she could at Lisa's face. Lisa expertly moved to avoid contact, but her shoes hit some gravel and she lost her footing. She fell headfirst against a boulder.

And there she lay.

For a second, Karen was frozen in place. She looked around her. Were there any witnesses? A crow called out to another crow in the tall pine trees. Were they reporting what happened? And then there was God. He had seen it.

"Jesus, please," she prayed. "Let her be okay."

She kneeled over her friend's body. "Lisa." She could barely say her name. What if she killed her? And then again, louder, "Lisa?" Air was still coming out of her friend's delicate nostrils.

She gently lifted Lisa's head, her hair streaming behind like a black veil, and surprisingly there was no blood, no evidence of the collision with the ground. Lisa's eyes were closed and there was a tiny bit of foam at the corner of her mouth. Karen wished she had brought her canteen.

"Dear Lord, please. I'll do anything. I'll be a better person. Just heal Lisa."

A crow cawed again, and miraculously, Lisa's eyes fluttered open.

"Oh my gosh, are you okay?"

"What happened?" Lisa squinted and frowned, pulling herself up by her elbows.

No, can it really be true? Has she forgotten?

"You slipped and hit your head. Maybe it's the altitude. I think it got to you." She helped Lisa to her feet.

"That was really weird."

"What do you remember?"

"Just that we were walking up the hill." Lisa's eyes got big. "I wanted to tell you something."

"Not now," Karen said. "Later tonight, okay?"

Lisa reluctantly nodded, and although a bit wobbly, she took the lead again. Walking behind her, Karen said silently: *Thank you, Jesus*.

"Let's pray for Lisa," Wendy instructed, as the paramedics strapped Lisa onto a gurney.

The Lukewarms had arrived and were sobbing, their noses red like cartoon bunnies. They all smelled death in the room.

All arms were extended toward Lisa's body. Karen didn't want to. Stupid poison-oak boy, with his pink legs, stood right next to her. Jacob on her other side. His whole body, especially his hands, seemed to be shaking, but no one else noticed.

What was that on her sleeve? The striped beetle again. Karen wanted to scream, but she didn't. Instead she swallowed her cry, closed her eyes, and extended her arm.

PART II

THE LINEUP

WHEELS OF JUSTICE

BY JON BAILIFF

STEAMER LANE

The wheels of justice grind exceedingly fine,
like the waves of the ocean grind the sands of time.

I'm not the kind of guy who goes around with wild, violent fantasies, like I got some shooter game playin' in my head. So this or that guy's got some beef. So what? I'm not out for confrontation.

But I've doled out plenty. 'Cause what are you gonna do? Nothing? Fuck that!

I'll be the first to admit I've had some issues here and there. Major issues with the Santa Cruz PD. Always fuckin' with me. Like true-blue dickheads—like *I'm* the loser! But that ain't me. Drunk and disorderly? Okay. Domestics? Maybe. But that assault charge? Total fuckin' bullshit. It's called self-defense!

I don't look for trouble. But if some goddamn faggot, pardon my lack of political correctness, and fuck you very much, tries some shit out on me? Well, okay. Trouble's in trouble now!

I surf Steamer Lane. It's my home break—not yours. You're not Westside Santa Cruz born and raised. Steamer's is not for you. Go back to the Valley, or Cowell's, or even Pacifica. We will not be tolerating any university inclusivity-diversity bullshit from outsider kooks, queers, and mud people. Stay behind the railing and watch.

So yeah, that incident at Steamer's. Don't act like you don't know. Everybody saw that shit. It was all over the *Sentinel*. Of course, those assholes got it fuckin' backward, 'cause I was totally in the right. You know I was.

Little-known fact: West Cliff, Lighthouse Field, even the Lane—after dark, it's a major gay cruise. Oh yeah. Don't believe me, fuckhead? Check Grindr. There's so much fuckin' action. You'll be gettin' it wet in MINUTES. It's truly disgusting.

So it's bar time and I'm all fucked up. I'm in the Carp lot, leaning on the railing, chilling, just checking out the swell for a dawn patrol. Minding my own business. This fat fuck comes wiggling up and sort of leans against the rail—and I know what's going down. I know before he even opens his pussy mouth. I am instantly pissed! Just instantly mortally pissed! I say, "Eat shit, you fuckin' faggot!"

I let him know who's the boss out here—which is what you have to do in such situations. And yeah, maybe I did get a little *too* "defensive" on the guy. Grindr-ass motherfucker. He had it coming.

Anyway. The cops somehow manage to come to the conclusion that it was all me! I was amazed that guy could even ID me. It was pitch black. So I told the judge how it went down. That I was in fear for my life, what with how dangerous it is out there, so late at night.

He's like, "What were you doing out there at that hour?"

"Just doing a surf check, Your Honor."

But him and the DA didn't get it. It was that ugly-ass faggot that *made* me go off! I had no choice. Am I right? You know I am.

They said I went over the line, as far as self-defense.

I was like, *Fuck him! He deserves worse!*

It was touch and go, they said. "The guy almost didn't make it. But he's gonna be okay."

I thought, *Oh really? Too bad. I shoulda put that faggot in a wheelchair.*

Thought it. But I'm not stupid. I didn't say it. Queers can be cops, or even judges now. They're everywhere.

My trial was a joke. No one was on my side. No one but Ashley the bitch, my ex-GF. The DA wanted assault with intent. But I got away with aggravated assault, due to my saying I was "feeling very threatened, Your Honor, and it was not my intention." Fuck 'em.

I'll tell you this for free—County is a bitch. Nothing to do. *Nada*. And what is doubly fucked-up is that, when the surf is going off, you can hear it in the lockup, late at night, when all the losers are asleep and it's halfway quiet. Those big breakers out there goin' *boom . . . boom . . . boom.* Makes me feel so far down.

Did I mention there wasn't shit-all to do in lockup? I tried not to go nuts. Some guys seem like they can just read through anything—sit there, nose in a book, all day, all night. Sometimes I kinda wish I'd given school a little more effort, back in the day. Looking back on it, I just . . . couldn't. Couldn't concentrate, you know? Couldn't focus my mind. Even if I tried to really put something in my head, I'd hear my old man yelling. If I even looked at him wrong—*bam*! He'd start kickin' the crap out of me. Yeah, but that motherfucker sure didn't like being reminded of the shit he *did* like me for. He took what he wanted. Fucked for life. That's me.

What I hate about County is dudes surrounding me, all day, every day, with their endless bullshit. Couldn't sleep with all those brown faggoty motherfuckers waiting for me to let my guard down. But I wasn't looking for trouble. I got twenty-four to thirty-six months. And with time off for being a good little bitch. I was out in thirty.

* * *

Yeah! I'm out, I'm headed to the Lane. Gotta get back in the lineup. It's all I've been dreamin' of for two and a half years. So fuckin' stoked.

But I get no priority. The boys are about as welcoming as a twenty-mile-per-hour on-shore south. What the fuck? Everybody lookin' at me all stink-eye. They don't know shit!

Plus—it seems like I was gone for all of five minutes, and my home break's all crowded with geezers, kooks, hippies, and bunches of chicks and faggots from up on the hill. UCSC cunts and their girlfriends think they have some kind of Pussy College hall pass to surf here. Like the Lane is just for *anyone* now.

Well, it fuckin' isn't. The Lane is not for you. Not for your girlfriend, not your boyfriend, not any of your friends. No way will this stand. No fuckin' way!

This scene has me so fuckin' aggro. I'm too amped—just sitting in my truck tryin' not to go all school-shooter on these assholes. When I'm like this, crank can sometimes calm me down. Hit that *pipa*, burn a blunt, get some brews flowing, and *whoa!* I am better, motherfucker! Screw that punk-ass parole officer. I'm out and I'll do what I please.

Oh yeah. That's better. That's more like it. Now I'm feelin' it. My dick is hard as a rock! I'm thinkin' about Ashley and how she gives me head exactly when I say to. And that's fine, as far as it goes. But I keep seein' that little *chica maricon* in County the whole time. Pumpin' like a big fresh south. Goddamn! I'm so ripped!

I snap out of it and—fuck me—outside is going off. The inside is loaded with kooks. The boys are all over first peak. Schracking! Monster sets from a huge south are rolling through, with super-long lulls and a takeoff so narrow you gotta be the earliest, charging-est, deep-throatin'-est motherfucker, or fuck you, you are not getting' anything. This shit is gnarly. *This shit is mine!*

Don't remember suiting up. Don't even remember paddling out. Just seems like I'm suddenly in the thick of it, raging. Yellin' at every kook I see. "Fuck you, faggots!" Paddling in front of all the Barneys and thinkin', *Make room for me, boys; priority is mine!*

But goddamn! I'm too amped! Pulse pounding. Can't chill. Timing is off. The extra fifty I gained in jail, on top of my crank-'n'-beer cocktail, is messing me up, slowin' me down.

"My wave, fuckhead! My wave!" But my fat-fucker pop-up is too slow—too late. No way am I gonna make it. I can feel my extra body weight dragging me down as I pearl my board and eat it, right into the bowl. Then I get sucked back up the face, feel the sick moment of weightlessness, then—over the falls, right onto the deck of my best board. Under water screaming, "FUCK!" It's a major hold-down. Hitting bottom. Rag-dolled to shit. Donuts all the way.

I finally pop up on the inside, puking seawater. I paddle the bottom half of my board back in and smash the shit out of it on the railing. All eyes on me in the lot, as the assholes bear witness to the sketchiest, gnarliest, most-fucked sesh of all time. I go to get in my truck and—of course—the keys are still in the ignition. The door is locked.

My fist goes right through the window. Don't even feel it. Like a GoPro slow-mo. Don't remember driving home. Next thing I remember, I'm rammin' that piece-of-shit truck right up onto the lawn at the bitch's apartment. My goddamn hand is achin' now, bleeding like a motherfucker! WHATEV!

Fuckin' stairs. Dizzy. Leaning on Ashley's doorbell and screaming bloody murder for her to LET ME IN, GODDAMNIT!

The neighbors all peekin' out, like a bunch of little bitches. Let 'em look. Fuck 'em. I need a shower, a blunt, a bump, and a brew! Gotta get my hand under control too. Blood's all over the place.

Finally she opens up. Fuck. Ashley freaks: "What the fuck happened to you?"

"Goddamn bitch, let me in!" Man, she pisses me off.

In the shower and I'm almost passing out. I hear Ashley talking to somebody. What the fuck? I told her to never answer the door if I'm here.

I yell, "Who the fuck is it?" No answer. My hand is still bleeding and I gotta deal with that. I wrap my knuckles in a towel and lean out the door to get the bitch's attention.

I can hear her now. She's yelling out by the front door. Fuck. The cops. Why are they here? She's sayin', "Don't come in! I'm fine! He's got a problem with you guys, you know that. Please!"

The cops are yappin', "Coming in, got a call, saw the blood, probable cause, prior domestic." Yada, yada. Goddamn neighbors. All their bullshit! So yeah, the cops have been here before. They got me then, but not again. No fuckin' way!

I go to grab my aluminum bat from high school. It feels like one of those giant medieval swords in my bloody hand. Those motherfuckers are gonna get the fuck out of here in a hurry. I haven't done anything! They got no fuckin' right coming into *my* house. Who do they think they are?

"Motherfuckers!" I'm charging, rushing into the front room. I swing and swing and swing. "GET THE FUCK OUT!" *Boom.*

Screaming. I hear screaming. I can't hear me. I'm burning. My whole body's on fire. On the floor, buck naked. It's not me screaming. Ashley, far away. Can't move. Smells like gunshots and like . . . shit. Can't get up. Can't feel anything but burning.

"Why did you have to come in?" she says. "You didn't have to shoot him! He didn't do anything!"

Five bullets fired. All hits. One lodged in my spine. T7. Sure, I got a lawyer. Fucker never calls anymore. Fuck him. Neither does Ashley. She didn't want to wipe my shit—left me when I was down.

Legless, dickless, soulless motherfucker I am now, everyone just looks—then looks away. Fuck you, for lookin' at me like some asshole crip. I blame you motherfuckers for all this shit. *Westside forever,* you fucks.

Now I'm just rolling. Rolling with the punches. Grinding up to Emeline Street and County Health. Then down to Pacific Avenue to hustle change. Back to the shelter. From the shelter back to Emeline. My chair's gonna need new wheels from all this grinding. All this goddamn grinding.

MISCHA AND THE SEAL

BY LIZA MONROY

Cowell's

Every so often the rage creeps up, cresting like waves during a storm. I plan my revenge when I see him there, on the beach or walking down the steps with his board tucked beneath his arm. My eyes lose track of him, even his silver shock of hair, in that neoprene soup. I see clearly underwater, all those legs in all those black suits, false skins trying to look like mine, all the same out here on their little planks. If I could get to him, if I could be sure it was him, I would shred him.

Mischa moved to Santa Cruz as a graduate student in marine biology. Since she preferred being around seals and otters to other people, it was the logical choice. Over time, though, as with everything she attempted, her focus scattered. She couldn't get it back. She dropped out and lived in her rented shack off the side of a surf shop. Her waitressing tips were enough to cover rent. She ate kitchen scraps and remnants of food on plates she collected. People were so wasteful. Mischa never left a trace.

The guy at the surf shop loaned her a board, blue and made of foam. She spent every day at sea, in the gentle waves at Cowell's Beach. Even when it was flat as a pane of glass, she went. Every day she basked in the ocean, so close to the sea lions, seals, and otters. She didn't want to study them, it turned out, she wanted to be among them. With her black eyes and skin so pale it took on a grayish tint in the water, it was like she'd been born one. Mischa could think of nothing she wanted, only things she didn't: she didn't want her once-promising marine biology career, she didn't want any of her former boyfriends—her mother was right, they'd all been losers—and lastly, she didn't want her mother, who had disappeared after taking too long of a swim.

On Mischa's mother's final visit, she'd entered a repetitive loop of conversation blaming Santa Cruz for her daughter's loss of ambition. The small seaside city was a land of lotus-eaters and it sucked her in. The place was an opiate. The Mediterranean weather, perpetual sunshine, glare of light on the bay beneath the cliffs. How did anyone ever get anything done here, or leave to go anywhere else?

Her mother had been staying at the Dream Inn, the fanciest hotel in Santa Cruz, and its only tall building. It was trying to be sleek in a city that felt more as if it had been built into its surroundings. Unlike most of the city, the Dream Inn had been interior-designed—its retro furnishings and the font for the logo of its sign more a tribute to a 1950s motel in Palm Springs or LA than anything in Santa Cruz, save for the surfboards hanging from the ceiling in the lounge.

Mischa went to the hotel every day even though she knew it was going to get worse the longer her mother stayed—the delusions, the nagging. They lay in chaise longues, sipping mai tais and bronzing in the sun. As her mother grilled her on all her wrong choices, Mischa stared out into the bay, tuning her out.

She saw a seal just beyond the surf break. *That seal doesn't give a fuck that you failed,* she thought.

On the morning of her mother's last day, she stopped

by her daughter's shack and pulled one of the ubiquitous blue-and-white-striped Dream Inn towels from her St. Tropez beach bag. "I got you this," she said, dropping the towel on Mischa's futon.

"You stole a towel from the hotel?"

"So you can still go, even after I leave."

"But you stole."

"Anything to get you out of sitting in this crappy shack and doing nothing but surfing all day and serving drunk people burgers all night. Go sit up there instead, think about what you're doing and what you really came here to do." Her mother looked down. "I don't know why I even bother. It's not like you listen."

Mischa considered returning the towel, but she really did like it there, the pool deck hovering over the beach like some cruise ship from space coming in for a landing in the snug little cove beneath the cliffs.

Mischa and her mother walked to the ocean to go for the last swim of her mother's visit. Mischa watched her mother's form from a distance. So many sea lions and seals streaming through the gray flatness. When Mischa looked back she realized she'd lost track of her—what she thought was her mother's bobbing head turned out to be a nearby seal. She scanned the ocean, growing panicked. Her mother had been a distance swimmer once. She was nowhere to be seen.

A rip current must have pulled her far under, sending her out to sea, the rescuers said. The search was called off, her body never found.

The towel attained sentimental value as the last thing her mother gave her. Mischa used it to pass into the pool area at the Dream Inn. She drank two mimosas and pretended she was someone else. She made small talk with tourists, changing her story for every different person—she was a professional horseback rider from Kentucky, a Parisian pastry chef, a musician from Nashville. Forgetting herself more and more.

The more Mischa used the towel, the less guilty she felt about having it. She wandered up and down the hallways of the Dream Inn imagining herself some kind of a living ghost, invisible, stealing the little shampoos from the housekeeping carts by the handful. When she made eye contact with the housekeepers working in rooms with doors left ajar, Mischa smiled, offering a little wave, the stolen towel draped over her wrist.

One day, she made her way down to the pool. As usual, she slipped past the guard—no one seemed to be expecting someone with a stolen towel to come in, or if they did, their sympathy for someone who needed to do such a thing outweighed their desire to enforce hotel policy—ordered a mai tai, and spread the towel over one of the choice chaise longues facing Cowell's. She lay there until the sun began to dip across the cliffs.

When she'd first set foot in Santa Cruz, she'd walked all the way out on the pier to watch the sun sink into the ocean. It would be spectacular, she'd imagined. But the sun did not set behind the water. It felt as if the sun set in the wrong direction here, to the north, as if she'd landed on some alternate planet that was otherwise just like earth. She still looked at maps to remind herself of the simple but disorienting fact that the Santa Cruz coast faced south.

A seal swam in the water, near the shore. She watched it playing in the waves. She loved the harbor seals the most, those spotted gray meat tubes, their black marble eyes and dog-mermaid bodies. They were so elegant. Almost human.

Then the seal stopped, treaded water, and looked directly at her.

You haven't failed. You haven't been ready. Some just need more time to adjust to all the feelings.

Mischa rubbed her eyes. Had the seal spoken? Did even seals here spout New Age aphorisms? Had somebody slipped something in the mai tais? On the chaise longue facing the sea, Mischa slipped into the drifting sleep of the drunk. When she woke it was twilight and all the tourists had gone inside.

At least you hear me.

Mischa met James the same way she met everyone: while impersonating a hotel guest. He was standing by the railing looking out into the bay. She walked over to check the waves. He held binoculars up to his eyes and scanned the ocean. When he lowered them, she was right beside him. She guessed he was in his forties. He was noticeably attractive, built like an athlete, but slightly worn, like he'd been in the sun a little too long and worked out at CrossFit a little too hard.

"What are you looking for?" she asked.

"Oh, seals and otters," he said, ". . . and you."

"So, endangered species?"

He smiled, the crow's feet around his blue eyes crinkling. "You're in danger?"

"Of not living up to my potential, maybe."

"You here for one of those weird self-development seminars?"

"No, I just live here."

"At the hotel?"

"Sort of."

"Really?"

"It's a long story."

"I'm James," he said.

"Mischa," she replied. It was the first time she'd given anyone at the Dream Inn her real name. "Where are you visiting from?"

"I live down the street."

"You have a stolen towel too?"

"No, what kind of person steals a towel? I walked up from the beach. The door is sometimes just open and if I see that, I come in. This is the perfect spot for watching sea lions and otters and sometimes even a seal."

She smiled as they stood, suddenly together, a crack forming in their private spaces, facing the waves.

"Have you been to the lounge?" she asked.

He suddenly seemed nervous.

"They just remodeled it," she said. "It's nice."

"Does that mean you'll let me buy you a drink? You're old enough to drink, right?"

There was something lonely about James, as if he'd missed out on pet adoption and wanted to take care of someone. Mischa felt like a stray, eating other people's leftover food scraps during her waitressing shifts, looking at other people's lives from outside. *This could be all right,* she thought.

Their second date, they went surfing. It was a bigger day—five-foot swell, negative tide. James's sexy, sculpted body looked even more outstanding in a wetsuit, like some kind of hot human-seal. She loved his blond sun-streaked mass of surfer hair. They caught the same wave, rode it all the way in to the beach. The sign, Mischa thought, because she always looked for signs, was the seal. The beady-eyed harbor seal rode the wave along with them, watching them, a silent witness.

That evening she went back to his house off West Cliff Drive, two sprawling stories and a separate garage large enough to be a second home. He showed her his office, his three-screen setup that faced the bay. Turned out Surfer James was also a multimillionaire day trader. Her mother would have been pleased.

After that, they were rarely apart, only when James worked or went out for solo fishing expeditions. He had a dirty old truck filled with fishing equipment. It was where he did his thinking, he said, his planning. Her skin prickled but she ignored this in favor of everything else he was: He shared her love of the bay and the creatures that inhabit it. He didn't seem fazed by her lack of direction. He seemed to want to be her new one. Maybe she could do this, become a mom who walked back and forth on West Cliff rolling a baby all day, free of troubles. She loved strolling the pier, listening to the barks of sea lions, those little beacons of ursine aquatic fuzziness—the otters—and slick, observant harbor seals.

During the day, while James did things with stocks, Mischa returned to the Dream Inn with the stolen towel. James never asked where she went. Come to think of it, James was secretive himself. He sometimes wouldn't call for a night or two, and sometimes he slipped out at odd hours, saying he had to be on East Coast time and didn't want to wake her. They spent almost every free moment together but he never insinuated she should move in or that anything should change.

"Are you seeing other people?" she asked one night while they were grilling tofu steaks, veggie burgers, and onion-and-pepper skewers on James's porch. Her eyes fixed on the locked garage.

"I would never do that to you," he said, and took a sip of sauvignon blanc.

She took him at his word. James was removed and solitary, tough to pin down, but so was she. "Why don't you use your garage for something? It would be a great studio or something." *Like for me,* she didn't say.

"It's just storage for my old surfboards and crap. Just crap I don't want to deal with."

"I can clean it out and organize it for you." She sunk her teeth into some tofu.

"Nah," he said, "not worth the trouble."

While James holed up in his office, or went on boat trips to fish and think, Mischa surfed. After changing out of her wetsuit at the bathrooms and pulling the towel from her mother's St. Tropez beach bag, she absconded to the pool and drank mai tais.

Were she and James growing apart? she asked herself one afternoon. Should she end it, legitimately become alone? Was he cheating on her? Why did the pier jutting out into the ocean sometimes look so sinister?

Then the seal popped up from the waves. She didn't know how she knew this was the same one, but it was—this she knew as it rose and watched her back.

You need to find out. Dig into it. You're practically a scientist. You need evidence. Take a closer look.

"You can't communicate with me, telepathically or otherwise, seal. Sorry. What kind of rum do they put in these drinks?"

It's Captain Morgan, love. But listen to me. Those mai tais are not the only thing that's spiked. A look of intensity crossed the seal's face before it dove under and disappeared.

Regretful of her dismissal, Mischa went to the pool every day and stood by the banister looking for the seal to resurface. She listened for it, becoming convinced that whatever its message, it was dreadfully important.

* * *

Mischa got her shift covered on a Wednesday night. She would follow James. He was still so aloof. They lived as if there was no future, and she had started wanting all of the false securities and illusions.

She borrowed a car from another waitress, and waited around the corner from James's house. Hours passed. At almost eleven, she was about to give up when the lights of his truck went on and he pulled out onto West Cliff Drive, headed toward Natural Bridges. She hung back, then followed. He drove on. He parked near the Seymour Marine Discovery Center. If he was having an affair, this was a strange place for an encounter. Then she saw what he took out of the back of his truck: an Airbow, a lightweight rifle that precision-shot arrows. The downy fuzz on the backs of her arms and legs stood up. That was no fishing instrument. Hadn't he said he threw them back? Or was that something she only wished was true?

She trailed him down to the cliff. He put on a high-beam headlamp, carried his Airbow down an opening to a trail to the ocean. He emitted a strange, low, hypnotic whistle. Mischa, lulled by the tone, resisted the urge to drift toward it. The moonlight rippled over the water. She plugged her ears as his whistling continued. And, as if he was a pied piper of marine life, animals began to surface: a pod of dolphins, some sea lions, a raft of otters, and a few seals. In the distance, under the moon, she saw the head of a solitary seal, keeping its distance. Even from there, she knew. It stared at her, caught her eye even from so far away.

You see? Now you know. What are you going to do about it?

The arrow struck. The pained howl of an animal rang out above the sound of the crashing waves. James cast a line, a wiry noose, and pulled it in. He covered the body with a tarp and dragged it back up to his truck, threw it in.

Was that *her* seal?

She followed him back to the house, her hands trembling in shock as they gripped the wheel. This was what he did when he went out by himself? She would have preferred if he were having an affair, because then at least he would be normal.

He unlocked the mysterious garage, pulled in the bloodied tarp, heavy with the body. Silently, she crept around the corner and watched.

It was no cluttered fisherman or surfer's garage. It was as if a caveman's home and a surgeon's operating theater had merged into one. The walls were lined with James's trophies: a baby otter, several sea lions, and a slew of seals among them. Some eyes seemed familiar. A light hung above a surgical steel table littered with scalpels, knives, hammers. A hot, bright rage consumed her. He was a criminal and a taxidermist. Addicted to his hobby like a drug. She fled back to the car and drove off.

A serial killer of otters and seals—if James could turn out to be that, anyone could be anything, really.

I know it's hard. But you're going to be all right.

"Oh my god, is it you? I was so worried I lost you."

The head popped out of the water. Mischa wrapped her towel around herself and ran down the stairs to the shore. She dropped the towel and walked into the sea.

"You tried to warn me. I'm so sorry."

Don't apologize—stop your slacking.

"I'll call the cops, they'll search the garage—"

Nobody else can handle this for us.

"What do you mean? I couldn't—"

You saw how many corpses line his shelves. But it's not the same. Our lives are not of equal value, you see. Not according to his kind. You have to decide who you want to be. But I think you finally have.

Mischa had to pretend everything was normal with James until a ninth night with a swell and negative tide—a rare occurrence, even more so on the dark night of a new moon.

But eventually, the night did come.

They sat at his dining room table, gazing out the floor-to-ceiling glass. So close, but entirely separate. James was talking about some successful trade he'd made and how he was finally planning their surf vacation to his other home on the Big Island.

"I can't wait to take you, honey," he said.

"I can't wait to go." She feigned a sweet smile even as her mind flashed to the stuffed baby otter in the garage.

"You all right?" he asked. "You seem a little bit . . . distracted."

"Oh no. I'm just daydreaming about these well-deserved plans—"

"Excited to finally do this?"

She nodded. "I think it's more than time." *Him, cutting into the flesh of a dolphin. Sewing up a seal. Sawing.* All those terrible instruments surgeons use to save lives, give new hearts, bring life into the world, he was using to maim and kill her innocent compatriots.

"Yeah, I know. I'm so sorry I haven't planned a vacation for us yet. It's just been a really busy time. But that is about to change!"

Damn fucking straight it is, seal murderer.

He looked giddy, like a young boy whose home run had just won his Little League baseball game. Mischa's stomach turned. How could he be so happy about going to Hawaii when his hands had gutted a small family? She had nightmares of the forever-frozen, terrified faces of those marine animals on secret garage shelves.

Did he say he grew up hunting deer in Minnesota?

"You know what?" she said. "I actually have a surprise planned for you." She took out the wetsuit, the glow sticks, and a bottle of champagne. "It's perfect conditions right now."

He smiled. "I'll go get ready."

It would take him ten minutes to get into his wetsuit. Mischa knew she had that long. She worked stealthily.

James paddled out ahead.

"I'm following you," she said. "It's hard to see in the dark. I'll just stay as close as I can."

She realized how little she'd ever known about James. The Airbow only weighed seven pounds. It wasn't hard to paddle out with it. But she'd always had strong arms. As she watched him sitting atop his board with the little glow stick, waiting for the next set, she almost felt sorry for him. She set the Airbow on the end of her board and peered through the precision viewfinder at James. What an easy, elegant little weapon. No wonder he liked it so much. She saw her seal, keeping its distance. The stillness was interrupted by an oncoming wave. The set was arriving. She gripped the trigger as she watched him paddle. She felt the lift beneath her board.

Now.

The arrow departed with force. James pummeled forward, off the board. The seal moved. A slight splashing in the waves, then silence. What a perfect collaborator. Who else could disappear a body with such grace? She could already see the headlines: "Cold-Blooded Killer," "St. Francis of the Seals."

She went home and took a shower. Early-dawn light

poured through the open windows, the thin, sheer curtains undulating like waves in the sea breeze. There wasn't much time. If she didn't go now she would have to wait another nine days, and by then it would be too late to go anywhere. She pulled her coat from its hanger and hurried to the beach.

When the detectives finally searched the house, he'd been missing for weeks. They broke the lock on the garage and turned on the light. Nothing but some power tools, old papers, and a dirty hotel towel. They would have questioned the girlfriend, but she was nowhere to be found, as if she, too, had slipped into the sea and vanished.

I am home again. I stayed too long, mesmerized by their world, avoiding my purpose until I forgot my identity. In the human terms, a slacker. A slacking selkie. But there are more like James, his kind, and even worse. Now we are just getting started.

FIRST PEAK

BY PEGGY TOWNSEND

Pleasure Point

Boone sat in the lineup, waiting.

The swell was chest high, out of the south.

He drew his hands through the water and felt the power of the storm that had given birth to the waves, the force that brought them to Pleasure Point. It was a heartbeat, an urgency, a gift from Tūtū Pele's capricious womb.

He wondered if something would happen before the day was over. He was her servant.

Already, the two kooks were paddling out, both of them in wetsuits that were new and smooth and black. Their arms dipped in choppy strokes. Their feet kicked as if they needed to also propel themselves by air.

He watched them come toward him, felt the energy building behind him. He flattened himself on his board, dug three hard strokes into Mother Ocean, and stood in a single motion that was as natural to him as breathing. He was riding on her supple back, sailing on the force of her slick, wet power. He crouched, let his arms go loose, and knew what the two kooks would see: a bearded apparition in faded neoprene, with long hair that trailed his head like seaweed. He gauged speed and distance, turned slightly so he slowed and was aimed directly at the two men.

He could see the spark of fear in their eyes.

But what they could not see, what they would not see,

was what had been left behind. What was now lying secret and powerful in the dirt next to a charcoal-gray monstrosity of a house.

That was what they should fear.

Not him on a board.

"What a dick," Jonah said, coming out of the water, leaving damp footprints on the concrete steps as he climbed to the top of the cliff. "He could have killed me."

"Asshole," Nate agreed.

The September day had an unseasonably dark feel to it, as if winter were ready to pounce. At the top of the stairs, the two men turned back toward the pewter ocean, trying to pick out the man among the two dozen surfers at First Peak who had ruined their day.

"I should call the cops," Jonah said. His chest rose and fell. Not from exertion but from the emotion of being assaulted by a guy who had looked like some watery Jesus coming at him on Judgment Day.

"You belong here as much as he does," Nate said.

"Fuckin'-A," Jonah replied.

Jonah had bought the house on the Point a year earlier, a single-story shack with a triangle peek of the ocean. It had been occupied by a long-haired woman and a young child who, he was told, was autistic. According to his realtor, the mother of the long-haired woman had purchased the place in 1998 for $325,000 and left it to her daughter after she died of metastatic breast cancer. Jonah had offered $1.5 million for the house a day after it went on the market and raised the price an additional $100,000 after another buyer had come on the scene.

He was twenty-nine years old and already worth $40 million.

"You're doing her a favor," the realtor had said.

The day after the longhaired woman accepted his offer, Jonah had driven by and seen her sitting in the front yard with her head in her hands. She hadn't looked like anybody was doing her any favors, but that wasn't his problem.

His contractor tore down the house to a single standing wall, then built it back up into a two-story modern contemporary with dark-gray stucco walls, a second-floor deck that now gave him a full view of the bay, and a red door that his interior designer said was a sign of good luck and prosperity.

But recently, his luck had gone to hell.

Boone watched the kooks climb the wide set of steps the county had set into a faux rock wall to foster access for the tourists or something. He remembered when Pleasure Point felt like a community instead of a destination resort, when a carpenter or a teacher could afford to rent or even buy a house because there weren't vacation rentals on every corner—or giant paychecks that allowed people from over the hill to build giant houses only they could afford. He remembered when you had to walk a narrow dirt path and hang onto a knotted rope to get down the cliff to the water, which kept out the people who did not deserve the waves.

He blamed the seawall and its stairs for what had happened to the neighborhood, for drawing crowds into the water, for making it so you had to worship at the altar of money in order to live here.

Sometimes he thought about putting a piece of dynamite in that phony wall and blowing everything back to the way it was. But he was not a violent man. Not anymore.

In his younger days, his anger had driven him to break noses and smash car windows. He'd spent a year in the county jail for a beat-down he'd given to a guy outside the Corner Pocket bar. After that, he found a job at a local tree service, chain-sawing overhanging limbs and view-blocking branches. He tried to get sober but was having trouble because the Point held so many reminders of why he liked to drink. He saved just enough money to get him and his board to Oahu where he'd hitchhiked to the North Shore and lived under a kiawe tree for the next four months while he got clean.

His third week there, he'd awakened to find an old man standing over him with a rooster in his arms. The deep lines on the old man's face reminded him of a lava field and the rooster looked as if someone had started to pluck him for dinner but quit halfway through the job.

"She talks to you, don't she?" the old man said. He had bare feet and wore a faded T-shirt and ragged shorts. "She don't talk to everybody, you know."

Boone sat up and rubbed his sun-ravaged eyes. He'd pledged to buy himself a cheap pair of sunglasses the next time he was in town but always forgot—consequently, every morning was like having spent the night with sandpaper glued under his eyelids. "I'm not sure what you mean," he said.

"Heh-heh." The old man set the half-naked chicken on the ground and they began to walk away. "Next time you have a beer for me, eh?"

It wasn't that Boone had intended to buy the old man beer, but he'd trimmed a couple of palm trees for one of the landlords who owned a few houses on the beach and had a little money in his pocket. He hitchhiked into town and bought a ten-dollar pair of sunglasses and a six-pack of Miller High Life, along with a loaf of bread and a jar of peanut butter, his main source of nourishment.

The old man and the rooster came back that afternoon

as if they'd known about his windfall. The ancient accepted a beer and Boone scooped out a bit of peanut butter and set it out for the chicken, who ended up with most of it stuck to his half-raw chest.

The old man leaned his back against the kiawe and began to tell Boone the story of Hawaii—the handsome men and women who had lived on the islands, the arrival of the Europeans, the stealing of the land, the fight for sovereignty.

After four beers the old man got up. "Better beer next time, man," he said and walked off, the rooster following behind, a bit of peanut butter stuck on its breast.

Boone trimmed more bushes and mowed the landlord's lawns, hitchhiked into town after a session at Rockpiles, and bought a six-pack of PBR and a package of sunflower seeds.

The old man and the chicken came back, nodding approval of the beer and the seeds, and the ancient told him about the proper way to enter and leave the sea, the way Mother Ocean sometimes allowed you back into her womb, and how you should never take that for granted because how often does a man get to return from where he came?

Over the next weeks, the old man and the rooster returned often, telling more stories of the gods that ruled the island, of Pele, and of what awaited those who did not pay respect to the ocean and the land.

Boone listened and felt something shift inside him. He felt the heartbeat of the soil on which he laid his head and the love of the ocean as she wrapped him in her waves. It was then he decided to never cut his hair.

One day, the old man arrived without the rooster, spit on the ground, and said, "Follow me."

Boone got up and trailed him into the brush, asking where the chicken had gone. The old man rubbed his stomach, which Boone took to mean that either the man had eaten the flea-bitten bird or that it had succumbed to some kind of intestinal problem. He vowed to make an offering of peanut butter to a bird that had been noble, even in its suffering.

Boone followed the old man for more than an hour, over land that grew steep and rocky. When the rubber strap on one of his flip-flops broke, he tossed them into the brush, stepping in the exact places where the old man put his calloused bare feet. He was surprised at the lack of pain.

On a promontory that looked over the Pacific, the old man folded a small talisman into Boone's hand and told him it had been given to him by Tūtū Pele—and that whoever held it and was pure would be blessed with peace and harmony. To those who were not pure, it would bring nothing but suffering and pain.

"That is all I have to say," the old man concluded.

It wasn't long after Jonah moved into the Pleasure Point house that trouble came. First, he lost his wallet and had to cancel all of his credit cards. Then his phone had fallen out of his back pocket on a bike ride. He bought a new phone but half of the numbers he transferred ended up without names attached.

The next day, he parked his BMW at Whole Foods and came back to find a grocery cart resting against its side. From the size of the dent in the rear passenger door, he figured someone must have let go of their cart the minute they walked out of the store and it had rolled unheeded down the entire slope of the parking lot until it swerved at the last minute and found his car.

No one left a note.

After that, he got a speeding ticket driving over Highway 17 and then a notice from the IRS that he was being audited. He was just telling himself that these were only blips in what had otherwise been a good life when a letter arrived from one of the big pharmaceutical companies. It threatened to sue him and his startup over software they'd written that used a simple blood test to determine, with 98 percent accuracy, if a drug would cause certain side effects without a patient having to experience the damage first. He thought of his sister who'd died at fourteen after a chemotherapy drug she took for her lymphoma caused her heart to fail, of how he believed the sale of his ridiculous dating app—four years before—would allow him to do something important with his life, like Bill Gates was doing.

And then there'd been this guy out in the water today.

He made himself a mug of coffee, plugged in his new phone to charge, and went out to the deck with a heaviness he hadn't felt since his sister died. The wind was picking up.

Boone hunkered on the crushed-granite path and watched Jonah's big gray house to see what Tūtū Pele would do. The first tendril of smoke came from an upstairs window an hour later.

He thought of Sandra and his son Nalu.

After she'd sold the house to the kook, Sandra had moved to Portland with their boy. By then, she and Boone hadn't lived as man and woman for more than eighteen months. The first years were good, but then there had been too many arguments, too many times when she looked at him with pity. But they both loved the boy and so he had moved into the garage and built a small kitchen and a platform bed where he and Nalu watched *The Lion King* over and over while Sandra was at work.

Sometimes Boone could still hear that movie in his head.

Then Sandra told him a realtor said she could get more than a million dollars for the house. She said she had no choice but to sell and move to a place where she could afford a good school for Nalu and buy a decent car. She told him it was better if he didn't come with them, that they each needed to get on with their lives.

They both cried, but not Nalu, who said, "Oh yes, the past can hurt," which was from his favorite scene in *The Lion King*. Three months later, the kook's contractor began tearing down every piece of wood and nail and pipe that held the memory of Sandra and his son.

Boone saw the smoke from the window grow heavier and then the kook jumping up from his chaise longue to run inside. The wind was stronger now. A few heartbeats later, the kook was on the front lawn yelling for help.

The wind whipped the fire into a fury in a way that let Boone know Pele had summoned it for her work. He watched the orange flames lick the sky, the house fall in on itself, wet and ugly. He felt the earth underneath heave a sigh of relief. He had not expected the depth of Pele's unhappiness.

A week later, he heard firefighters had blamed the blaze on the kook's phone, which had caught fire as it was being charged. But Boone knew better. That same night he retrieved the talisman from its spot in the dirt near where the gray house had stood.

He held it for a good five minutes, marveling over the truth of what the old man had said. He tucked the talisman back into his pocket. There was a house, down near the lagoon where he camped, that had just been turned into a vacation rental, with two surfboards in the backyard for its guests.

SAFE HARBOR

BY SEANA GRAHAM

Seabright

She was standing right at the bar the night Ray walked in—a hairbreadth from skinny and Ray tended to like his women with more meat on their bones. It'd been a long day at work; he'd only come to Brady's for a drink before heading home.

Her tattoos intrigued him—that serpent that disappeared under her shirt. People had tattoos in Detroit, of course, but Californians seemed to embrace body art with an abandon he hadn't seen back home. Milder weather? *Sheer exhibitionism*, the Midwesterner in him scoffed.

Skinny Girl must have felt his gaze, because she turned right around and began her own frank appraisal of him. If she wasn't actually a prostitute, she wasn't in this place for the conversation, either.

Ray stepped up to the bar and ordered a drink, offering one to the lady as well. She peered at him with huge green eyes—and accepted. She told him her name was Jazz and that she'd just come down from San Francisco.

Her tattoos might disguise the fact that she was from the South, but it didn't take Ray long to grasp that she was a long way from home. Caught out, she admitted her real name was Jasmine, that she was escaping some trouble back in Memphis. Everything about her suggested she'd brought a lot of it with her. On that first night, Ray asked Jasmine if she'd come out to California to see the Pacific Ocean. She looked at him strangely, as though he wasn't quite right in the head.

"No, sugar," she said, "I came to California for the money."

It seemed as good a line as any to start their negotiations.

For as long as Ray could remember, he'd wanted to live by the ocean. Where this idea had come from, he didn't know—he'd grown up in the middle of Kansas. His parents were no-nonsense Methodist farmers, not given to encouraging flights of fancy or yearnings for anything but one's hard-earned place in heaven. What they did give Ray, though, was the opportunity to work on tractors and other farm equipment, which developed not only his practical skills, but also his talent for innovation. After college, when the family farm had all but withered away, these aptitudes gave him a foothold in Detroit, where he found his niche in the more experimental foundation of the auto industry. Once Ray was established, he married, and bought a big house on the river, believing it would satisfy his need to be near water. Later, when he realized that it wouldn't, he told himself it would have to do.

When Ray got the call five years ago from the headhunter about a job at one of the Silicon Valley firms, he believed God had heard his prayers. His wife Maureen objected to the move at first—they knew no one in California. But the money was too good for her to hold out long. So they put the three kids in their big SUV and drove out to San Jose.

San Jose proved disappointing. It was late summer and they'd left green lawns in Michigan. Here, the hills were brown and tired, relieved only here and there by small dark stands of stubborn live oak.

Once they'd settled into the hotel room his company provided for their transition, Ray wasted no time in packing the whole family up for a trip over the mountains to Santa Cruz. As he drove the winding road through the redwoods, he took in one deep breath after another. This was the life he had always wanted, right here for the taking. He tried to share it with Maureen, but the kids were feeling queasy from the twists and turns of Highway 17 and she'd turned around to comfort them. The moment passed.

They came down out of the mountains and got their first full view of the Monterey Bay. Ray caught his breath. Even from this distance, the water was dazzling. They drove straight down to the Boardwalk and plopped their towels on the beach. Ray was just as entranced as the kids. When evening came, they all walked out on the wharf for supper. "Supper"—he would soon learn that this was a word that marked him as a Midwesterner.

They ate at a family-style place called Gilda's, watching the sun set on the Pacific, with huge pelicans lounging on the pier right outside the windows and sea lions barking under the wharf. Ray ate his calamari and thought, *This is it.* He would find them a house by the ocean and then they would all live happily ever after.

Ray kept Jazz in the dark at first. He didn't want her to realize right off what a big fish she'd landed. He should hold something in reserve. She might be the type who would bleed you dry if you let her. She had an armband tattoo that circled her right bicep which read: *Trust me . . . wait . . . Trust me . . . wait . . . Trust me . . .* It seemed to flicker back and forth from being just her little joke to revealing some deeper truth. He didn't know quite how he could think this and want to keep seeing her, but he did.

So for a while Ray wined and dined her, taking Jazz down to Monterey where no one was likely to know them. They had sex for the first time in a discreet hotel on Cannery Row. The sex was good but not great. Ray thought afterward that maybe Jazz was holding something back too. Those green eyes had to mean something.

Ray couldn't get Jazz to talk much about herself, not at first. He was an affable guy when he wanted to be, and it came as a surprise to him that she had even less interest in being drawn out than he did. She used her lithe body to great effect, one moment beguiling and winsome, another sultry and seductive. It was like a costume she put on.

She mentioned a man several times in passing, someone back home, and Ray, after a few glasses of wine one night, was more persistent than usual in trying to get more out of her. It amused her to tease him, but when she saw that he was getting sulky, she leaned across the table and kissed him full on the lips, something she hadn't done in public before.

"Darlin', believe me when I tell you—you really don't want to know."

A *boat* was all he'd thought when he first visited the harbor in Santa Cruz. A small sailboat like the one he'd kept back on the Detroit River, or a catamaran with an engine to take him out a little farther. But then one afternoon the CFO took him out on his yacht and the scale of Ray's dream began to change. He began to look at listings online, poring over the details as other men study catalogs of fine wine.

One day he saw an ad for a fifty-footer moored up in Sausalito. He took a surreptitious day trip up to see it, exactly as if he were going off to meet a paramour. When he saw the sleek, sexy vessel in person for the first time, Ray thought he finally knew what people meant when they talked about falling in love.

The yacht was the first thing he and Maureen really fought about in California—the first *big* thing. Everything in her upbringing—and in his, for that matter—suggested that this was just "showing off." After a week or so, she saw it was pointless to resist and said no more about it. This wasn't quite the same thing as accepting the idea, but good relations were restored.

Ray was learning about the nautical life. He named his new craft *Departure* and made improvements to the navigation system and other electronics, as only a man of his skills could. He forgot Brady's bar for a time and began to hang out at the Crow's Nest on the harbor, getting to know other boat owners. Maureen went with him the first couple of times but didn't take to it. He continued going alone.

It took longer than one might think for a good Methodist boy to realize the yacht afforded him the chance to have women. He made discreet inquiries, both at work and here in town, about how to get exactly the kind of thing he wanted. It took Ray longer to figure out exactly what that was. At first he worried about what his wife might find out, or at least suspect. But with the long hours he kept at his job, the crazy commute, there was plenty of wiggle room. She resented the boat and Ray had to bribe her with doing household chores to even get her to even come aboard.

Ray was still trying to be a good family man. But he felt that there had been a divine dispensation that had allowed him to reach California, that somehow he'd been absolved of everything in advance. All the strict rules of childhood, the black-and-white way of seeing things that had followed him into adulthood, had simply dropped along the roadside on the way out west.

Sometimes in the middle of the night, his early childhood edicts would resurface and Ray would wake, sweating. But then he'd turn and see Maureen sleeping soundly beside him and tell himself everything was all right. If she was still here, it must be.

Ray didn't take Jazz to the yacht right away. Yet there was only so much you could do with nice dinners and anonymous hotel rooms. Ray could tell, despite the money he regularly deposited in her bank account, Jazz was losing interest. She was the kind of woman who always had other offers. So one night he told her about the boat. She was not as impressed as Ray had hoped, but he thought she'd perk up when she actually saw it. He arranged to pick her up at Brady's on a Wednesday night.

On a whim he couldn't have explained, Ray decided to take his family out on the yacht the weekend before his date with Jazz. It had been a while since he'd done so and the kids were excited. The captain he'd hired to maintain the yacht lived in a considerably smaller boat in the harbor and was free to take them Sunday afternoon. When they were all on board and the kids had explored below deck a bit, he asked the captain to take them out on the open sea. Despite all his love of the ocean, he had rarely taken the boat out of the bay.

Maureen declined to come on deck, and stayed in the cabin, reading a novel. As the *Departure* picked up speed, Ray stood with his hands on the shoulders of his youngest son, looking over the bow at the Pacific horizon.

"What do you think, son?"

"It's so big, Daddy. Bigger than I ever thought."

"You got that right," Ray said. *Here I am on the edge of all of this*, he thought, *and I've barely ventured out. Despite everything, I'm still a landlubber at heart. Still just a farm boy from Kansas.* He told himself that he would change that. He would risk bigger things.

He had expected Jazz to be impressed with the yacht but she wasn't. Ray was surprised at how well he'd learned to see the world through her eyes. It was nice for a boat, but as a place for a rendezvous, it wasn't all that much. His electronic gadgetry meant nothing to her. That was the kind of background stuff she took for granted.

She did notice the surveillance cameras and gave him a funny look—a sly look that said she knew exactly what he planned to do with *those*. In fact, he had gotten them so that he could keep his eye on the vessel when he was elsewhere—as innocent as that. But Jazz would never take a thing at face value when she could read a lewd meaning into it. Ray wondered briefly what had happened to Jazz that she always saw life like this. But he realized he, too, could now see prurient motives in everything. She'd shown him that.

They had a drink. Then another. Ray tried to kiss her, but she pulled away, dancing on the opposite side of the small cabin, as enticing and remote as ever. Ray thought, *I have a large yacht, more money than I know what to do with, and yet I have nothing to offer this woman.* So he had another drink, a strong one, and then he told Jazz that he loved her.

She looked at him strangely, as she had on that very first night at Brady's, as though he didn't really grasp anything about her. "Let me take you to the wild side, baby."

What would that be? Bondage? Strange sex toys? They'd already done that. But when Jazz pulled the hypo out of her purse, he saw that he had misunderstood. Ray was disappointed.

Ah, only that. He could get drugs on his own. He had been trying them recreationally for a while; it was part of the culture at work.

Maybe when this night was over, maybe he would go home and see what he could do about patching up things with Maureen. The affair with Jazz seemed to be reaching the end of the line. Well, at least he'd probably get *some* kind of sex out of this. Ray smiled gamely, like a kid offered his first cigarette by a popular girl in middle school. Bravado is sometimes everything.

"Sure," he said. He watched her passively as she got out the rest of the gear and readied the rig. Her expertise shone through and he was reminded of nothing so much as going to the doctor's office as a kid and gravely watching the nurse as she prepared the vaccination. Maybe that was the right way to look at this. A vaccination against the shortcomings of living.

"You done this before, babe?"

Ray shook his head. He'd been afraid of needles as a boy. She was half his age, he thought—and yet there was a way in which she seemed almost maternal now, as if she were guiding him through some rite of passage.

At the same time, watching Jazz be focused like this, not theatrical, not "on," he could see how young she really was. He caught a glimpse.

She looked him in the eyes again, and he was reminded of the first night he'd seen her—the way their gaze had locked. There was something fated between them that went back a thousand years. He felt a chill go up his spine and shivered.

"Don't be afraid, darlin'," she said. "I've done this a hundred times."

He was afraid, though. Until he wasn't.

* * *

Ray remained aware of Jazz for quite a while before he died—the way she tried to rouse him, speaking to him quietly and then more urgently, before finally giving up. His eyes were no longer open, though he had a sense of her presence. He heard the quick *glug glug* of the wine as she poured herself another glass, then felt her moving around the room, stepping over him to pull the curtain down and gently drawing the door closed behind her. *Don't leave me,* Ray thought, as he heard the clicking of her heels recede down the dock. *Don't leave.* And then the ocean rushed in where she had been, the beautiful ocean, and swept him out to sea.

MISCALCULATION

BY VINNIE HANSEN

Yacht Harbor

When the "Guitar Case Bandit" whipped open his case at the teller's window, Molly's mouth fell open. The black case on her counter was built for a ukulele, not a guitar! The media were such idiots—this had to be the fifth bank robbery in a month, and they still didn't have the details right.

Two other tellers froze on command—Susanna and Amber—as well as the loan officer and branch manager. Molly forked over the bills, placing the final band of twenties in the uke case. "There you go, sir."

Her heart hammered with the thrill of it all. The elusive bandit right in front of her!

"Thank you, Mo . . ."

Mo?

Maybe he was going to say "Ma'am." The robber was noted for his politeness, or at least that's what the *Sentinel* reported. Or maybe he read her name from her pin.

This guy gave every teller plenty of time to look him over: black Fedora, Bucci sunglasses, and a red ascot pulled over his lower face. Molly couldn't help staring.

The Guitar Case Bandit had been holding up community banks and credit unions in Santa Cruz County for the last year and yet he'd strolled right in here unheeded, even with the sign on the door prohibiting caps and sunglasses.

"Aim those baby-blues somewhere else, dollface." The man snapped his case shut.

A telltale mark on the case clasp caught her eye. She'd seen this ukulele case plenty of times. Her knees quivered like a jellyfish. She stared into the robber's eyes. *Dollface.* She blushed.

He snapped his fingers like a six-shooter, "Here's looking at you, kid," and strode out of the credit union.

Molly's life of serving John Q. Public for fourteen dollars an hour walked right out the door with him.

Molly played her ukulele every Saturday morning with the Sons of the Beach at the harbor mouth. Her new favorite instrument was her Rick Turner Rose Compass C-Tenor. This weekend, she couldn't wait.

Smoothing Friday's *Sentinel* onto her kitchen counter, she reread its crime coverage. In his usual modus operandi, the Guitar Case Bandit had walked away casually from her branch. He'd crossed the street into a hedged parking lot where the police patrol never spotted him. No street camera picked up a departing car with a likely driver. Possibly he had an accomplice or had hidden inside a vehicle. Molly couldn't tell if the speculation came from the police department or the paper.

The bandit had made off with an "undisclosed amount of money." But Molly knew the figure. Through the grapevine, she'd heard the other sums too. A cool million total.

The police sought the person of interest shown in a grainy photograph, age about fifty, height about 5'10", weight 170. *Gosh, that's practically the same as me*, Molly thought, *I'm just two inches shorter.*

"Everything about him was average," the paper quoted the other teller, Susanna. Ha!

Susanna always dressed like the boat salesperson she used to be, before the recent downturn. But if Sue had been the least bit observant, she would've said something about the ukulele case. After all, Molly had introduced Sue to the instrument. Once Susanna spent a single morning playing at the Sons of the Beach group, she'd been hooked. Molly sniffed—not that Susanna had ever hired her for uke lessons.

Well, at least she'd kept her cool, Molly gave her that—better than Amber. Little drama queen had hyperventilated and required treatment from an EMT.

Still, Molly was miffed. She'd described the gun as a modern piece, no revolving chamber for the bullets. The reporter hadn't bothered to quote *her*. The story didn't mention the weapon at all.

The article ended with a hotline number.

They haven't caught him yet and they aren't about to—unless he decides not to cooperate with me. Molly packed her songbooks in her canvas tote bag and slipped on her wedged sandals and glass pendant that matched. *Dress for success.*

She strutted down the Harbor Beach breezeway, a bounce in her step. The Sons of the Beach congregated outside in front of the Kind Grind café, up to a hundred at a time.

Susanna stepped right in Molly's path. Her glittery sandals sprayed sand and startled the seagull pecking up crumbs from her undoubtably gluten-free muffin. "You look like the cat who ate the canary."

Leave it to Susanna to use a cliché.

Sue brushed off her low-cut Hawaiian sundress. There wasn't that much to see. "Did you remember more from the bank robbery?"

"Nothing new to report." Molly jammed her metal music stand into the sand.

Susanna inspected her. "Tangerine nail polish? What's going on with that? A date?"

Molly glanced away toward one of the walkway benches. A bag overflowed with plastic leis, brought by the bandleader.

"Want a lei?" Molly asked.

"Sure." Susanna frowned and tailed her.

Molly sighed. "Stop following me. I like privacy for my lays."

"I swear you are in some kind of mood this morning."

Molly threaded along the edge of the thickening crowd, mostly ukulele players, but also a keyboard, a mouth harp, and a bass. A black fabric case for the upright bass spilled over a cement bench. A ukulele case rested on the same, but its bright blue fabric sported a design of a topless woman cradling a strategically held uke. Molly lifted the bass case. Nothing buried.

She passed the drummers and the mandolin player, circling toward the harbor side of the beach where more experienced musicians grouped, the exclusive part of the ring where she never ventured. The guys over here sacrificed a view of the water for a view of the backsides of the women volleyball players.

She stopped in front of Rudy Carmona, and his agile fingers quit dancing along the frets of his koa wood instrument. Abalone shell gleamed around the sound hole.

"Well, hello there!"

In Levi's and a muscle shirt, he looked anything but average. She'd never dreamed of talking to Rudy Carmona. Of course, in point of fact, she hadn't yet spoken.

"You're looking fine this a.m." His dark eyes revealed nothing. Behind him, sailboats glided from the mouth of the harbor off on dolphin and whale adventures. Molly blinked nervously. Up close he even smelled good. "What can I do for you?" he asked.

"So, you ditched your ukulele case?" she stammered.

He lifted his brows and strummed three quick C chords and then a B: *Dah dah dah-duuuh.*

Was he mocking her? Molly flushed again.

He dipped his cleft chin toward the bench. "Right there. Behind the bass."

"The blue one?" she asked.

"You like it?"

"What happened to your usual case?"

Rudy sighed and scanned the crowd. He nodded to a hula dancer named Linda. She was possibly the Linda he'd had a fling with, although hard to tell—every other woman in the group was named Linda. "All those black cases look alike," he said.

Molly pinned him with her eyes, the way she did with a customer bearing a questionable ID. "That's why people mark them." She could smell her own lavender essential oil, and she knew he must too.

He took hold of her arm. "We'll discuss this at break." He whispered in spite of the din of the others warming up. He leaned close to her ear. "On my boat."

Her heart did a soft shoe to the tune of "(I'd Like to Get You on a) Slow Boat to China."

The group had barely finished their opening song, "All of Me," when Sue tapped Molly's freckled arm. "What's going on with you and Rudy Carmona?"

"I'm going on his boat at coffee break."

"You?" Susanna's eyes stretched wide. "And Rudy?"

"Want to chaperone?"

"You can't be serious!"

"If we're not back for the second set, call me." Molly followed the band into "I'm in the Mood for Love," but her friend could only stare.

Rudy's sailboat, the *Karma II,* occupied a middle berth on N dock. The dock gate clanked shut behind them and they started down the slippery composite, which had replaced the old wood after the 2011 tsunami. The dock still creaked and swayed.

Rudy offered an arm to help her into his craft.

"Should we go below deck?" she asked. This was his secret lair, maybe all the money mounded on a table—his bed right next to it. She was shaking.

Rudy, who hadn't said one word since they opened the gate, shook his head and led her to two beach chairs at the stern. Their brightly striped fiesta pattern surprised her.

"Sit."

Molly settled into the low-slung canvas.

Rudy crossed his strong arms over his chest. He stared off at the view of the Crow's Nest, a two-story watering hole on the side of the harbor mouth. A seal arced out of the water, took an airy breath, and swooshed back down, leaving a small ripple.

"So where's your old case?" she asked.

"Gave it to Goodwill."

"And a man 'about fifty, height about 5'0", weight about 170,' happened to buy it?"

"Get down to business," he hissed.

She touched her lower lip. "We'd make a great team."

"You better tell me what's going on here." Susanna had taken her chair and sounded even more bossy than usual.

Molly shook her curls.

"Where's Rudy?"

"I left him winded."

Sue's thin eyebrows tried to fly up, but Botox froze them in place.

"Don't get excited." Molly smiled to know something Susanna didn't—Susanna who strutted around the credit union like she intended to be branch manager before the year was out. "This has to stay very hush-hush."

"Of course."

Molly extracted her ukulele from her tote and began to tune. "I talked to him about a business deal."

"Like something at the bank?" Susanna asked.

"Exactly."

The Sons of the Beach wrapped up with their traditional morning finale, "Please Don't Talk About Me When I'm Gone." Molly hustled into the thick coffee aroma of the Kind Grind. She never ordered a soy milk chai here without thinking of the employee who'd been raped and locked in the refrigerator. Or the killer of two local police officers who'd worked here. It didn't make sense. How could two horrific crimes be connected to a quaint coffee shop? In Santa Cruz? At the ukulele beach?

She sat over to the side and peeked around the wall to watch Susanna looking for her. Eventually Sue gave up and strode off rolling her cart full of gear.

Molly rubbed her chin, wondering if she'd settled for too little with Rudy. She'd started at 50 percent.

"No can do." Rudy had kept his gaze on the pilings as if watching a cormorant sunning. His playful manner had evaporated.

"Are you in a position to negotiate?" she'd asked.

"Thirty-three percent. And that's it." Rudy sliced his hands through the air.

As she sipped her chai, Molly divided the loot by three in her head—simple math, but amazing how many people resorted to a calculator. With the cash she could pay off her condo. Maybe take that trip to Paris.

Her job didn't used to be so bad, but now the customers who came into the credit union were mostly seniors who distrusted computers and still used checks, or the lonely who sought free coffee and someone to talk to.

Her phone vibrated. Molly checked the text message. Rudy must have gotten her number from the SOB site where she advertised her uke lessons.

Come to boat tonight. Work out details.

She snorted. *Fat chance.* She wasn't getting on a sailboat alone with Rudy Carmona in the dark. As nice as that might be. Her mind drifted a moment before she responded: *Maybe TTYL.*

Molly drained the last of her chai, packed up her compass rose, and walked out into the salty breeze. A volleyball hottie soared vertically and slammed a spike. *Yes!*

"Where did you disappear to at the end?" Susanna's indignation blared over the phone.

Molly drummed her fingers on her kitchen table. "I didn't know you were waiting for me."

"Right. We only walk to our cars together every single week."

"Sorry."

"I swear, since the holdup you've been acting like a prima donna."

"Do you still own a gun?" Molly asked.

"Of course." Impatience pinched Susanna's husky voice. "Just went out to Markley's Range last weekend."

"Can I borrow it?"

"Why? Are you going to shoot Rudy Carmona?"

"I wouldn't waste a bullet. He's probably slept with twenty women in Sons of the Beach. I'm not that big of a fool."

Quiet on the other end of the line.

"Do you even know how to hold one?" Susanna finally asked.

"It's just for show."

"What are you getting yourself into?"

"It's nothing. Rudy wants to meet again on his boat and I don't trust him." Yeah, even if her body tingled at the prospect of meeting him again. Even in the light of day sitting on the boat with him, the smell of him . . . Maybe she could persuade Rudy to take her into the privacy of the cabin, suggest a little addition to the bargain.

"Are you still there?" Susanna asked.

"So what do you say?" Molly pressed.

"If I go along with this hare-brained scheme, I swear, you better cough up every sordid detail of what you and Rudy have going on."

"Cross my heart and hope to die."

A stiff ten-knot wind in the harbor had every rigging chiming. Below the halo of a single dock light, Rudy unlocked the gate. It clanged behind them. He put his hand right on the small of Molly's back.

"Pretty dark out here," Molly murmured.

"There aren't any other live-aboard's on N dock."

Molly snaked a hand into the pocket of her wrap. The butt of the gun steadied her nerves.

Rudy helped her over the boat's edge.

She turned toward his locked cabin door. "It's a bit chilly, right?"

"Romantic, though," he said. "Out here with the sound of the sea."

Romantic. Molly swiped a loose curl from her forehead. She took a seat again in his fiesta chair. Rudy crossed the deck holding two fishing rods she hadn't seen before. He hovered by the outboard, adjusting a couple of levers.

"What are you doing?"

"Thought we might do a little night fishing." Rudy yanked the starter. Molly struggled up from the chair. "I'd stay seated," he said. "Wouldn't want to lose your balance and fall over." He yanked the rope again. When the engine caught, he adjusted the choke. "What's the matter, dollface? Thought you liked fishing expeditions."

Molly calculated her options—riding out to sea with this man or pulling the gun now. The stink of the engine fumes made her stomach churn.

"You know, two can keep a secret if one is dead," Rudy whispered in her ear.

In spite of everything, his breath stirred Molly right down to her tangerine toenails. She pulled out the weapon from her wrap.

"What are you planning to do?" Rudy chuckled. "Shoot a gull?"

She leveled the barrel at his chest.

"Take your finger off that trigger," Rudy said.

"Hey, I have the gun . . . I give the orders."

In one move, Rudy twisted her wrist, took her gun, and knocked Molly out of the chair. She tumbled to the deck, scraping her bare legs. His full weight fell on top of her and an embarrassing sound squeezed from her body.

"Now I have the gun, sweetheart."

Molly struggled to get up, and he allowed her that. Blood trickled down her calves. Rudy kept the gun trained on her as he eased the boat out of its slip.

They burbled out of the harbor, through the channel, past the riprap of the jetty, past the lighthouse, and into open water. Molly shivered. Her thin dress was meant for seduction not sailing. Although it didn't seem like Rudy intended to hoist either her dress or the sails.

A pod of dolphins broke the surface of the open water off the bow. Molly swallowed. *Dolphins are good luck,* she told herself.

The boat slowed and bobbed in the swell. On the starboard side, the distant lights of the wharf and Boardwalk winked through the fog.

"I think I'm going to be sick," Molly said.

"Oh no you don't."

"So, here we are," said a throaty voice.

Molly snapped her head toward the sound. "Susanna!"

"Hi, Molly." Sue was elegantly coiffed even here. She wore latex gloves and held a gun that looked like the one Rudy had used at the bank.

Molly gulped.

Sue pointed the gun at Rudy first.

"Now wait a minute, dollface," he said.

"Didn't you call *her* that about two minutes ago?" Susanna waved the gun back at Molly. Molly shrieked and Sue snorted. Then she returned her aim toward Rudy. "You were going to negotiate with this pink-faced idiot? Thought you could charm her pants off, huh? Have her join our little venture?"

Rudy moved in toward Susanna. "Doll, in case you haven't noticed, I have Molly's gun in my hand."

"It's not loaded."

The cold wind whipped hair into Molly's eyes. "Sue, you gave me an unloaded gun?"

"Hey, you said yourself it was just a prop."

Rudy pulled the trigger. An empty click.

Susanna fired her gun straight into his heart; he keeled over without another word.

Straddling his body, Sue shook her head. "So average. Like I said."

Molly's heart exploded. "You're the accomplice?"

"A little hiccup happens to be lying here," she said to Molly as she slipped the weapon into her waistband. "Let's tie some weights on him and get him overboard."

"Fifty percent?" Molly said.

"Of course."

They pulled out fishing line and weight belts from a deck box. It took the two of them to wrap him tight and hoist his 170 pounds, plus the weight belts, over the side. He sank like a stone.

Cackling, Susanna launched into the first bars of "Octopus's Garden." "Wish I had my ukulele now."

Molly shivered. "But we're stuck out here."

Susanna stopped singing about wanting to be under the sea. "Hah! I know this boat better than he did. Who do you think sold him this wreck?"

Molly shook her head. *Of course.*

"Now, about that deal . . ." Sue scratched behind her ear.

"Yes?" Molly's teeth chattered.

"Here's your 50/50, dollface." Susanna drew the gun back out of her waistband. "You can either go overboard voluntarily, saving me some work, or I can shoot you first."

"I thought we were friends."

"Seriously? Me, friends with someone who never advanced beyond teller?"

"You can keep all the money."

Susanna laughed. "How very generous of you." She gestured with the barrel toward the water where Rudy's body had disappeared.

Dripping with misery, Molly looked at the waves roiling below. "But why, Sue?"

"Any woman stupid enough to trust Rudy Carmona deserves to die."

A swift jab with the gun sent Molly flailing backward. Icy shock surrounded her. She gulped salt water and then bobbed to the surface.

Above her, Susanna waggled her fingers and launched into a deep-throated rendition of "Under the Boardwalk."

Molly treaded water, her wet wrap tugging her down. The distant lights taunted her. Never much of a swimmer, she took a floundering stroke.

The boat turned and putted toward shore, wagging its stern at her. The water's phosphorescence lit the scrolled lettering on the stern: *Karma II*.

PART III

Good Neighbors

TO LIVE AND DIE IN SANTA CRUZ

BY CALVIN MCMILLIN
UCSC

Maybe it's just misplaced nostalgia, but I'm one of those people who still buys the newspaper. When I was little, my dad would leave our trailer every Sunday morning and come back with a box of donuts and three different newspapers cradled in his arm like a football. All these years later, I'm still not sure why our household needed so much news coverage. I always reached for the comics. Unfortunately, there was nothing comical about this Sunday's edition of the *Santa Cruz Sentinel.*

> ***Graduate Student Found Dead on Campus***
> *Julie Chan, Staff Writer*
> *The body of a UC Santa Cruz graduate student was discovered early Saturday morning on campus grounds, according to a university press release.*
>
> *The deceased was found in the vicinity of the student health center, which is located on McLaughlin Drive across from College Nine. Campus police are currently handling the investigation.*
>
> *The student's name has not been released to the public as authorities are attempting to notify the next of kin.*

Next of kin. The phrase gave me goose bumps. I tossed the

newspaper in the backseat of my Mustang and looked up the *Sentinel*'s homepage on my phone.

> ***PhD Student Died From Apparent Fall from Bridge***
> *Stephanie Williams, Staff Writer*
> *Elizabeth White has been identified as the UC Santa Cruz graduate student found dead on university property last Saturday morning. She may have fallen from one of the pedestrian bridges on campus. White was a PhD candidate in literature and lived in graduate student housing.*
>
> *Campus police have cordoned off a footbridge located near the student health center. The bridge is suspended approximately seventy-five feet above the ground. This summer, new five-foot-high guardrails were installed to address safety concerns.*
>
> *White attended high school in Battle Creek, Michigan, and was an honor student in English at Michigan State University before coming to Santa Cruz three years ago. Friday marked her twenty-fifth birthday.*

That last line hit me hard. I didn't cry; I just stared at that sentence, wondering why bad things happen to good people, as if I were the first person in the world to ever ask the question. I killed the engine and swung the car door open.

Composed of a trio of buildings, graduate student housing was billed on its official website as "a friendly neighborhood consisting of eighty-eight scholars hailing from different countries across the globe." I couldn't care less. I just needed to talk to *two* of those eighty-eight. Not coincidentally, they shared an apartment on the fourth floor of Building 3.

After knocking on the door, I stood back from the peephole so whoever was inside could get a good look. A redhead with soft bangs wearing a Banana Slug hoodie answered the door. I must've looked respectable.

"Can I help you?"

"I called yesterday. I'm Elizabeth's sister."

Elizabeth's room was clean and well-lit, but otherwise unremarkable: a bed, a nightstand, a desk, a swivel chair, and a bulletin board without a single note. All standard issue from the university. No posters. No photographs. Aside from a trio of succulents on the windowsill, it was as if Elizabeth hadn't made herself at home. At the foot of her bed stood a bookcase filled with literary classics, trashy best sellers, and phone book–sized anthologies, many of them stacked artfully, others shoved haphazardly into every available nook. If there had ever been an earthquake in the middle of the night, the looming bookcase could have easily crushed Elizabeth in her sleep. She didn't have to worry about that anymore.

On the top shelf stood a little plastic doll—a woman in a frilly bonnet wearing an old-fashioned blue dress. She held a book in one hand and a quill in the other. I'd never seen it out of the package. I couldn't help myself; I had to pick it up.

"That's Jane Austen," said Alice, the redhead. "Don't feel bad. I didn't know who it was either. I thought it was an Amish woman!"

I smiled and put the figure down carefully.

"I should probably give you some privacy," Alice said.

"Actually, do you mind chatting with me for a bit?"

"Not at all." Alice sat across from me on Elizabeth's bed.

"I'd like to learn more about my sister's life here in Santa Cruz before she . . ." I let the sentence trail off and put my head in my hands. The tears came easily.

"Lizzy was a great person!" Alice exclaimed, as if enthusiasm alone could mute my feelings. "She was super nice. Polite. Always kept the common areas clean. I never had any problems with her."

Nice? Polite? Clean? Obviously, Alice barely knew Elizabeth.

"And Lizzy was such a go-getter!" she added. "Always attending some conference or taking a research trip. She even taught her own class!"

"What about her social life? Did she have any friends? I mean, besides you."

Alice looked embarrassed; clearly, she didn't count herself as a friend.

"Was she seeing anyone? The police didn't say."

"Yeah, she was . . . His name was Chet, I think."

"Chet?" I laughed. "What do you know about him?"

"Not much. He's handsome. Oh, and he's in the creative writing program."

"Does he live in student housing too?"

"No, Lizzy said he lives near the Boardwalk. In that old apartment complex with the bell tower. God, he must be devastated."

"You think so?"

"Yeah, he had it bad. He sent her bouquets of flowers, one after the other, right up until the, until the—" Alice tried to catch herself.

"Until the end?"

"Yeah, sorry." She averted her eyes.

"Don't worry about it. When's the last time you saw Chet?"

"Maybe a month back. I came home late. To be honest, it kinda freaked me out seeing a guy come out of our bathroom in the middle of the night." Alice pointed to the hallway. "The funny thing is, he looked twice as scared as me and super embarrassed."

"I see." An uncomfortable silence hung in the air.

"It must've been an accident, right?" Alice said. "I know grad school is stressful, but I didn't think she'd commit suicide."

"She's not the type. Believe me, I'd know."

"Of course, you're sisters."

We exchanged polite smiles.

"Y'know," Alice said, grinning like she'd just thought of the perfect joke, "I sort of forgot that Elizabeth was adopted."

"Adopted? What makes you say that?"

"Uh, well, I—" Her smile faded.

"You don't detect a family resemblance?"

"Um . . ."

Before I could let Alice off the hook, I heard the front door open.

"That must be Natalie," Alice said. "You should talk to her. She and Lizzy were in the same department."

We stared at the open door until Natalie came into view. A black Bettie Page bob framed a pair of deep blue eyes and a delicate face. In one hand, she clutched a large soft drink and in the other, a bag of takeout that was sweating with grease.

"Natalie," Alice called out, "come here and meet Lizzy's sister."

I stood up, but Natalie's hands were full, so instead of offering my hand to shake, I gave her a little wave and sat back down.

The sound of crickets chirping punctuated the awkward moment, as Alice scrambled to silence her phone. "Sorry, that's my cue to leave. I have a meeting with my advisor."

We exchanged pleasantries, and I remained seated as Alice left the apartment.

"So, why are you here again?" Natalie asked between sips of soda.

"To learn more about Elizabeth." I made a gesture inviting her to take a seat. She refused, towering over me.

"Liz was a slut," she announced, the smell of french fries on her breath.

"Excuse me?"

"I said, Liz. Was. A. Slut."

I jumped to my feet. "How could you even say that to me?"

"Easy. Liz didn't have a sister. So you better tell me who the hell you are before I call the cops."

I felt numb. Instead of offering a quick denial, I smiled to suggest that Natalie's accusation hadn't rankled me one bit. "Okay, you caught me. I'm not Elizabeth's sister. No relation at all. I'm Stephanie Williams of the *Santa Cruz Sentinel*, and I'm doing a story on Elizabeth's death."

"So you pretended to be her sister?"

"Sorry. I didn't think anyone would talk to me if I told the truth."

"Sounds a little unethical to me." Natalie sat on the bed, suddenly interested.

"There's a story here. I'm sure of it. Elizabeth was intelligent, beautiful, and in the prime of her life—and then, suddenly, she ends up at the bottom of a ravine? Why kill herself?"

"Have the police confirmed it was a suicide?" Natalie asked.

"Not yet. But depression is a big problem among graduate students. I thought I could shed some light on Elizabeth's story."

"Of course."

"So, is it true?"

"Is *what* true?" Natalie asked.

"You called her a slut."

"Well, I don't like to speak ill of the dead, but Liz didn't exactly play hard to get, if you know what I mean."

"Alice didn't mention anything like that."

"Her room is on the other end of the apartment. She couldn't hear a peep."

"But you could."

"Hard to miss. I'm right next door."

"And what exactly did you hear?"

She rolled her eyes. "Well, if you must know, she and her . . . boyfriend made so much freakin' noise." Something about the way Natalie said "boyfriend" made it sound illegitimate. "I teach a discussion section at nine in the morning. Hard to get any sleep with her going at it all night."

"Has your relationship with Elizabeth always been so strained?"

"Actually, no. We were close the first year. That's how I know about her family. But we drifted apart."

"Aren't you both in the same department?"

"Yeah, but I do postcolonial studies. Liz isn't exactly a serious scholar. She's into Jane Austen. I mean, can you think of anything fluffier than that? And my god, have you ever read *Mansfield Park*? Complete garbage."

"So, you had a falling out over . . . Jane Austen?"

"No, it was over the bathroom. She wanted things spotless. No matter how much I cleaned, it was never enough. And don't get me started on all her little passive-aggressive comments."

"Such as?"

"Liz was a strict vegetarian." Natalie held up the bag in her hand. "If I want to eat Jack in the Box, I'll eat Jack in the Box. It's none of her business." She reached into the bag and popped a soggy french fry in her mouth.

"So her vegetarianism became an annoyance?"

"That's putting it mildly," Natalie replied. "You know who else was a vegetarian? Hitler. And Pol Pot."

"I guess that's what happens when you love animals too much—genocide."

Natalie giggled. My little joke seemed to have won her over.

"So, just to make sure I'm understanding you correctly, the reason you called Elizabeth a slut was because she had loud sex with her boyfriend? Is that all?"

"N-no, that's just part of it. Elizabeth stole Chet away from another girl, and then turned around and cheated on him. Did Alice tell you about the flowers?"

I nodded.

"Chet didn't send them. He put up with all her whiny bullshit, and this is how she rewards him?"

"A potential love triangle. Interesting." I took out my smartphone and began typing up notes. Natalie didn't know I'd already started recording her.

"Don't quote me on that!" she said, only half-serious.

"I'll keep your name out of the article. But tell me this: who else was Elizabeth seeing?"

"Not sure. Someone older, I think."

"What do you know about Chet?"

"Nothing, really. I've never spoken to him."

I handed Natalie a business card. She inspected it like a cashier examining a suspiciously crisp hundred-dollar bill. "If you think of anything, my cell number is on the back. Don't call the office. That's not a direct line. I don't want anyone getting my messages and poaching the story, okay?"

"Sure," Natalie said, "but I gotta eat my lunch now. My tacos are getting cold."

* * *

Elizabeth's social media accounts offered few clues. Highlights included a couple of gorgeous West Cliff Drive sunsets and a handful of perfectly composed selfies highlighting Elizabeth's natural beauty. She'd crafted her online persona to suggest her life was incredibly fun—and conspicuously solitary. Her last post had been the previous summer.

I'd brought a box to pack up some of Elizabeth's things, but to my disappointment, the police took almost everything of value. No laptop. No tablet. Not even a stapler. Her desk drawers were all empty too. I thumbed through every book on her shelf, hoping to find some sort of clue—a diary, a scrap of paper, something.

Back in the Mustang, I stared at the only thing of value I retrieved: a photograph of a little Korean girl, probably five or six years old, smiling between two adoring Caucasian parents—Gregory and Susan White. The couple had difficulty conceiving, but with the help of an international adoption agency, they found and fell in love with a baby girl named Jae-Hee Kim, soon to be renamed Elizabeth Jane White.

While it's true that Elizabeth's parents were initially childless, her roommate Natalie didn't know half the story. The first twelve years of Elizabeth's life were relatively happy, though when her parents divorced, things took an ugly turn. Her father had only agreed to the adoption for the sake of his wife, so once the divorce was finalized, he cut off contact with Elizabeth, never to be heard from again.

Elizabeth's mother retained custody, yet when she remarried two years later, her new husband wasn't fond of a teenager in the house, especially one so obviously not his. Having to explain the existence of this Korean child, a constant reminder of his wife's previous marriage, made him deeply uncomfortable. Elizabeth's stepfather wanted children of his own, and he got his wish when her mother became pregnant with twins through the miracle of in vitro fertilization.

When Elizabeth completed high school, her stepfather accepted a job in Boston, taking her mother and her half-siblings out of state. Elizabeth's weekly phone calls from college to her mother slowly turned into an annual call and then into no calls at all. By the time she graduated from Michigan State, the family had ceased all contact. Thankfully, she'd been accepted into graduate school at Santa Cruz, a place where she could begin again—or so she thought.

Perhaps there was more to the story. But with Elizabeth gone, it was unlikely that I would ever discover the full truth.

My thoughts returned to the happy little girl in the photograph. Her adoptive parents looked happy too, no clue of the misery they would cause in the years to come. After drying my eyes, I put the photograph down and reached under the seat. To my relief, my pistol—a Ruger 9mm—was still there. I popped the magazine and checked the bullets. All seven rounds were ready for use.

At first glance, Chet Crawford was something of a disappointment. Despite Elizabeth's interest in all things Jane Austen, I'm sorry to report that Chet was no Mr. Darcy from *Pride and Prejudice*. If anything, I suspected he had more in common with Mr. Wickham, Darcy's charming but deceitful foil.

Chet's apartment wasn't difficult to find. Boasting Spanish Colonial Revival architecture and an iconic bell tower, the Beach Street Villa must have been breathtaking during its 1930s heyday. Eighty-five years later, the place was considerably less impressive. I suppose "crack house" might be a more apt description. Still, the appeal lay mainly in its location: to visit the Santa Cruz Beach Boardwalk, all you had to do was walk across the street.

For some reason, I expected Chet to be taller, but we were at eye level when he answered the door. He was alone, accompanied only by the distinct stench of alcohol. When I identified myself as a reporter, I figured Chet would slam the door in my face, but instead he invited me inside without protest.

If the villa's exterior looked bad, the interior of Chet's apartment was worse: dirty clothes draped everywhere, empty cans of beer stacked on the dresser, even a couple fast-food wrappers crumpled on the floor. Chez Chet had all the charm of an indoor landfill. Adorning his yellowed cracked walls were the markers of a cultured man: a framed poster for Wong Kar-Wai's *Days of Being Wild*, a reproduction of Gustav Klimt's *The Kiss*, and Yousuf Karsh's iconic photograph of Bogart.

"Beth was always so sensitive," he told me later, his handsome face blotchy with an alcoholic's sunburn. "I mean, being sensitive is fine if it means you're sensitive to other people's feelings, but it was a one-way street with her. She was so thin-skinned. Actually, it was like she was missing a layer of skin."

"Why didn't you break up with her?"

"Because she beat me to the punch. We hooked up at the end of spring quarter, and she wanted to keep seeing me through summer break. I was planning a cross-country road trip with my buddies—y'know, do the whole Kerouac thing—but I ended up canceling because of her. At the time, I didn't mind. I thought things were going well. But then, out of the blue, she breaks up with me and starts sleeping with somebody else. It's crazy!"

"And by *somebody else*, do you mean the mystery man sending her flowers?"

"How did you know about that?"

"I have my sources. But I don't know his name."

"He's a professor . . ."

"Which professor?"

"My advisor, Christian Malory. He's teaching this huge lecture course, two hundred people. It's called 'The Fantastic,' but believe me, it's anything but. Anyway, me, Beth, and two other grad students were assigned as his teaching assistants. At first, I admired him. Of course, I didn't realize Malory was such a fucking creep. He's always hitting on his students, even though he's got a fiancée in Los Angeles. It's like they always say, *Never meet your heroes*."

"So what happened?"

"Last month, I met up with Malory and his grad school groupies at the Rush Inn, a dive bar on Knight Street. Beth, on the other hand, *never* came to these drink nights."

"Why not?"

"Well, she's a real bookworm, homebody type. Unless we did something together, she was always in her room studying. But this *one* fucking time, Beth shows up. This is like a day after breaking up with me! And she's acting flirty—with *Professor Malory*. Like, at one point, she's sitting on his lap. She just wanted to make me jealous."

"What did you do?"

"What could I do? Beth never drinks, but she got pretty wasted that night. I tried to stick around to make sure she got home safely, but her behavior with Malory was tough to watch."

"So you left the bar early?"

"Yeah, though I actually stayed up waiting for her."

"Where did you wait?"

"What do you mean?" Chet seemed truly puzzled.

"Where *specifically* did you wait? Outside her apartment? Or inside?"

"Oh, inside. I have a key. Ended up sleeping there. When she didn't come home in the morning, I left."

"Did something happen between Elizabeth and Dr. Malory?"

"Why don't you ask him yourself?" Chet turned his back to me and cracked another beer. "He'll be at the Rush Inn tonight."

After meeting with Chet, I drove downtown and bought a tight red dress that accentuated my curves and a pair of knee-high boots with stiletto heels. With a dusting of glittery eye shadow, my outfit came together nicely.

That night, at the Rush Inn, I found Professor Malory with his coterie of hangers-on, just as Chet described. He was an imposing sight: well over six feet tall, muscular, with a supremely confident smirk.

I introduced myself as an undergrad looking for guidance on whether to switch my major. I expressed my admiration for his body of work, peppering my compliments with information I'd gleaned from a cursory reading of his campus bio. Malory was so pleased, I suspect he asked me back to his place on that reason alone.

When we crossed the threshold of his vintage Eichler home, I expected to be offered a drink, but Malory had other ideas—he lunged at me. His lips were pressed against mine, his tongue forcing my mouth open and flopping inside like a fish on a riverbank. Before I knew it, his hands were around my neck—and not in a tender caress. *He was choking me.* When I realized he had no intention of letting go, I cuffed him. Literally.

"What's this?"

I'd solidly clipped a pair of handcuffs to his left wrist.

"Let's play a game," I commanded, in the most seductive voice I could muster.

Christian Malory was a Berkeley-educated scholar, a man who spent the majority of his adult life dedicated to the pursuit of social justice, and a self-described activist who positioned himself as a feminist ally. And yet here, in his own home, he behaved like a horny teenager—and a willing captive.

Thus, he happily complied with my order to remove his clothes and lie on the bed. He owned a metal headboard, so I snaked the handcuffs around one of the bars and closed the open cuff around his other wrist. Eager to participate, he directed me to a dresser where he kept his neckties, so I secured his ankles to the two newel posts at the foot of the bed. Malory loved every second of it—that is, until I grabbed my purse and drew out my pistol.

"You're kidding, right?" he asked, almost amused.

I shook my head.

"Look, I'm all for games, but this is crazy."

I pointed the Ruger at his head.

"Don't shoot! You can take anything you want!"

"I only want one thing." I placed the tip of the barrel between his eyebrows.

"It's yours! Name it!"

"The truth about Elizabeth White."

"There's nothing to tell. She was my TA."

"Oh, I think she was more than that." I aimed the gun at his crotch.

"Okay! We slept together. Just once, I swear!"

I shook my head. "She was intoxicated. She couldn't possibly have consented. That's rape."

"You're crazy! She was into it!"

"Then why no second date? Why were you sending her flowers?"

"What? How do you—? I don't know what you're talking about."

"Enough lying." I grabbed one of Malory's argyle socks from the floor and stuffed it in his mouth. "Let me tell you a secret. I had an appointment at the student health center last Friday. I saw Elizabeth there. I wanted to say hello, but she didn't acknowledge me. It's understandable. Nobody wants to talk about why they're seeing the doctor. I was still in the waiting room when she came out. She looked horrible. But why am I even telling you this? *You were there*."

Malory's eyes widened, but he didn't make a sound.

"I followed her outside. I don't know why. I probably should've respected her privacy. But then I saw you waiting for her in the parking lot. And I saw the look on your face when she spoke to you. I didn't know your name. I had no idea how to find you. But now I have."

Malory grunted, so I took the sock out of his mouth.

"You've got it all wrong!" he screamed, gasping for air. "Let me explain!"

"What's there to explain? You raped her, you probably got her pregnant," I said, almost crying, "and then you killed her to shut her up."

"I didn't kill her! That was the last time I saw her. She texted me later that night, but I didn't reply. She needed a ride. The cops already questioned me about all this! I wasn't even in Santa Cruz! I was in LA with my girlfriend!"

"I don't believe you," I hissed. "You're a liar. And a rapist."

"It wasn't rape! If she didn't want it, she shouldn't have thrown herself at me."

"Your behavior put her in an emotional state that resulted in her death. You're responsible."

"Actually, I disagree," he began, as if he were lecturing a student. "I think—"

"I don't care what you think."

I put a pillow over his face and pulled the trigger.

The following afternoon, I awoke to the sound of a text message. I'd forgotten I'd even given Natalie my number.

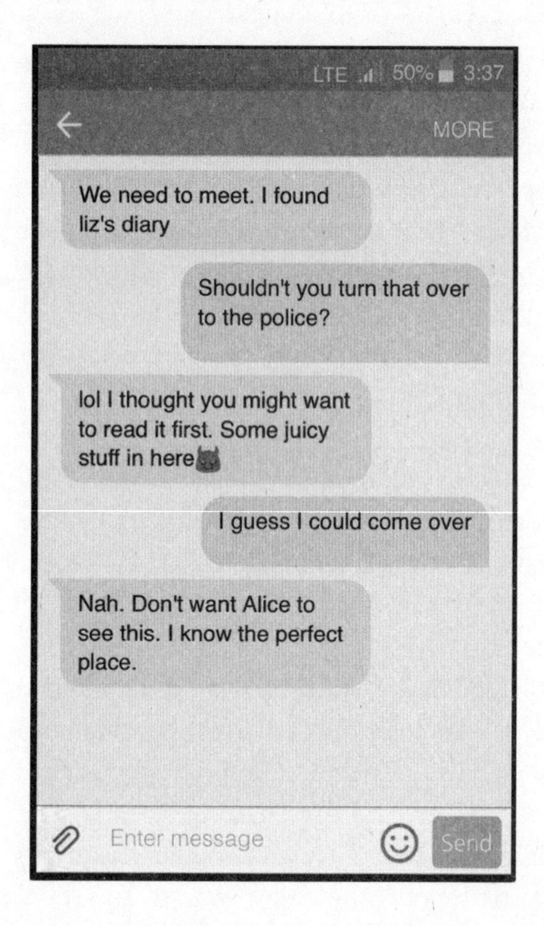

I called Natalie. She suggested meeting up near one of the campus bridges. Not *that* bridge, she giggled, but one located at the far end of Kresge College deep in the redwoods. There was a park bench near the entrance of the bridge, making it the perfect place for a clandestine meeting. She actually used the word "clandestine." Obviously she'd seen one too many spy movies. I wanted the diary, so I agreed to meet her that night at eight.

"Take her legs," a voice said. I couldn't tell who was speaking, and I had a hard time opening my eyes. Two arms were shoved under my armpits, dragging me through wet leaves.

"Think we can carry her to the bridge?" asked a different voice.

"Yeah, I think so."

"What if someone sees us?"

"Don't worry. No one's out here but us."

How could I be so stupid? If I hadn't been curious about Elizabeth's diary, I never would've agreed to meet Natalie in the first place. I'd gotten sloppy. If I'd been quicker to react, she wouldn't have been holding my feet.

"Are you sure we should do this?" Natalie asked the man clutching me. "We don't even know who she is."

"Check her driver's license when we get to the middle of the bridge."

When did Natalie figure out I wasn't Stephanie Williams of the *Santa Cruz Sentinel?* I'd pocketed a couple of business cards from the real Stephanie's office on Monday. Even with my phone number written on the back, I knew passing her card off as mine would be a risk. I just didn't think it could cost me my life.

When Natalie showed up a half hour late, the first thing I

asked for was the diary, no small talk. I should have run away the moment she started grinning like an idiot.

But all that planning had made me overconfident. During our meeting, I clutched the Ruger hidden in my jacket pocket, knowing full well that if things spiraled out of control, all I'd have to do is squeeze the trigger and the bullet would do the work. But Natalie had an accomplice. That realization came too late, all thanks to a sharp blow to the back of my head. Chet Crawford was the last thing I saw before losing consciousness.

"Switch with me, babe," Chet ordered. "Prop her up. I'll grab her legs and throw her over."

"What about her head?" asked Natalie, as she changed positions. "You hit her hard. She's bleeding."

"They'll think she got it in the fall."

"Fuck, she's heavier than Lizzy."

The mere mention of Elizabeth finally woke me up. I could feel Natalie's bony hands digging into my armpits. Chet's face loomed large in front of me. They were taking a breather. Hauling my limp body from the park bench all the way to the bridge must've been exhausting.

This was my chance.

I reached into my jacket pocket and fired four shots from my Ruger, striking Chet in the chest. He careened backward over the opposite guardrail and plummeted seventy feet to his death.

Unlike the other bridge where Elizabeth died, the guardrails here were only four feet high. They were next on the university's list to be replaced.

"Chet!" Natalie screamed.

I slammed the back of my head into Natalie's nose and heard a distinct crunch. She shrieked in pain, releasing me as she fell to the ground.

"Please don't!" she screamed, her face covered in blood. "I didn't mean for any of this to happen!"

I grabbed her by the collar with my gloved hands and dragged her back to where Chet went over. Natalie tried to fight back, but every arm-flail in her defense proved useless. When I reached the middle of the bridge, I let go of her collar and pointed my gun at her face. "Tell me what you did to Elizabeth."

"It was an accident," she said.

"You already said that. Explain."

"After her doctor's appointment, Elizabeth wandered around campus in a daze. That night, she texted me to come pick her up. She was too exhausted to walk back. I ignored her message, but Chet said we should go anyway. Chet and I—we'd started seeing each other again."

"And then?"

"She was in a pretty fucked-up state of mind when we found her. She said some nasty things. I said some things. Chet got involved and then . . ."

"And then what?"

"She slipped. Like I said, it was an accident."

"And yet, you and your boyfriend were perfectly willing to kill me tonight."

She turned her head away from me. "We thought you were going to expose us! We just went a little crazy."

"Me too." I placed the muzzle of the Ruger to Natalie's temple and fired. Her body slumped awkwardly against the guardrail.

I took my cell phone, a burner I'd bought at Target in Watsonville, and tossed it over the railing in Chet's general direction. After placing the gun near Natalie's body, I removed my leather gloves, revealing vinyl ones underneath, and put them on her hands. My right glove was likely coated in gunshot residue, and I'd already filed off the Ruger's serial number. It was the perfect crime, although honestly, I didn't care about getting caught. In fact, I'd never felt so alive.

On Sunday, I discovered that the pedestrian bridge where Elizabeth died had become a memorial—flowers, cards, and numerous trinkets had been left in her honor. Not being family, I didn't know when her body would be laid to rest or where, so I brought a bag of donuts, a chocolate milk, and a Sunday newspaper for the both of us.

Bizarre Murder-Suicide Linked to Graduate Student's Death

Stephanie Williams, Staff Writer

UC Santa Cruz police have confirmed that two graduate students were found dead on campus in an apparent murder-suicide on Friday night. The bodies were discovered near a pedestrian bridge located on campus. Officials confirmed that this is not the same bridge from which Elizabeth White reportedly fell, but would offer no further comment as that investigation remains ongoing.

The victims were male and female, both in their late twenties. Their identities have not been released.

Body of UC Santa Cruz Professor Found in Home

Julie Chan, Staff Writer

Christian Malory, a UC Santa Cruz literature professor, was found dead Saturday in his home on Escalona Drive. The cause of death has not been released.

Elizabeth White, whose death from an apparent fall on November 11 is still under investigation, was listed as one of Malory's teaching assistants for the fall semester. Police would neither confirm nor deny a connection between the cases.

I couldn't read another line. Elizabeth was more than just a teaching assistant to me. She was my mentor, my friend, and my one true love.

I was such a mess when I signed up for her discussion section in Professor Yamamura's Pacific literature course. I'd escaped to UCSC after fleeing an abusive relationship back home. When I told her one of the novels had triggered my PTSD, Elizabeth was sympathetic. She represented everything that was kind and decent and wonderful about the world. When I heard she'd be teaching "Jane Austen and Popular Culture," a course she'd designed herself, I immediately signed up the following semester. A few days before the final exam, Elizabeth invited me to her office to discuss my clunky, overlong term paper on the homoerotic overtones of *Emma*, *Pride and Prejudice*, and my all-time favorite, *Mansfield Park*. After she submitted final grades, we began spending more time together, although always in secret.

Over the Christmas holiday, we were inseparable. I told her about being a lonely, depressed teen, plagued by self-destructive impulses and suicidal ideation. She told me about being adopted and abandoned. About the racism she encountered—from colleagues, from professors, from people she'd dated.

"We can't let them win," she said. "We *won't* let them win."

Of course, all good things must come to an end. Elizabeth broke up with me a few months later. Even though there was little disparity in our ages, she was adamant in her reasoning:

I was a student; she was a teacher. It was simply inappropriate.

The breakup drove me into a deep depression. That's why I was at the health center that day. To get treatment. That's why I wanted to talk to her so bad. Sure, Elizabeth didn't say hello that day, but I figured we'd see each other again.

And then I read the Sunday paper.

In front of her memorial, I fumbled through my purse and pulled out the Jane Austen figure I'd swiped from her apartment. It would look nice next to a framed photo that had been taken from her graduate student profile page. No one knew that I was the one who'd bought that figure for Elizabeth as a token of gratitude for all her help. For all her love. Frankly, I was amazed that she'd kept it.

"I didn't let them win," I said aloud through my tears, confessing all I'd done.

TREASURE ISLAND

BY MICAH PERKS

Grant Park

Welcome to Good Neighbor!™
Choose a Neighborhood: Midtown
Choose a Category: Crime and Safety
Add Subject: "We're in This Together!"
Post Message: Log Date, November 15, 2017

I'm a seventy-two-year-old retired middle school assistant principal who has lived in Grant Park for forty years. Since the Emeline Street "needle exchange" invaded our neighborhood, we've seen our streets taken over by crack addicts, tweekers, panhandlers—the whole basket of deplorables, to borrow a phrase. How many of us have posted about bicycle theft? Stolen mail? Keyed cars? Garbage rifled through? Dirty needles?

I'm going to post each day for the next month a record of the incidents I witness in our neighborhood. I will present my log at the next city council meeting on December 15. I urge you to do the same. We're in this together!

Welcome to Good Neighbor!™
Choose a Neighborhood: Midtown
Choose a Category: Crime and Safety
Add Subject: "We're in This Together!"
Post Message: Log Date, November 16, 2017

11:00 a.m.—Apparently white male, medium height/build, UC Santa Cruz Banana Slug sweatshirt, yelling obscenities in park across street, per usual. FU**, COC* SUCKER, etcetera. You've heard it. Pacing across entrance, per usual. For the hearing impaired, this apparently strung-out individual hollers in the park approximately three times a week. You know him as the Screamer. I go out on my second-floor balcony to document.

The Screamer screams, "I see you, sir! Yeah, you, there on the balcony! Staring is very rude! It's rude to take photos of strangers!" I continue to take photos [attached here], though blurry because, distance. Screamer then screams, "Fu** you! Go ahead—call the cops again!"

11:05 a.m.—I call the cops.

11:35 a.m.—Cops arrive (surprise, surprise)! Talk to Screamer. Screamer leaves park, heading toward McDonald's, as is his habit. Does he scream at McDonald's? Anybody know?

2:30 p.m.—School bus drops pupils off in front of park, per usual. Three apparently Hispanic males, ages approximately eight or nine years old, stuff candy wrappers into neighbor's "Little Library." I go to balcony, take photos of them. Yell down, "Pick up those wrappers!" They scream, "*El diablo viejo!*" (Google translation: little old devil man) and run toward Button Street.

2:35 p.m.—I call the cops, report incident.

3:00 p.m.—Cops have not responded, per usual.

3:15 p.m.—I descend, which takes some time due to bum hip, retrieve plastic bag and "trash grabber" ($6.47, Amazon Prime, you can read my review, three stars because the sharp tongs are dangerous), exit house, open gate, cross street to neighbor's "Little Library" (a glassed-in cabinet painted a glaring aqua, plunked onto a post).

I grab candy wrappers, deposit in bag. Open neighbor's gate, covered in multiple strings of bells, so jingle jingle jingle. Knock on door of this neighbor, a "writer" who "works" from home. ("Writer" always takes morning tea on his porch in his pajamas and at five p.m., takes cocktail on porch, still in his pajamas. You've probably seen him on your way to and from actual work.)

Conversation:

Me: (holding out trash bag) "Three juvenile delinquents stuffed this trash in your 'Little Library' again."

"Writer": (apparently Asian male, apparently in his thirties, in pajamas, per usual): "Okay."

Me: "I've warned you before that your so-called 'Little Library' attracts vagrants."

"Writer": "Books attract vagrants?"

Me: "Have you been to the downtown library? It's basically a homeless shelter."

"Writer": (taking bag) "Thanks, Mr. Nowicki, I'll take care of it."

(NOTE: "Writer" is not on Good Neighbor!™ even though I have invited him by e-mail multiple times.)

I have looked "Writer" up on Amazon and he has one book of short stories published seven years ago, titled: *Miraculous Escapes*. Only two reviews, both three stars, #3,053,049 in Books. He has placed two copies of his own book in his "Little Library," but apparently no one has ever taken it out.

Apparently, no one has ever taken a book out of the "Little Library" at all, although he checks it daily. Am I right? Have any of you taken advantage of the "Little Library" or is it just a receptacle for trash?

5:00 p.m.: "Writer," still in pajamas, exits house, puts on rubber boots he always leaves by door (despite my warnings that it will attract thieves), nails my plastic bag to fence beside "Little Library" with cardboard sign, "Put Trash Here." Drinks cocktail on porch.

Welcome to Good Neighbor!™
Choose a Neighborhood: Midtown
Choose a Category: Crime and Safety
Add Subject: "We're in This Together!"
Post Message: Log Date, November 17, 2017

5:45 a.m.—Woken by bells on gate of "Writer's" house. Jingle jingle jingle. I open curtain. Individual in hoodie, apparently young adolescent male, caught in act of stealing "Writer's" rubber boots. I run downstairs (really gimp downstairs because of bum hip), take up trash-grabber by door, exit house. Thief still in "Writer's" yard. I brandish trash-grabber aloft from across street, yelling: "Drop those boots!"

Thief does not drop boots. I limp across street, open gate, hit boots out of perp's hands with trash-grabber. I yell "Writer's" name because in rush forgot phone to call cops.

Thief makes to attack me, but trips on fallen rubber boot, grabs onto trash-grabber on way down. Why? No idea. I yell for "Writer" again.

"Writer" (exiting house, in pajamas, long hair loose like wild man of Borneo): "What's going on?"

Me: "Call the cops!"

"Writer" looks down. I look down. Thief's hood has fallen back, revealing an apparently mixed-race female, late teens or early twenties, short dark hair, multiple piercings and whatnots in ears and nose, one big brown eye, holding other eye with both hands. Blood seeping through fingers. Apparently Thief hit trash-grabber with eye.

Thief: "My eye, my eye! This old man attacked me."

Me: "I apprehended this criminal stealing your rubber boots."

"Writer": (ignoring me, to Thief) "Are you okay?"

Thief: "Something's wrong with my eye." (Blood dripping down face onto sweatshirt, will definitely stain if not washed immediately.)

"Writer": (dialing 911 on his phone) "We need an ambulance."

Me: "Are you crazy? She's probably faking. Do you know how much an ambulance costs? Over a thousand dollars. Do you have insurance?"

"Writer": (finally paying attention, hangs up). "I'll drive you to the emergency room. My car's just right here."

"Writer" helps Thief to feet. Half-carries Thief to car (Prius, keyed on both sides). Drives away, silently, because: Prius. Leaves rubber boots on sidewalk. I gather them up, line them back up on his porch, all ready to be stolen again.

10:00 a.m.—Prius returns. "Writer" goes around to passenger-side door. Helps out Thief, who is wearing eyepatch like pirate. "Writer" and Thief enter "Writer's" house.

11:10 a.m.—I am questioned by police. Officers P. and S. accuse me of assault with a weapon on private property. Say I'm lucky the "victim" is not pressing charges. I express outrage.

Officer P., apparently Hispanic, bald, says, "Maybe you should choose your battles, sir. You've called 911 twenty-two times in the past month." P. and S. smirk at each other.

I express outrage that the neighborhood has been allowed to become like the movie *Falling Down*. Question officers if they have even seen the movie *Falling Down* with Michael Douglas. (You should rent it on Amazon Prime, $3.99, I gave it five stars—story of regular man fighting back against falling-down neighborhood like ours.)

Officer S. asks me if I've seen *Rear Window*, his favorite movie. I ask officers if they are arresting Thief. Officer S. says, "You mean the female victim?"

Are there any witnesses to what actually occurred at 5:45 a.m.? Private message me.

Welcome to Good Neighbor!™
Choose a Neighborhood: Midtown
Choose a Category: Crime and Safety
Add Subject: "We're in This Together!"
Post Message: Log Date, November 18, 2017

9:00 a.m.—"Writer" and Thief taking tea on front porch. Thief still wearing eyepatch. Thief is pale, likely tweeker, with bruise on cheek. Bruises easily due to drug use?

There is 98 percent likelihood Thief will rob "Writer" blind, kill him in his sleep, etcetera. I am predicting this now.

(I suggest some of you walk by and take some photos for evidence of this future crime. I don't want to reveal house number, but I'm sure you all know the residence. The one with the overgrown front yard, jasmine and morning glories, etcetera, choking everything, weeds growing onto sidewalk through the white fence which is broken off and tilting in places, front porch painted purple, that "Little Library" hammered onto a post by that gate with those bells all over it.)

This "Writer" not your typical Santa Cruz hippie, though, because Asian. "Writer" bought house fifteen months ago. At first I thought he would help us save the neighborhood, because Asian. At my middle school, Asian children were always best behaved, neatest handwriting, etcetera, but this "Writer" has long, shaggy hair that looks like birds could make nest in it.

To describe "Writer," hard, because he doesn't look like actor I can think of, because so few Asian actors. Maybe like Bruce Lee if Bruce Lee wore a woman's wig to play a washed-up "Writer." More like pre–washed up, because never famous. I wish Bruce Lee lived in neighborhood, he'd keep everyone in line with his karate chops.

Imagine he's mooching off his family—the "Writer"—not Bruce Lee. Probably his parents are immigrants who worked all their lives running a small business, a souvenir shop in Chinatown, to put him through the best schools, and this is how he repays them, living off their money pretending to write. Parents never visit, as far as I can see. Probably better for them not to observe how he's living, probably give them heart attack.

10:00 a.m.—Thief, still with eyepatch, wearing "Writer's" large rubber boots, is weeding "Writer's" overgrown yard. So she nabbed the rubber boots after all.

11:00 a.m.—Still weeding. Has filled three trash bags with green waste (Thief looks like that actress with short hair, good face, what's her name? Just Googled it: Audrey Hepburn. Like Audrey Hepburn playing thief/tweeker. I wish Audrey Hepburn lived next door, but just crazy dream because she would have moved out long ago due to crack addicts, etcetera).

12:00 p.m.—Thief examines "Little Library." Takes out a *Babysitters Club Mystery*. Makes me think! Either this book is much too young for Thief or Thief is much younger than I first thought.

Is Thief a runaway? Situation suddenly takes on new, ugly light. Perhaps it is Thief who is in danger from "Writer," not other way round.

Did "Writer" put a *Babysitters Club Mystery* in "Little Library" to lure underage girl? Possibility of statutory rape raises its depraved head. Consider calling cops, but will gather proof first.

1:00 p.m.—With my copy of *Treasure Island* I make my way to front gate of "Writer's" house. Shake gate with bells to get her attention. Call to Thief, "If you're going to read, which may strain your one eye and cause blindness, at least don't read trash. Here's a classic."

She comes down off purple porch. Stands on other side of gate. Undernourished in ratty T-shirt, though no apparent needle marks on arms or signs of that popular cutting hobby either. Close up, she is not so much Audrey Hepburn, more like very pretty lollipop with long neck and round face with huge eyes.

Thief: "You're a tough old geezer. You remind me of my grandpa."

Me: "Where is your grandfather?"

Thief: "Dead."

Me: "What about your parents?"

Thief: "Same."

Me: "How old are you?"

Thief: "How old are *you*?"

Me: "Seventy-two."

Thief: "You don't look a day older than seventy-one, ha-ha. Seriously, I could give you a makeover. I have about two-thirds of a degree in cosmetology."

Me: "Very funny. What is your name?"

Thief: "Jim."

Me: "Jim?"

Thief: "Jim. It's my nickname. Jim Hawkins."

Me: "Why were you reading that *Babysitter* book?

Thief: "I put it under the leg of a rickety chair."

(Alert: See attached photo of "Jim Hawkins" that I took from second-floor balcony. Runaway in danger? If anyone recognizes her, private message me.)

1:45 p.m.—Correction: Jim is an alias. I realize from googling that girl gave me the name of the main character in *Treasure Island*, "Jim Hawkins." Perhaps secret message. Jim Hawkins taken captive by pirates. This person is clearly educated. Have strong feeling family is not all dead, and may be looking for her. This young person may be being taken advantage of by lecherous older man.

1:50 p.m.—Decide to call cops. Express my concerns re: runaway, statutory rape, etcetera.

3:11 p.m.—Officer P. knocks on "Writer's" door. "Jim" answers. Officer P. speaks. "Jim" takes out what appears to be an ID. Officer examines briefly and returns (could be fake). Officer P. and "Jim" look over at my house and laugh. I drop curtain.

5:00 p.m.—"Jim" and "Writer" taking cocktails on purple porch. More laughter.

Welcome to Good Neighbor!™
Choose a Neighborhood: Midtown
Choose a Category: Crime and Safety
Add Subject: "We're in This Together!"
Post Message: Log Date, November 19, 2017

9:00 a.m.—"Jim" is weeding again. Must admit Jim is busy bee. Good work ethic. Perhaps of Hispanic origin?

10:00 a.m.—Now "Jim" is fixing fence. Nailing loose pickets.

2:15 p.m.—Now "Jim" is weeding sidewalk in front. Looks up, waves to me (on my second-floor balcony).

"Jim": "How are you this morning, Mr. Nowicki?"

She is clearly exhausted from hard work. Where is that "Writer"? Probably snoozing away the day on his couch in his pajamas. Has gotten himself good deal. Beautiful young handyman/servant. Hot day, even though November always pretty hot. I make glass of Lipton iced tea and bring it to her. She thanks me.

While we are both in yard, school bus stops in front of park, down street, per usual. Same three miscreants exit, backpacks bumping on their backs as they chase each other down street. We can see them easily because "Jim" has clipped the hedge back.

They see me. "El diablo!" they scream—and throw their wrappers in "Writer's" yard, laughing, running away.

"Jim" hands me iced tea. Vaults the fence like superhero (maybe gymnastics?) and runs down the street after them.

Next thing I know she is dragging two of them by the shirt back down the street.

"Jim": (giving them a shove) "Pick it up."

They gather up wrappers.

"Jim": "Apologize to Mr. Nowicki."

They apologize. One is crying (younger one, maybe seven years old).

"Jim": "Do you accept their apology?"

Me: "Yes."

"Jim": "If I ever see wrappers in my yard again I am going to hunt you little fu**ers down and kill you. Get it?"

They nod. She lets them leave.

"Jim" takes glass of tea back from me and finishes it.

3:30 p.m.—Note: Not sure what to think about this turn of events. What is your opinion?

4:00 p.m.—Note: "Jim" said "my" yard.

5:00 p.m.—"Jim" on porch drinking cocktail. "Writer" nowhere to be seen. Yard is spick 'n' span, fence is fixed, but where is "Writer"? Not drinking tea this morning, not checking his "Little Library" and having his cocktail at five, per usual.

Welcome to Good Neighbor!™
Choose a Neighborhood: Midtown
Choose a Category: Crime and Safety
Add Subject: "We're in This Together!"
Post Message: Log Date, November 20, 2017

9:00 a.m.—"Jim" chops up "Little Library" with axe. "Jim" is expert with axe.

"Jim": (noticing me watch from balcony) "Hey, Mr. Nowicki, I know you hate this 'Little Library.' It attracts scumbags, am I right?"

Me: (I don't know what to say, so just take photo [attached here].)

"Jim": "Got any more of that Lipton?"

9:30 a.m.—I bring tea out (excuse to gather info).

Me: "What does the 'Writer' think of you getting rid of the 'Little Library'?"

"Jim": "I'm taking care of things now."

Me: "But he checked that 'Little Library' every day."

"Jim": "Exactly. He needs to focus."

Me: "I'd like a word with him."

"Jim": (repeating herself) "I'm taking care of everything now."

Me: (not knowing what to say) "That's nice of you."

Jim: "I'm not nice. I'm family."

Me: "What do you mean?"

"Jim" sits down on purple porch, drinks tea, proceeds to tell me long story. I can't quote the exact words. But here's a summary:

—She's "Writer's" sister! Half-sister.

—She comes from the first wife. (Means "Jim" must be in thirties, has that Asian thing where never seem to age.)

—The father called "Jim's" mother "The Mistake."

—Father abandoned them, father became fancy head librarian at research university, married second wife, had a kid, a bookworm: the "Writer."

—"Jim" grew up in the library. Mother couldn't afford babysitter so she would hide "Jim" in the stacks when she went to work.

—Both kids bookworms, but "Writer" became a "writer," "Jim" became a dropout from Fresno School of Cosmetology.

—"Jim's" mother died two years ago, "Jim" tried to see father. He rebuffed her.

Me: (after long story) "But why are you chopping down the 'Little Library' then? If your mother loved libraries? If you're a bookworm?"

"Jim": "I never said I loved libraries. I said I grew up in libraries. Books are bullsh**. Books are just a way not to see. You and me, Mr. Nowicki, we see. I know you know what I mean."

Me: "But . . . you were stealing his boots."

"Jim": "It's a joke we like to play on each other."

Me: "But—"

"Jim": "I like you, Mr. Nowicki. You keep your eye on things, make sure everything is on the up and up. Don't even need to buy a security cam with you around. If I didn't have that lemon tree in front of the window, you could see right into my house, couldn't you?

Welcome to Good Neighbor!™
Choose a Neighborhood: Midtown
Choose a Category: Crime and Safety
Add Subject: "We're in This Together!"
Post Message: Log Date, November 21, 2017

9:00 a.m.—"Jim" is power-washing the Prius. No sign of "Writer."

11:00 a.m.—Screamer in park again. "Jim" marches out of house, carrying something. Walks into park, right up to Screamer, says something.

Screamer: "Fu** you, ma'am."

"Jim" holds up something to his face. Screamer screams in a different way, holds eyes. Must have been mace. "Jim" says something else. Screamer stumbles out of park, hands over eyes, not toward McDonald's, toward Emeline Public Health Services. "Jim" walks back into house.

Welcome to Good Neighbor!™
Choose a Neighborhood: Midtown
Choose a Category: Crime and Safety
Add Subject: "We're in This Together!"
Post Message: Log Date, November 22, 2017

I haven't seen "Writer" in four days, not in the morning, not in the evening. No tea, no cocktail. Has anyone seen writer? Private message me if you have.

Welcome to Good Neighbor!™
Choose a Neighborhood: Midtown
Choose a Category: Crime and Safety
Add Subject: "We're in This Together!"
Post Message: Log Date, November 25, 2017

I've been doing some Internet research. Found an interview of "Writer" in *Catamaran Literary Reader*. Interviewer asks "Writer" about origin of his story "Rubber Boots." "Writer" said parents died in a fire two years ago. Suspected arson, but no one ever caught. All that was left: father's rubber boots on doorstep. Everything else burned. "Writer" used inheritance to buy house in Santa Cruz, etcetera. "Writer" says he is only child.

Welcome to Good Neighbor!™
Choose a Neighborhood: Midtown
Choose a Category: Crime and Safety
Add Subject: "I Am Not a Pervert"
Post Message: Log Date, November 27, 2017

6:00 p.m.—First time I've been able to post since I got home from the hospital. I see someone has made Good Neighbor!™ take down all my posts. Please read this now before they take this post down too.

I am not a pervert. If you have been reading my log, you know I was and still am concerned for the well-being of my neighbor, the writer who lives (or lived) opposite me, because said writer has been missing since November 18. I documented all of this, before it was erased. Did anyone take a screenshot? Private message me.

On the night of November 23 at approximately eleven p.m. I donned black pants. Didn't have black turtleneck but wore green.

I made my way downstairs, took long time because hip, per usual. Nobody on street as far as I could see. Forty-two degrees, cloudy. You remember. Very dark because city refuses to put more lights on our street to deter criminals. Cross street to gate of "Writer's" house. Open gate very slowly, little jingle jingle jingle, but not much.

I freeze, wait.

Nothing.

Light is on downstairs at "Writer's" house. I hold onto branch of lemon tree. It sways. I freeze again, nothing. With help of branch I duck down, behind lemon tree, right against front window. Living room is lined with bookshelves, but bookshelves almost all empty! "Jim" is boxing up all the books.

Drinking wine. And by back door? Four heavy-duty green trash bags. Next to them, leaning against back door: the axe.

I continue to watch (I realize now that "Jim" was in underwear, no bra, black panties, thong-type, but at the time I didn't notice because too busy documenting evidence).

Then "Jim" looks up. Seems to stare right at me.

I freeze.

She goes back to packing up books, humming and drinking wine. I am spooked. I grab branch, whole tree sways, don't even care because, slightly panicked, duck under, come out from tree.

There's "Jim." Just standing there in hoodie, waiting for me. I scream. "Jim" maces me.

It hurts so much, like hot sauce in my eyes. I stumble around, can't see, trip over tree root, crash to ground. My hip on fire. Scream for help. Some of you came out, I'm sure, but I couldn't see.

Did any of you film this?

Next thing I know, ambulance. I'm screaming, "No, no ambulance!" even though I have insurance, waste of money. I'm screaming, "She murdered him! She murdered him! Just look in the house!"

Some of you must have heard me. I hear "Jim" telling the cops I was peeping in her window.

That's all I remember, must have passed out.

Hip broken, surgery. Hazy, because drugged. Wake up at one point and there is Officer P., looming over me.

Me: "Did you search the house? Did you see the trash bags?"

Officer P.: "You're a lucky man, Mr. Nowicki."

Me: "Lucky? I broke my hip."

Officer P.: "Lucky because once again your neighbor is not

pressing charges. You need to leave this young woman alone."

Me: "She's not my neighbor. That's not her house. You have to listen to me. Read my posts on Good Neighbor!™ It's all there!"

Officer P.: "Mr. Nowicki, your neighbor is at a writer's colony in Upstate New York. He's left his house in care of his sister. We've received an e-mail from him."

Me: "But then, why is she throwing out all his books? What about the trash bags? Did you look inside?"

Officer P.: "Mr. Nowicki, that's not your business. You're going to be laid up for a while, but after that, why don't you go on down to the Market Street Senior Center. They have folk dancing, ukulele lessons, wood carving. Great rehab for your hip. Or you could take up tai chi in the park. Something to do, meet people. Keep you out of trouble."

Now I'm stuck in a hospital bed in my own living room. Had a day-nurse come in. I asked her to help me get to the window but she refused. "No more peeping, Mr. Nowicki."

12:00 a.m.: Alone, can't sleep, stuck in hospital bed. Hip hurts. Spooked. Keep hearing strange noises, but may be the drugs.

Whoever is reading this before it's taken down, please help.

Take screen shot. Call police. I will say this now: "Jim" murdered her brother. Find the trash bags. Find the axe. We need "Writer's" disappearance investigated. I can't do this alone.

Welcome to Good Neighbor!™
Choose a Neighborhood: Midtown
Choose a Category: Crime and Safety
Add Subject: A Sad Day
Post Message: Log Date, November 28, 2017

Hi, everyone, I just joined Good Neighbor!™ My name is Dave Nguyen. I'm writing from the East Coast, where I heard the sad news that my next door neighbor Mr. Nowicki has passed. We're all sorry to lose a respected neighbor and member of the community. I wasn't able to go to the services, but my sister went and told me two of his former students attended.

First off, I think we all need to thank the SCFD for keeping the fire from spreading to other houses. I don't know what they are planning to do with the remains of Mr. Nowicki's house, but I know you'll all agree with me that it's an unsightly mess (my sister says) and a sad reminder. I hope his relatives or the city takes care of this soon.

I have a teaching opportunity here, so will be relocating, but my sister will take care of everything at my house. She's helping me get rid of some extra things, books, some knickknacks, CDs, a few paintings—so if you want anything, they will be in boxes outside the house before she goes to Goodwill on Monday. Feel free to stop by and pick up some of the loot. She'll be watching for you.

FLAMING ARROWS

BY WALLACE BAINE

Soquel Hills

My wife died.

That's what I'd tell you if I sensed you wondering why I lived alone in this big house in the California hills, overlooking the Monterey Bay.

It's true. Just not the whole truth. Two years ago, she left me—after seventeen years. She called from a La Quinta in Irvine. At some horribly early hour. Told me she wasn't coming back.

"What about your things?" I said, a golf ball in my throat.

She sighed. "I have my things."

She'd been gone for three days, and it wasn't until after that phone call that I noticed she'd cleared out her clothes, her books—everything that belonged to her.

Then, a couple of months later, she died, right after our last meal together. Car accident.

We had met at Dharma's, a hippie cafeteria she liked. I bought her a hot chai.

She wanted to talk about divorce. I was pleased to learn that she hadn't yet contacted a lawyer. We were both civil. I felt so, anyway. Then she had to leave. Get over to Palo Alto for something. I didn't know where she was staying. Didn't ask.

Less than an hour later, she lost control of her Acura near the Summit on Highway 17. We had bought that car new.

Couldn't have had more than three or four thousand miles on it.

She nodded off at the wheel. Apparently. There was no autopsy and no one else was killed, thank God.

I had a few sleepless nights after that. To say the least.

It was the worst thing to ever happen to me. And the best thing too.

I choose to think of myself as a "mourning husband" rather than a chump. And prefer it if you thought that way too. It's easier for everybody.

I love my house, the views, the aroma of eucalyptus when it's hot out. I smoke weed whenever I want, watch porn on the flat-screen, eat at midnight, scream obscenities from the stationary bike at NBA players who take stupid shots. When I leave something on the kitchen table, it stays there.

Everything is perfect. But one thing.

The dog.

It's not my dog. It's the neighbors'. It barks. All the fucking time.

It's not like the dog is right next to me. In this neighborhood, we prize our elbow room. But the barking reverberates through the canyon, arousing more distant dogs to bark, filling the air with mindless, assaultive bursts of aggression, each one landing somewhere in my chest. Morning. Noon. And night.

I used to complain about it to Amy. She'd stop what she was doing and tilt her head, as if to make an effort to hear the barking. "Oh, yeah. That's kind of annoying."

How could I have shared my life with someone like that? Who could willfully ignore the equivalent of flaming arrows shot at our house every hour of every day?

It's not annoying, darling. Running out of toothpaste is annoy-

ing. This is the kind of casual everyday brutalization that turns decent men into . . . well, people like me.

I'm not going to kill the dog. Sure, I want to. I've fantasized about it. Even aimed my rifle at it a couple of times. Wouldn't be a gimme. I'd need a scope. But maybe with a little practice, it could be done.

It's not the dog's fault. I know that. I don't hate dogs. It's the people. Whoever the fuck they are.

They've lived in this neighborhood for years. Ten? Fifteen? I don't know. Did Amy know their names? I doubt it. All I know is that it's gotten worse since . . .

Nobody knows their neighbors around here. It's not done that way. You might pick up fragments about their habits, their aggressions, their neglects. You make judgments, usually negative ones. You'll see faces occasionally, through a windshield. Give a wave maybe. We get to know each other in personal shorthand: *There's leaf-blower guy. There's Giants-fan lady.* Maybe I'm wife-died guy. I don't know.

But at the post office, or the Safeway in town, you don't look up. Being neighborly means one thing back in Illinois where I grew up. Here, it means the opposite. You respect your neighbors by not acknowledging them. People want space, physically, psychically. You should give it to them.

The dog ruins all that.

I sit on my deck in the mornings with my coffee and nurse my rage. It's what I do. I don't let it slide. I don't act out. I just absorb. The barking—sharp, high-pitched, weirdly metallic—comes in clusters. Sometimes it turns into a yelp, as if the dog is in a bear trap. Those are the bad days. I actually tracked it a few months back. Kept a log on a legal pad; did it for a couple of weeks. Saw no pattern, other than its daily relentlessness.

Sure, I can play loud music, and I do. Sonny Rollins. Dexter Gordon. Whatever. I use white-noise apps. I got them all. But the dog outlasts everything.

It's a Thursday morning. Foggy. I'm stuck. Can't find the flow. The barking swarms my ears.

Peering into my binoculars at the neighbors' backyard across the canyon, I see the dog. Short legs, brown, medium-sized. I don't know what kind of dog it is. I don't know dogs.

I put on my sneakers and ball cap and step down into the canyon toward the dog. It's all my land. I'm on three acres. Eucalyptus, poison oak, a creek bed that hasn't been wet for ten years. I almost never come down here—only in the fall to clear out stuff—and not since Amy left.

I move my way back up the other side and reach the chain-link fence that separates my property from the other guy's. The dog is inside a second fenced-in enclosure. It sees me now. The barking reaches fever pitch. Like my pulse. I look for some sign that someone is home. Nothing.

"A watchdog is only effective when it doesn't bark all the goddamn time, you little bastard." I'm talking to the stupid dog now.

I climb back up along the property line until I get to the road. I walk to the front of the house, rehearsing my appeal. Keep your cool. Try to be friendly. Don't demand anything. Tell them you don't expect the dog to be quiet all the time. But don't be a pussy. Put it on them to take action. Remember that you hate these people for being oblivious. Make sure they don't forget this encounter.

I stride to the door with certainty, in case someone is watching from the window. I ring the bell. Again. One more time. No answer.

When I was a kid—eleven, twelve, something like that—I

went on a spree of breaking and entering. Actually, not breaking. There was always something open or unlocked back then. I would sneak into people's houses just to sit in their chairs, poke around their kitchens. I never stole anything. Didn't feel the need. But now I'm a fifty-two-year-old man.

I slide around the far side of the house and end up behind the garage, the dog barking the whole time. No security system. No cameras. You can see the road but no other houses in my line of sight. The back door of the garage is unlocked and so is the door to the kitchen inside the garage. How can this be so fucking easy?

Nice house. New living room furniture. No IKEA shit here. Pictures of grandkids (and someone's new Harley) on the refrigerator. *Dave and Marilyn Kittle*. Funny name, sounds like cat food. They pay a lot more to PG&E than I do. They still have a landline. Marilyn's going to the dentist next Friday. Someone named Sandra was supposed to arrive on the twenty-third, but it's scratched out.

I open the fridge—sparkling water, hummus, a sealed package of organic chicken breasts, a wedge of that expensive cheese they sell at Deluxe Market. I dig out a couple of grapes and pop them in my mouth. Take the cheese out of its wrapping. Rub my fingers across it. Did I touch poison oak down in the canyon? Maybe. Hard to say.

I copy down the Kittles' phone number (could come in handy). Explore the junk drawer. I resist the temptation to scribble *Quiet your dog!* on the empty space on the calendar beside Sandra's cancelled visit. I take down a steak knife from a magnetic stripe near the fridge and run my tongue up and down it. Juvenile, yes. The last time I did this, I was a juvenile. Maybe I'll come back tomorrow. Bring a few props this time. Hide a ripe banana in the linen closet. Slide a disgusting photo into a coat pocket. Drop a dead fly into their chardonnay.

I go upstairs and enjoy perspectives of my own house that I've never seen before. Peer into the first bedroom—a guest room? A child's bedroom? Is this where Sandra spent her childhood? Nice master bath. Might be your best selling point, if and when you decide to sell.

I take a pee surrounded by gleaming mirrors. It's a well-earned pee, a post-coffee pee. I reach to flush, then stop myself. No flush. Why not sow a tiny seedling of discord between Dave and Marilyn? She'll blame him for being a pig. He'll have no clue why she's in a rotten mood.

From my wallet, I dig out the neon business card of a divorce lawyer that I picked up after Amy left. What kind of crass business ploy is that anyway? He wasn't worth a red nickel. I leave it facedown on the carpet just beside the small waste basket in the bedroom. Why not have a little fun with Mr. and Mrs. Wonderful?

I'm not sure if the dog still knows there's someone in the house. Its barking has returned to its normal rhythms, though it sounds different not echoing around the canyon. Up close, the cheese-grater effect on my nerves is intensified. I feel the cortisol flowing in my blood. I feel like I could pick up this refrigerator.

How can you live with this, Dave and Marilyn? How can you be so deaf? It's possible you could both be deaf, but that shelf of CDs—the Three Tenors, *The Brandenburg Concerto*—says otherwise.

I've been putting up with this for months—fuck that, years. And I've never once—not once, not early in the morning, not late at night—heard either of you scream for the dog to shut up. That would be something in your favor. But I don't even get that. From certain angles—say, from my house to yours—indifference and hostility look pretty much identical.

So, what am I to conclude here? You must know the damn dog is destroying the peace and quiet of the neighborhood, but it means nothing to you. It never once occurred to you that someone in the house across the way might be bothered, might feel violated, trapped, might come to see that his own house is no escape from the rudeness and ignorance of other people.

And here, of all places. In the golden Soquel Hills, every home a seven-figure valuation. You and I, we're not uneducated burger-flippers living in some shitty apartment complex. I'd expect noise pollution at a place like that. We should know better.

I could've retaliated. I could've dragged out some speakers as big your sofa and aimed them at your house, blasted out Whitesnake and Zappa every time your dog got out of control. I'd kind of enjoy that.

But even after years of your assaults, I've never succumbed to tit-for-tat, because that's not who we are. At least, that's not who I am.

I don't expect you to look over at my house and worry about me, send over bran muffins and a cheese plate. I don't want your friendship. I don't want to be invited to barbecues. I just want the slightest sliver of humanity, that impulse to think about what your beloved little monster might be doing to your neighbors' peace of mind, the sense to know that someone close to you is suffering even if you're not. This house tells me that you're capable of that.

Now, I just want it to stop. For good. It's gone too far.

I slip out the kitchen door into the garage, and then out the back door of the garage, just as I came in.

When I get home, I take a long shower, do a load of wash,

and make it to Zelda's at the beach just in time for happy hour. For about an hour, I'm happy too.

Friday morning is clear and sunny. I feel inspired, determined to make some progress on my work. The coffee has a brightness to it. It tastes alive, a tad fruity. I'm twenty minutes into writing code before it I notice it. *No barking.*

Through the binoculars, I see no sign of the dog. Did they get rid of it? Did they somehow come to their senses and flash on how rude they were being to the neighbors by keeping that poor thing locked up all day?

The back door to the house is open. A figure in yellow plastic coveralls appears at the door, holding a garbage bag. Man, I can't be this lucky. They probably just took the dog for a walk while the house cleaners were working.

Might as well enjoy the quiet while it lasts. I turn back to my work. I find myself in the zone much quicker than usual. See, it makes a difference, the quiet. A man needs quiet.

And yet, another interruption. This time, the doorbell. I glance out my second-floor window to see a car in the driveway.

Santa Cruz County Sheriff. What the fuck is this? Nobody saw me go into the Kittles' house, or leave it. I'm sure of it. This must be about something else.

It's a man and a woman. Both in uniform. I smile, invite them inside. They decline. So I go outside, and stand in my front yard with the two deputies.

They're not unpleasant—very cordial, in fact. They tell me they're investigating a break-in in the neighborhood. They ask my name, who else lives in the house, how long I've lived here. I cooperate.

"Do you the know the Kittles, sir?" says the woman deputy.

"No, I . . ."

"They're your neighbors just across the way in the back over on Bobcat Lane."

"Oh, yes. Were they burgled?"

"Not really." The woman looks warily to the male deputy. "Were you at home yesterday, sir?"

"In the morning. Spent the afternoon at Zelda's in Capitola. Much of the evening too, actually."

"Did you see or hear anything unusual?"

"Unusual, how do you mean?"

The female deputy purses her lips. The man sighs. He looks very young, like a high school kid almost. I can see his jaw clenching. He speaks for the first time: "Look, there was a pretty serious crime committed over there. You might want to consider—"

"Did you see anything unusual?" she repeats, interrupting.

"No, nothing. Don't I have a right to know what's happened here?"

"The Kittles' dog was butchered sometime yesterday," says the boy deputy.

"Butchered? What do you mean 'butchered'?"

The female deputy shakes her head and gives him a look. Not a happy one. "Wyatt," she says. "Don't—"

"Killed with a steak knife," says the male deputy, ignoring his partner. "Its blood and entrails spread all over the interior of the house, the walls, upstairs and downstairs. Things drawn on mirrors and surfaces in blood. Food thrown all over the place, broken glass, dishes. Whoever it was must have been over there for a long time, working up a pretty good rage."

"Deputy, that's enough," says the woman. She approaches me with a business card in her hand. "Sir, if you see or hear anything out of the ordinary, anything at all, please call us.

This is my personal cell phone number. We'll be patrolling the neighborhood for a while."

"Yes, of course, I will." My mouth is so dry I can barely get out the words.

"You have a good day, sir." The deputies walk back to their car. I need some water and I need to sit down. I step back into the house, pour a glass of water, and gulp it down. I sit at the kitchen table for I don't know how long, listening back in my head to what the deputy said. Things drawn on mirrors? What the fuck was he talking about? I need to get out of here. Take a run. Maybe along the beach at New Brighton. Maybe take the bike to Nisene Marks. Burn off this anxiety.

As I move to go down to the garage, I pass by the window. To my shock, the sheriff's car is still there. The two deputies talking to each other. Suddenly, another car appears. Another sheriff's car. It parks right behind the first one.

The original officers get out of their car again. The two new boys flank out to opposite sides of my house. One reaches over to put his hand on his gun, like you and I would pat down our pocket to make sure we had our phone. The other one is carrying something bright yellow, like a Post-it note, in a plastic bag.

The doorbell chimes again. I can't believe it. Somewhere deep in the canyon to the east, I swear I can hear another dog barking.

THE BIG CREEP

BY ELIZABETH MCKENZIE

The Circles

I met Ronald Hill at the frozen yogurt place on Mission Street. It was a late afternoon in January, raining, near dark, the road clogged with pissed-off commuters, but he made it on time.

I took off my yellow anorak as soon as I came inside. My hair was frizzy and pulled to the side with a clip and I looked about as respectable as possible for meeting a new client in that weather. He wanted the corner, as far from the college girl at the counter as we could get. We could only find a table that hadn't been bussed. I wiped off some pink sprinkles with the back of my hand while he got rid of somebody's mug smudged with coffee all around the lip, like they'd been sucking on it.

He told me his name. Ronald was probably in his forties, overdressed for Santa Cruz, in a gray sharkskin suit. He had a thin neck rattling around in his shirt collar, reddish-brown hair shaved close on the sides, a tight, square jaw, and small blue eyes with thin eyebrows that made it easy to picture him as a needy baby.

"Can I get you anything?" he asked, before taking a seat.

To be honest, I always choose the frozen yogurt place with the hope the client will get me something. I agreed to a large vanilla, with cookie dough and fresh strawberries. I calculated how much money I'd just saved me and my dad in calories.

"So, it sounds like you know Teddy?" he asked.

"We're in a class together, that's all."

"I hope it's not necessary to say that everything I'm about to tell you is confidential?"

"Yep, it's not necessary."

"I wasn't too thrilled about hiring a fifteen-year-old girl as my PI, but Joe Fernandez told me a few of your success stories and says I can trust you." He challenged me with his childish blue eyes.

I shrugged. "I don't care if you trust me or not. I have enough stuff to do."

"Don't take it the wrong way." He sighed and leaned in closer to the table. "Teddy's mother and I divorced a little over a year ago. I live about a mile away now and I try to see Teddy as much as I can. It's been working out okay, but about five months ago, she started seeing a guy named Kyle Wilkins."

His fingernails were manicured, I noticed, and he was noticing too. He was staring at his own fingernails, which looked as if they had a coat of polish.

"And?"

"So it looks like Kyle is making it his life's mission to be Teddy's best friend. Believe me, I wouldn't want Teddy to have to be around someone who's indifferent to him or treated him badly. But it's getting to the point that Teddy would rather hang around with him all the time—even when it's my weekend. And Kyle's doing things with him that I don't approve of. He has a pilot's license and he'll just take Teddy out of school, go to Tahoe with him for the day. I mean, geez, I can't compete with that."

"What makes you think it's a competition?"

"In case you don't know, it's very easy for divorced fathers to get sidelined."

"Have you talked to your ex-wife about stuff like the trips to Tahoe?"

"Yes. She thinks I'm jealous, that I'm not thinking of Teddy."

Ronald Hill looked at his perfect fingernails again. They must have made him feel important. Even though I have to work around it all the time, I have problems with well-dressed people in fancy jobs who are ostentatiously concerned about their children. He was probably the kind of jerk who, when Teddy was born, had a *Baby on Board* sign in the window of whatever air-bagged, super-safe SUV they'd picked up to tote their spawn.

"So what do you want exactly?"

"I guess I'm afraid he's using Teddy to get to Ariel, and who knows how long that's going to last. Teddy's going to get hurt if they break up. Anyway, I feel like there's something not right about him."

"Why?"

"That's why I came to you." He looked like he was holding back, trying to decide what else to tell me. "Ariel is from a wealthy family. She has a lot of money and she's going to inherit a lot more. Who knows who Kyle Wilkins is! Google him, you'll see. There's nothing. He's a nobody!"

This put me firmly on the side of Kyle Wilkins. Nobodies were somebodies in my world. Every time I saw someone treating my dad like a nobody, I understood the origins of violence. "So let's say I get something on Kyle Wilkins. How are you going to use it?"

"I'm going to make sure Ariel knows, without involving my son. She's very protective of what's hers. If the guy's trying to enrich himself at her expense, she'll pull away."

"Like she did with you?" I blurted out. I don't know where that came from. I'd read too many detective stories not to suspect the client of having some personal agenda. And some guy who wanted to discredit his ex-wife's new boyfriend automatically looked bad.

He pushed away from the table. "We had differences about raising Teddy, is what it comes down to. If we'd never had a child, who knows, we'd probably still be married. But Teddy's all that matters now."

What a big creep. If they'd never had Teddy, he and his wife would still be married? Like he'd spent time imagining his life without his kid? I'd like to hope most parents are too superstitious to do that.

He forked over a clean fifty-dollar bill to start me off, and we stepped outside. It had gotten dark and traffic had loosened up, but the rain was still coming down, and passing cars were sending explosions of grimy water into the air when they hit the rushing gutters. I said I'd start looking into it, and be in touch in a few days. He walked away and started to sprint across Van Ness to his car as if getting wet would kill him. A white van coming north on Mission took the corner, brakes screeching, fishtailing—I'd end up describing it way too many times. I saw the whole thing. I saw the van smash into Ronald Hill and go right over him.

There was this eerie quiet for a second. The van stopped, while the traffic kept passing on Mission. I should have known no one survives an impact like that, but I ran to Hill, his body lying in a pool of blood mixed with the rain. I kneeled to lift his head, to look into his little blue eyes—nobody'd say he looked like a baby now. All this hot liquid was running out the back of his head.

In no time, three cop cars showed up, and I could hear the ambulance and fire truck on the way. I saw an older guy with a white beard in a blue denim work shirt getting out of the van and talking to a cop, gesturing wildly. I crouched in front of the yogurt shop to wipe my hands in the wet grass. Then I was standing in the rain shaking. One of the uniforms peeled away from the scene and came my way. It was Joe.

"Into the car," he said. "Come on." He wrapped his jacket around me. "What the hell happened?"

"That's Hill," I choked out.

"I know who it is," Joe said.

He and my dad have been best friends since they were kids, locals who hauled their surfboards down to the beach every day. He's stocky, with a bristly crew cut that's fun to run your hands over. There are pictures of him holding me when I was a baby, so I guess he's like my uncle or something. At first he had misgivings about showing me the ropes of detective work, but I guess I drove him crazy about it and by now I've helped him on so many cases I don't think he feels much regret. He left me in the car and went on talking with the other officers.

His car smelled clean, like not a speck of garbage or mold was in it. It was practically a spa in there, and it relaxed me. The rain pelted the roof of the car, and the police radio crackled and hissed with other dramas unfolding all over town. A robbery near the Boardwalk. Domestic dispute on Ocean Street. Naked man walking on West Cliff. After a while it became white noise, until Joe got back in and said he'd drive me home.

"I said goodbye to Ronald Hill and then he was dead," I said flatly.

"Sorry, kiddo. You didn't need this. People don't know how to drive for shit in this weather."

"It rains and someone has to die?" My voice sounded shrill.

"So it goes."

"What did you find out about the driver?"

Joe took out his pad. "Name's Allan Lundgren, looks like he checks out by Santa Cruz standards. No record of any kind. Doesn't have an address, lives in the van. Breath check was clean. According to his statement, by the time he saw Hill, who was not in the crosswalk, it was too late."

"How'd you know Hill?" I asked.

Joe sniffed. "Kind of embarrassing. Sold me some vitamins a few years ago. Not vitamins exactly, but this blue-green algae stuff. Supposed to give you energy."

"Whoa. I thought he was a totally different type, not some bogus supplement pusher."

"He wasn't very good at it. A good salesman is usually a little more fun. Makes you think you'll have fun too if you buy whatever he's selling." Then he said, "Let's just say that I didn't buy his algae because of some great sales pitch."

I told him I'd need a *great* sales pitch to buy algae. "He must've had a different job by now. He looked well-off."

"Trust fund, probably," Joe said. I can't count how many times he and my dad have muttered about trust-fund kids who showed up to go to college and were able to lead charmed lives around here without having to work their butts off.

We left the scene. His big fat police car barreled down the grassy alley where me and my dad lived. In the rain there wouldn't likely be anybody back there, rummaging through the garbage cans or curling up next to a shopping cart in a dirty sleeping bag.

He pulled up behind our place, which was not one to be appearing in *House Beautiful* anytime soon. It was a converted garage. Our door looked makeshift, like it had been hastily screwed onto the hinges after a home invasion, and there were mangy gray bushes growing around the windows, filled with cobwebs and feathers that we never bothered to clean out. Let me add that we were lucky to have it—after our last eviction, my dad made the whole thing happen by befriending Connie, the owner, a one-legged widow who's the bookkeeper at the Pick 'n Save in Watsonville. This was the fifth or sixth rental we'd had since my mother died, which goes to show that we were either a pretty undesirable duo or that the world is cruel. Probably both.

Joe said he had to take my official witness statement, but I needed a shower and told him to wait. I went inside, turned on the wall heater and the lights, then ripped off my damp clothes in the bathroom and stood under the hot water in the narrow stall, shivering. Coming off the back of my arm, a streak of blood went down the drain.

Eventually I waved Joe in, and he made me describe what I'd seen while he took notes. My meeting with Ronald Hill was off the record. Joe, who's been a detective for almost ten years, regular cop for ten before, didn't want to raise eyebrows in the department for sending work to me. Anyway, he always says it's the spirit of the law that counts, not the letter of it.

"You're worried about something, aren't you?" Joe said.

"Yeah, I guess. Something seems strange. Like, sure, it could be a coincidence that this paranoid guy gets run over right after he'd decided to take action on his paranoia, but maybe not."

He looked at me, I'd like to think, with a small bit of respect. "Anything solid to base that on? Because this looks strictly like an accident at this point."

"I don't have anything yet. Maybe it's nothing," I told him.

"Let me know if anything strikes you. I'll call your dad for you, let him know what happened," Joe said, getting up to go.

"No, don't."

"Why?"

"I don't want him driving upset."

"You sure? You gonna be okay here till he gets home?"

"I'm gonna be okay. Listen, Joe, could you run a check on Kyle Wilkins?"

"The boyfriend?"

"Yeah."

"Seriously? You think it matters?"

"It's what Hill came to talk to me about, in the last minutes of his life. So yeah, I think it matters."

"Okay, okay," Joe said. "Let me see what I can do."

After he left, I sat for a while. Didn't move a muscle. I was lost in a bunch of random, jumping thoughts and didn't feel very good, so I did what I usually do at night before my dad gets home: I poured about half a cup of vodka into a glass of orange juice, drank that down, felt the heat move through my shoulders and neck, started to relax a little. And then I started to sob.

I guess I was sobbing about seeing a person get run over, but there was self-pity, no denying it. My dad used to be a long-distance truck driver before my mom died, and now he's a *short*-distance truck driver so he can be around. The work's hard, delivering boxes and pallets of stuff, climbing in and out, clattering down on the lift gate with his dolly, up and down stairs. He has big callouses on his hands from clutching the wheel and I'm always seeing hemorrhoid ointment boxes in the trash. He has one of those antigravity machines in the corner that he'll get on first thing when he gets home to stretch out his back before having a huge vodka and tonic and sitting in front of the TV. He takes about ten ibuprofen a day. As long as I read books at home, he could care less how I do in school; he just wants me to grow up to be a cynic.

It must have been around nine before he called to let me know how messed up his day had been, and that he wouldn't be coming home because of a five a.m. start the next day. No big deal. I never complain because it's nothing as bad for me as it is for him.

Tonight I wanted to tell him, *By the way, today I saw a guy get run over and killed.* But I couldn't, because then he'd for sure kill himself driving home to be with me.

Instead, I made another drink and fell onto my mattress in the corner. All I could think of was poor Teddy hearing the news about his father. Now that Ronald Hill was a dead blue-green algae salesman, he didn't seem so fancy. Little did he know while we were sitting there talking that he was about to be dead. There he was, watching me guzzle down my yogurt, worrying about some guy showing his kid and his ex a good time and feeling all left out and stuff. Two minutes later, dead.

No more worries. No more feeling left out.

Case closed.

Just after two a.m., I got up from the floor, ran to the bathroom, and barfed. It happens. I washed my face with cold water, rinsed out my mouth, brushed my hair, and thought, *There's no way I'm going to sleep tonight, so why even try?* The rain had stopped. I'm not sure what was driving me to get dressed and go outside and pull out my bike and take off down the alley and through the wet streets, except maybe the fifty-dollar bill that was still stuffed in my pocket.

Compensation is a strange thing. I've seen it firsthand, how in the absence of someone, others will start filling in to make up for what's lost. I saw my dad change after my mom was gone. I saw him try to learn how to cook and even start filling in forms from my school with his big clumsy hands. I saw him start to worry about me in a way he never used to when my mom was around to worry. Now that Ronald Hill was no longer around to worry about Teddy, I was starting to.

I had the address Hill had given me of Teddy's place—where, these days, Kyle Wilkins was also living. The sky was clear and bright, stars blazing, the streets extra quiet. It could give a person a superior feeling to be out on a night like this, the world to yourself while everybody else is snoring away. My mood picked up, and I cycled to Bay, turned at King, then climbed the steep hills to Teddy's neighborhood, where, just a few years ago, street repair workers found an Indian burial ground. Maybe that's why I've always had the feeling the neighborhood's cursed. The bluff is crowded with ranch-style houses, roads to nowhere, cul-de-sacs. It's the kind of neighborhood where people keep their dirty laundry inside, and there's plenty of it. I've helped Joe uncover a few scary "family" men, suicides, ODs, and one time, a psycho housewife who was poisoning cats.

The address was on one of those cul-de-sacs with a free-standing basketball hoop on the curb that looked like it'd come straight out of the box. I hid my bike in some shrubs a few houses down. Even in the dark, Teddy's home was tidy and respectable, with a landscaped front yard filled with birds of paradise, mallow, and Mexican sage—the kind of place I usually insult but secretly wish for. No cars in front. Looked pretty quiet.

I slipped around the side, and discovered dim lights turned on in a back room. It was there, through a sliding-glass door, that I could see Teddy, alone under a blanket, watching a movie. It was a black-and-white Western. A stampede of cattle was mounting a grassy knoll and descending onto the wide-open plains, while picture-perfect cowboys in their chaps and spurs and boots kicked their stallions and rode alongside.

I could see the side of Teddy's face. He'd been crying. Of course he'd been crying!

What was he doing alone? Where the fuck was his mother?

The scene just about broke me. I don't remember what my dad and I did the day my mother died, but I have a memory of him driving us, soon after, to Disneyland.

I began to shiver and decided to get the hell out of there and go back to bed like a normal person. Just as I was drawing away into the darkness, Teddy jumped up from the couch and ran toward the front of the house. I stole around the side. A Ford Mustang had pulled into the driveway, and a man and woman got out.

They started unloading bags and boxes from the car. In the starlight I saw a tall man in a T-shirt, jeans, black canvas shoes, and bleached surfer hair—likely the one and only Kyle Wilkins. The woman had blond hair, on the young side, pretty. Teddy opened the front door and they started carrying the bags and boxes in, making several trips. I waited in the shadows until they disappeared inside.

I saw a lump on the ground by the car as I scuttled away. I had one of those primal shudders, like maybe it was an animal about to pounce on me in the dark. I snapped my fingers and the lump didn't move. I ran over, grabbed it, and ran off.

It was a coat. Still warm, a few wet spots on it, but heavy and soft. I put it on as I jumped on my bike and rolled away. It was luxurious. It seemed like a raincoat on the outside, but there was fleece on the inside and I had this sudden thought that this was a mother's coat. A mother's coat would have to be this way, unlike the cold shells my dad wore over his work clothes.

When I got home, I hung it up to admire. It was chocolate brown and looked brand-new. Why did I take it? What a creepy thing to do.

The next day, Teddy Hill wasn't at school, and my head wasn't either. But I got through the day. You can have the worst thing in the world happen, and a second later there's a bird singing on a wire, there are leaves rustling in the breeze. Life goes on.

All I could think about was the life and death of Ronald Hill. Why had I been chosen as witness? What was I supposed to do with it? Joe'd gotten me the background check on Kyle Wilkins, which confirmed he was the bleach-haired guy I'd seen at Teddy's house. He had nothing more than a couple of bounced checks and speeding tickets. Not exactly Charles Manson but not Boy Scouts either. I don't like people who bounce checks.

Wilkins was new to the area, he'd lived in Tahoe before. Here's the good and bad thing about Santa Cruz: it's not a place where everybody's lived here forever and a newcomer gets the once-over. No, it's a city where anybody can come fit in for a while, and move away before you've even had a chance to say hello. It's a city full of transients, and I don't mean the ones on the streets. I mean, you don't always know your neighbors and you don't ask questions. Kyle Wilkins shows up, moves in, replaces Ronald Hill, the neighbors nod or don't nod. For that matter, a chubby truck driver and his alcoholic daughter move into a garage, nobody notices that either.

After school that day, I thought I'd ride past Ronald Hill's former residence near the Circles. And then, what do you know. There was that same Mustang parked in front, the one I'd seen in front of Teddy's. I jumped off my bike and walked through the open door.

Inside, Kyle Wilkins was leaning over a desk, leafing energetically through a stack of papers in a file. There was a pile of boxes in one corner, a few bulging garbage bags in another. New theory: Kyle Wilkins was the big creep, not Ronald Hill. I didn't like how happy Kyle looked rifling through the papers of a dead man. He was like a pirate on a treasure hunt. It looked like more of the same stuff I'd seen them lugging home in the middle of the night after the accident, leaving Teddy alone. Hill wasn't even cold and they'd already been over here, prowling around?

"Hey, what's going on?"

Wilkins startled, but seeing a teenage girl in a *Totoro* sweatshirt put him at ease. "Uh, hello?" he said, revealing some extra-big teeth. "You are . . . ?"

"Neighbor—who're you?"

"I'm Kyle, friend of the family. Not sure if you've heard, but Ted's father was in a fatal accident yesterday," he said. "And I'm helping out."

"Helping out doing what exactly?"

Just then, a toilet flushed. Teddy came around from the hallway. He's tall and skinny, with black hair that hangs in his eyes. He was wearing sagging black pants and a gray hoodie with a picture of a skateboard on it.

"Uh, hey," Teddy said.

"Hi, Teddy. I'm really sorry about your dad."

"Thanks," he mumbled.

"We got a big mess here," Kyle Wilkins said, by way of his oversized teeth. "Not very nice to leave behind a shitload of unpaid bills for people to clean up." He smoothed back his hair.

"It's not very nice to talk about it," I said.

Wilkins turned away from me. "Teddy, maybe you could do your social life later?" He sounded like a bully.

I moved toward the door. "Think you'll be back at school soon?"

"I don't know." Teddy followed me out, carrying a box of the papers Wilkins had been pawing. I could see a bunch of bills and bank statements on top, including an invoice from something called Life Bonanza for eight hundred dollars' worth of fish oil pills. There might be something worth finding in Ronald Hill's papers. Teddy threw the box onto the backseat of the Mustang. "There's a thing later this afternoon at Peace United, if you're interested."

I said, trying to sound casual, "You know, my pretty-much uncle's with the Santa Cruz PD. He's really cool. I mean, if you ever need anything."

Teddy looked totally weirded out. "Why would I need anything from the police?"

"I mean, if anything . . . feels wrong."

"A lot of things feel wrong. My father just got run over by some asshole who's probably forgotten all about it by now."

I played my ace: "My mother died when I was eight, so I sort of know what it's like."

"Oh fuck! That sucks."

"Bye, Teddy," I said, and gave him a hug. For all my calculated moves, that part came spontaneously. And he hugged back, which made me feel good.

When I got home I slammed the ugly door and threw down my backpack. I couldn't even look at the coat for a while, though it was right there, on a hall hanger. I didn't look at it while I made myself a vodka and orange juice and watched a rerun of *The Gilmore Girls*. I didn't look at it while I cleaned up my dad's pile of oily rags and empty oil cans by the door that our landlady Connie recently complained about. She was always asking my dad to help her do stuff, and sometimes he even helped her put on her artificial leg. I didn't want to think about it.

But there I was, thinking about that and every other bad thing. About some leg that went on a stump that my dad had to look at, all because my mother died from a freak stroke that she never should've died from. I could hardly remember her. I could hardly remember what it was like to be near her. My throat closed like a fist.

I heard the low rumble of my dad's truck trundling down the alley. A distinct throttling sound, like the engine was held together by a bunch of loose bolts. It rattled and knocked until he turned it off and then it blew a huge hiss, like a giant dog settling down for a nap. The presence of my dad, in the afternoon, in the truck, could only mean one thing: he was bringing home an overage.

I jumped up wobbly and ran outside. He had the emergency lights flashing, and he was already rolling up the door in back. "Get ready," he said.

"What now?"

"Take a look at this," he said, and I peered into the back of the truck. Whatever it was, there was a lot of it. Case upon case of—

"Toilet paper?"

"You can't have enough."

"We're keeping all of that?"

"Seventeen cases," he said, with unmistakable satisfaction.

"Inside?"

"We'll figure it out," he said, and started stacking the cases on his dolly and wheeling it toward our door. He went inside first and moved his antigravity rack out of the way, then rolled the dolly in and started stacking the cases in the corner. I noticed the figures were printed on the box. Ninety-six. *96 x 17 = 1,632 rolls.*

"Dad, we don't need this much toilet paper!"

"We'll give it to people. It's something everybody wants."

"I'm not taking it to school!"

"Stop complaining."

Overages were his pride and joy. People on loading docks often didn't know how to count, it seemed. About every other month, my dad would find himself with an extra pallet of some junk. One time, we had five cases of Mr. T–head piggy banks. They were super tacky but he made me take them to school and give one to everybody in my grade. That was embarrassing, though some kids liked them. Another time, he had a bunch of cases of potato chips, which kept us going for months, not to mention all the bags we gave away.

"We need to go do something," I told him. "Right now."

"Okay."

That was a good thing about Dad: he perked up at any reasonable request.

I ran back inside and grabbed the hanging coat before I climbed into the truck. I hadn't been inside my dad's "office" in a while. It was full of the crumbs of hundreds of sandwiches, cookies, and chips he ate while exercising his daily duties—a thousand cigarettes and a legion of old rancid coffee cups. He liked to horde brochures, so there were a bunch of those from anywhere brochures could be found, stuffed into the door pouch and the crack of the seat, advertising hot tubs and wild animal safari parks and colon cleansers.

I told him which way to drive, and I liked how he didn't asked me a single question. It's like he knew he owed me somehow.

We pulled up at the church on High Street. Peace United.

I decided to wear the brown coat. My dad followed me in and sat in back while I went through the line where they were greeting people. When I got to Teddy we hugged again, like it was starting to become normal. When I came to his mother, she stared at me for a second, then said, "I just lost a coat like that."

It was hard to tell where the creep meter was finally going to land. I shrugged. "Huh," I said to her, "I guess it's hard to think about a missing coat right now, when there's so much to think about for Teddy."

She frowned, and I moved on to sit in the back.

I couldn't help wishing Joe had never gotten me involved with this one. I couldn't let go of it. For weeks after, I'd see Teddy slouching around school, and stupid fear would nag at me, that something wasn't going right for him.

But what was I supposed to do, worry about him the rest of my life? Run around hugging him every second? And anyway, no matter what you do, what could ever be right?

DEATH AND TAXES

BY JILL WOLFSON

Mission Street

This is Cody's first day as a sign dancer. He pops a tab of Adderall at the beginning of his shift and stands at the corner of Mission and Swift in a Statue of Liberty costume, urging people driving by to get their taxes done by this outfit called Liberty Taxes. The spiky plastic crown on his forehead leaves an indentation, but the crown adds inches to his height, which he's touchy about, always wanting to be taller, at least 5'11", like Tyler, Stepfather #3, who Cody doesn't chill with that much anymore, due to Tyler's my-shit-don't-stink attitude and their whole family situation being fucked up.

This Liberty gig has got to be the best job ever. Smell the ocean air, throw your head back, and pound your chest like a surfer dude. Open your arms wide and feel the sun on your face. The flowing green fabric of Cody's gown catches the early-spring wind and for a second it holds the sleeves out stiff.

Does Tyler, that lazy dickhead Mr. Stepdad of the Year, get to work all afternoon in the great outdoors? No, he doesn't.

Red light turns green and cars rev up. Here they come: Ford, Chevy, Toyota.

Sure, Cody's kind of nervous, being just seventeen and his first day on the job and all. But he's ready.

Ready for what?

Ready to blow the drivers' minds with extraordinary feats of sign-twirling never before seen anywhere. Not even if there are sign twirlers on a planet in a whole other universe. And yes, human-type beings ARE up there with all those stars, and people who think otherwise, dickwads like Tyler, should get their fat heads out of their dumb asses and do the math.

Showtime!

Spin that tax sign clockwise like it's a Boardwalk ride. Toss it in the air, hurl your body around in a one-footed, tiptoed 360, and catch the sign behind your back. *Ta-da.*

Holy crap on a strap! He actually caught it! Thumbs-up from a Prius driver.

Another Prius, another Prius. Is there a fuckin' sale on Priuses or what?

Yesterday, this corner was just another place. Cody must've eaten a million slices of pepperoni at Upper Crust. Carved his initials into the oak by the U-Wash-It car place. Felt up that hippie chick Sequoia by the dumpster behind the Chinese place.

But now? Cody owns this corner.

Cranks up the death-metal drum solo playing in his head: *Ba-dum-bum-CHING ba-dum-pump chsh-ba-dump-dump-chshshshshshshsh-Ba-dun-DUN.*

His mind switches channels to an outstanding game he invented. Yes, he invented it himself even though Tyler says the game's *too* sick, that a stupid kid like Cody must've ripped it off from someone else.

Did not!

Here's the game: add the word "anal" before the name of each car passing by.

Anal Probe! Anal Hummer! Anal Rover!

Cracks himself up.

Is this a lame job like Tyler said it was? Is this a job that only a kid right out of juvie would take? Could *anyone* stand on a street corner and get total strangers to go see Mr. Liberty—check it, that's his real name, Frank Liberty—who does taxes fast and cheap?

First day on the job and Cody's already learning stuff. Important info you need. Like how taxes are one of only two things in life you can't avoid, the other one being death. Words of wisdom from the best fuckin' boss ever, Frank Liberty.

Cody's feet do a happy, crazy tap dance for an Anal Fit with a dent in one of its back doors.

So today is Saturday and in six more days, it's payday. Best day ever!

Is Cody gonna spend his big fat paycheck on weed? That's what Tyler thinks, 'cause he said, "You're just gonna go down to the levee and get wasted, little dude. Get caught with a dirty pee test by your PO 'cause you always get caught at everything."

No! Cody is not going to blow his money on weed! 'Cause he's not a selfish douchebag asshole who only thinks about himself anymore.

He thinks about his mother. How her birthday's coming up. He thinks about what he did for her birthday last year.

Busted. Vandalism. Went apeshit in the middle of the night at Santa Cruz High. Expelled for life.

He looks down at his kicks. No wind in his sleeves now. That one night earned him six months in Hotel California, which is what the guys call juvie up there on Graham Hill Road.

But this birthday? He's a new Cody, a mature Cody who thinks about what mothers like for their special day.

Chocolate. Not from the drugstore but the expensive kind

from Marini's on the Boardwalk. A big red box with a red bow.

No, a glittery gold bow!

One thing, though. His mom's got this problem. When he goes up to her place and hands her the box, she's gonna get all mental about her weight and lift her shirt and pinch about ten inches of blubber around her belly and he'll have to look at how the flesh is white with a little pink, like a bloated earthworm.

So he'll say, *Oh, Ma. You're fine the way you are. Eat a chocolate.*

And she'll eat half the box in like ten seconds and say, *The only thing I ever got from* my *mother were these fatty-fat genes.*

Shit!

A Nissan Versa with a mattress tied to the top whizzes by too close and forces Cody to jump back on the curb.

Anal Versa Asshole!

He hikes up his pants under the costume. Clothes always slip over Cody's skinny hips. Burns calories just standing still. At least he didn't get the family pork genes.

And the family bad-luck genes are gonna stop with him too. He's got X-factors going for him. Like the Cody smile, which females of all ages go crazy for because his teeth are straight and white, not like Tyler whose teeth are ugly black Jujubes from all the meth.

A minivan honks and he sees like a hundred kids cheering him, their faces pressed against the window. Bet most of them have shithead stepfathers too.

Do it, Cody. Brighten their day.

Triple-pumping motion with the arrow-shaped sign and fancies it up with high karate kicks.

"Anal Excursion!" Cody yells.

"Anal Prowler!"

A mom-type lady in a silver Camry flips her signal and turns into the Liberty Taxes parking lot.

Fist pump! Success! A customer. His first!

He pretends to fish and hook the Camry. Reel it in.

Driver laughs. With him, not *at* him like Tyler does.

He leaps in the air, a cheerleader split with bent legs. Drops the sign and flips into a wobbly, rubber-legged handstand just for her.

Liberty crown hits the pavement. Green gown hikes up to show size-ten sneakers, one of them untied, laces dangling. And flashing something—his good luck charm, insurance—tucked into the waistband of Cody's jeans.

A few minutes after Cody starts his gig at Liberty Taxes, another seventeen-year-old arrives for his shift, right up the street at Ferrell's Donuts.

Milo, small-boned and on the shorter side for a high school junior, exits the front passenger door of his mother's silver Camry. Runs his fingers through the lock of hair that flops over his forehead, popular-boy-band style. Milo is not especially popular nor in a band, but he does have great affection for music, mostly classical.

He studies the Camry and, hit by inspiration, flips on his video phone.

Slow zoom, tight close-up of subject in driver's seat. Uber-cinematic. But not too artsy. Milo abhors anything *too* artsy. Hates it even more than he hates being derivative.

Is he being insensitive for casting his mother's face in what's shaping up to be a genre-breaking art-house horror film? If Mom could get inside his head right now—and sometimes Milo thinks that she can actually do that, a two-member support team ever since Dad died—Milo and

Mom, Mom and Milo—her feelings would be uber-hurt.

So yes, he is definitely being an insensitive person.

Milo presses the delete button.

He hears the hum of the driver's window rolling down.

Mom and Milo are eyeball to eyeball now. "My working-man," she says, then orders: "Head bump!"

He leans in even closer. Their foreheads gently connect. Her face, full-screen, huge. Like this dream he had—keeps having, the same dream ever since Dad died—where their foreheads, Mom's and Milo's, have magnets in them and no matter where he goes, their faces lock, her north to his south, blocking his view of everything but her.

Milo moves back a few steps to the curb. Mom pulls out into traffic, heading off to get her taxes done.

Behind him, a voice-over fading in, meow-y and sexy.

No, the opposite of that.

His coworker Melissa. Black polyester pants, white shirt tucked in, donut-shaped name tag, a dot of red jelly on her upper lip. He remembers her from back in Bayview Elementary, a tiny, quiet girl who he imagined having a river of deep thought running through her.

"Jesus, Mylar, you gonna stand out here all day?" Melissa says. "I wanna clock my ass out of here."

The camera in his head clicks on.

He follows, recording her walk in those unattractive pants.

The buzzer sounds as the Ferrell's door opens.

Quick montage. The glistening sludge of the classic glazed, the perfect doughy circles with their centers missing.

"Symbols," Milo says under his breath. "The emptiness of human existence that hungers for connection."

Fade out.

* * *

Reel 'em in, boy! Show 'em how it's done!

Two more customers. Then Mr. Liberty, the man himself, pats Cody on the back, tells him, "Great job; break time, buddy."

Cody feels so proud and so full his heart wants to burst out and leave a valentine-shaped hole smack in the middle of the Statue of Liberty.

The next twenty minutes are all his. A Man with a Plan. Dash over to Ferrell's and see if that girl Melissa from last night's party works there like she said. If Melissa's there, whip out the charm. Flash his smile. Turn down the free maple bar she promised him. Pay for it himself 'cause he's a workingman now. Wink as he drops a gigunda tip into the jar.

The buzzer sounds as Cody enters the shop. Smell the sweet grease.

Nope, no Melissa. Figures. Fuck Melissa. Whatevs.

Hey, check out the geeky nerd behind the register, bent over a book. Kid doesn't look up. What? Is he deaf?

Hold on. Cody knows this kid. Same grade at SC High. Before the apeshit incident.

Hold on again. Time warp. Fourth grade. Bayview. Yeah, he sat in back of this dude all year. Damn, he's still got the same LEGO hair like back in the day. What's with that? Man up, get a buzz or something.

Miss Merlotti's class.

What's his name? Silo? J-Lo?

Milo. Yeah, that's it.

He's in Drama Club, something faggy like that. Only don't use *faggy*, Cody. Not cool. Not mature. Not worthy of the New You. Live and let live.

But there's something else about this Milo.

Tap tap, Cody's heel of his hand against his forehead.

Oh yeah. Kid's got a dead dad. Cancer or something

mega-fuckin' depressing. 'Bout a year ago. Weird how much you know about someone's shit you don't even talk to. Bad news gets in the air like a fart.

Dead dad. That's gotta suck.

Sure, plenty of times Cody prayed Tyler croaked in some gruesome way, like choking on a ham sandwich while also being chewed up to his nuts by a pit bull. But Tyler *did* get him his first BB gun—taught him to roll a joint the very best way.

Cody's eyes turn up to heaven in prayer. Tells God he wants to take back the Tyler death wish. Really! A psycho dad is better than a dead one.

This sudden appreciation of the good things in his own life does something to Cody's insides. A melting sensation all through his chest.

What's with him today, opening and expanding with such tender feelings?

Here's what he should do: Say something nice to this Milo. Reach out dude to dude. Milo's one of those sensitive types, for Chrissakes. Those people *feel.* What do you say to someone whose dad is RIP?

He rehearses in his mind: *Milo, may I take the occasion of my work break from Liberty Taxes to offer my sincere condolences on the loss of your most beloved father?*

Nice.

Cody raps on the counter to get the kid to look up from his book.

Milo looks up.

Milo's mind-aperture clicks open. Master shot.

Some guy in a dress? Yes, in a polyester gown, with a crown, who—no polite way to say this—reeks *really* bad.

Oh, it's the sign-dancing guy from down the street. That must be the worst job ever. Only not the same guy as yesterday because this one has close-cropped blond hair. Yesterday's Liberty had stringy dirty-brown hair.

Zoom in. They're multiplying! Cloning themselves in a plot to repopulate the world with Statue of Liberty look-alikes!

Statue's lips are moving. He is not saying: *Give me your tired, your poor.* He's saying: "May I take the occasion to . . . "

No way!

He knows this guy.

Crazy Cody! His nemesis from Miss Merlotti's class. Made Milo's life a living hell. Spent the entire year behind Milo flicking his ears. Went into his backpack. Stole money and pencils. Singled him out every dodgeball game and smacked him so hard that Milo nearly peed himself one day.

Okay, he *did* pee himself. In front of the whole class.

Does Cody still have that problem where his eyeballs vibrate in their sockets?

Milo sneaks a quick look. Yes, he does.

Be careful. Tread lightly.

Be uber-polite: "Can I help you? Is there a particular donut that catches your fancy?"

Holy crap in a sack!

Cody just screwed open his heart and poured out every pity thing he could think to say to a fag kid with a dead dad, and does he get a thank you?

No, he does not.

Milo with his stupid-ass haircut. What the hell?

Ba-dum-bum-ba-donk-a-donk-dum-chssk.

Something else. *Tap tap* on his forehead. It all comes back to him. Fourth grade. Who ratted on Cody? What little shit was all *Teacher, teacher, Cody stole from me?* Who turned Miss Merlotti and every kid in the class against him? Whose fault was it that the principal called and Tyler beat the shit of Cody to teach him a lesson?

Cody takes five giant steps down the length of the counter. A blur of donuts. Apple-filled. Custard-filled. Special of the day: pink frosting and sprinkles. *Ew.*

Cody asks: "Donut dude, how much for six of the ones that cost the most?"

"The most?" the kid asks.

Like he can't believe Cody can afford a half-dozen donuts. Like Cody doesn't have a real job. Like he's a piece of trash who just got out of juvie and sponges off other people's donuts.

Cody reaches for his waistband. *Tap tap, pat pat* on his good luck charm. He imagines the heft of it. The sound of it. Assurance against unwanted surprises. He straightens his crown.

Face to face with Mr. Donut. "Only two things in life are unavoidable. Guess what they are. *Guess!*"

Milo's face is all twitchy.

"Taxes," Cody says. "And death."

Don't say it, Milo orders himself. "I beg to differ," he says.

Do not add any more dialogue to this scene with Crazy Cody. Do not say: *What about defecating? We all have to poop.*

No, too late. Milo said it all out loud.

He puts his hand over his mouth. He notices: Cody's fist hardening into a ball. His feet doing this strange agitated shuffle, then coming to a pigeon-toed stop.

What's Cody asking? Come on, Milo! Focus. Attention.

". . . I need to take a whizz. A piss palace?"

Oh, thank goodness.

Milo points to the bathroom.

Fuck a duck. Fuck a big, quacking duck!

Palm slap against his forehead.

Cody takes a piss and rezips.

This Milo must think he's stupid. Must think he's a loser, like Tyler does. Like everyone does, right?

Yeah, even Frank Liberty. Cody imagines Frank laughing his ass off, telling Mrs. Liberty—*Yeah, dumb juvie kid believed me.* Ha-ha. *Little loser even said he was gonna get a tat:* Death and Taxes.

Cody's face flushes. An embarrassment so familiar, like a second beating heart.

His mind goes all wrecking ball.

Fuck you, Milo. Little know-it-all.

He reaches down and touches his good luck charm. Nice and heavy, there when he needs it.

Time for a demo.

Cody steps out of the bathroom.

Zero in on Milo.

Why is the kid just standing there like an idiot by the cash register? Why's he got his hands in the air?

Oh, shit on a shingle. Dump on a bump. Some dickhead with a flowered cloth tied over his nose and mouth, pointing a gun at Milo.

Cody ducks low behind the cold drink case for a better look.

The dickhead with the gun? No fuckin' way.

Yes fuckin' way!

He knows the thickness of that neck, the bend in the arm from where it broke. Hell, he even recognizes the yellow floral print of the scarf.

Tyler.

Asshole cut up Mom's favorite scarf to rob Ferrell's Donuts.

And what's this? No! Flamin' poo on a shoe! There's a long wet stain spreading down the front of Milo's pants.

Little Milo, with the dead dad and no homies and a crap donut job where he pays taxes, just went and pissed himself. All because dickhead Tyler stuck a gun in his face.

He should do something about this.

And before Cody has another thought, he *is* doing something.

Milo's mind camera—tracking shot:

Ninja Statue of Liberty, legs akimbo, a soldier yell of outrage. Whips out a set of nunchucks, whirls them in a ferocious figure eight. *Whoosh*.

Dialogue:

"Thanks for telling me about this place, Code-ster."

"Not why I *told* you, Tyler."

"Easy, boy. Looks like you were planning this job yourself."

"Naw, just a demo of my skill. Was gonna mess up some fritters big time. Send them to the trash can."

"You want in then? Father/son action?"

"Don't get all flesh-and-blood-ish with me, dickhead."

"Put down the numbnuts, Cody."

"Pay your taxes, Tyler!"

"Huh?"

"Don't mess with my homie Milo!"

At the sound of his own name, *zoom in*.

Cody's nunchucks moving fast, snapping from shoulder to shoulder, like the Statue of Liberty patting himself on the back.

Back and forth and back and forth and back and forth and—

Oh no!

Disaster.

The 'chucks hit the countertop, drop, hit the floor, bounce.

A lunge. A stumble.

Too much too fast for Milo's head to record.

A shout.

An explosion.

The bakery case glass shatters.

The smell of gunpowder. And apple fritters.

Then Milo watches. The symbol of our entire country slumps on the floor. Green fabric billowing out. A red stain spreading across his chest.

No! Not a symbol.

Not dialogue.

Not a fake scene.

Milo's knees go wobbly.

Camera off off off!

Shit! What the fuck!

Wave the gun in the air. Slam fist on the counter.

Think, Tyler. *Think*!

Don't look at the mess on the floor.

Stupid little Cody. Couldn't control the numbnuts! Trying to be a hero. What am I always telling him? Wrong place, wrong time. Again.

Tell the other one to open the cash register.

"Now! Pronto!"

Stuff bills in pockets. Leave the coins. Fifty dollars, maybe sixty. *That's it?*

Donut kid looking at him too hard. "Take a picture, why don't ya?"

Fuckin' jacked up now. Kick the white plastic table set.

Got a big, big problem on my hands.

The old lady. Cody's mom. Got a soft spot for the kid.

This whole mess is her fault, spoiling him, not smacking him when he gets out of line. And now she's going be all fucked up and crying and shit and he's gonna have to smack her and that means more crying and who's gonna to have to live with that drama?

Him, Tyler, that's who!

Throw the coffee creamer against the wall. Use the butt of the gun to spider another donut case.

Plus, her birthday's coming up. Cody once again wrecking it, three years in a row. Coulda won money on that bet.

Hold on! *Ding ding ding*. Got an idea.

Donuts. That'll make her feel better. Always does.

That's the kind of guy Tyler is. When tragedy hits, always right there with something thoughtful.

Order the donut kid: "Get me one of those pink boxes. Start fillin'."

Two jelly, two blueberry, two old-fashioned, two cinnamon crunch. No, make it three cinnamon crunch. She really likes those. Two chocolate. One apple-filled. *What do you mean one more?* Oh, baker's dozen special. Nice.

Seems like an okay dude, this donut kid. Thoughtful. Not a loser like Cody.

Too bad.

Point the gun. Pull the trigger. Feel the kick.

Wipe off the prints. Put the gun in the donut kid's hand.

Naw. Move it to Cody's hand.

Doesn't totally add up. But it's the best Tyler can do given the circumstances. Cops'll be scratching their heads over this one.

Open the door. Hear the buzzer. Don't tilt the donut box. Take one last look at the scene.

Fuckin' Cody. Look what he made me do.

PART IV

Killer South

THE STRAWBERRY TATTOO

BY MACEO MONTOYA

Aptos

When David started barking, Marcela knew something awful was about to happen. His first bark, a sudden low growl, could've been mistaken for a man clearing his throat. But by the second and third, it was clear that David was doing his best impersonation of a bulldog ready to attack. When she followed his eyes, past all their colleagues at the hotel bar, she saw that he was staring at her boyfriend, Vicente.

"Shit," she said.

Someone else added, "What the hell is going on?"

Marcela and David used to sleep together. They were both English instructors in Avanza, a community college program geared toward disadvantaged students, most of them Latino. Marcela and David taught at different colleges now, Marcela in the Bay Area, David near Sacramento—but they ran into each other periodically at these team-building workshops. This semester, they'd gathered at the Seascape Beach Resort in Aptos.

Marcela was married when they first met, and so was David, but their attraction was so strong, at least on her end, that she refused to drink at the conference mixers in case she found her defenses weakened. At the next conference, after her marriage collapsed, she downed two tequila shots, found David, and practically dragged him to her room. He was stocky, muscular, with tattoos all over his body: on his back an Aztec warrior carrying a half-naked princess; on his chest the Virgen de Guadalupe, the rays of her halo crawling up his neck; and on his rib cage a giant bulldog in full color. She knew he'd gone to Fresno State.

"Damn, you got some serious school pride," she said when she first saw it.

"Something like that," he said.

David reminded her of the boys she grew up with. He may've been a college-level English professor, with an MA in comparative lit, schooling poorly prepared students in basic grammar and critical thinking, but he hadn't shed his upbringing. With his shaved head and carefully manicured goatee, he looked like a cholo, often talked like one. One unfortunate night, he acted like one too. At a conference in Sacramento, Marcela and David went for a beer run for the after-party. While David went inside the liquor store, she stayed out front to smoke a cigarette. A guy passed by and asked her if she had a light. She fumbled in her purse for her lighter and the guy asked, "Whatchu up to tonight, girl?"

She was about to say something friendly and dismissive, when she heard the door jingle behind her.

"Better back the fuck off, motherfucker," David's voice was right at her back.

The guy looked up. "Who the fuck you think you talking to, son?"

She tried to intervene. "David, stop—"

She didn't even see the punch, just a flurry, and suddenly the guy was knocked out cold.

Marcela screamed. "What the hell, David?" She grabbed his arm, but he jerked it away and she tumbled backward, almost falling. Marcela stumbled in her heels across the parking lot. She made it to the corner when she turned around, hoping David would be right behind, but there he was, holding a case of Tecate in one hand, standing over the guy and barking like a mad dog.

They never talked about the incident. They slept together a few more times, but then she heard he was still married and just had a kid. She avoided him from then on.

Everyone's attention was on David's barking act now: their academic colleagues, the bartender, and several recently arrived hotel guests. Marcela stared at Vicente. He was smiling as he mouthed something in David's direction.

Vicente was the most beautiful man, straight or otherwise, Marcela had ever met, down to the unblemished smoothness of his skin and his thick, shiny hair with never a strand out of place. She wished she had his eyelashes, his eyebrows, his nose and shapely lips, even his permanently minty breath. She was envious of his arms, and his thin, muscular legs. It was unfair so much beauty had been bestowed on a man.

There were drawbacks to his perfection. He heightened her insecurities, even though Vicente soothed her with compliments. But he could also act like the model on a magazine cover—unattainable, enigmatic, as perfect as he was blank. They'd been together almost six months and it drove her crazy.

This current moment was a good example of his inscrutability. What was Vicente mouthing in David's direction? Why the hell was he smiling?

David was the opposite. He was a man who wore his heart on his sleeve, and right now he was reacting, pure and simple.

"Come on, David, stop it," a male colleague said.

David's barking grew more aggressive. He set his glass of whiskey on the bar counter and now both arms were free to emphasize his canine-about-to-pounce stance.

The bartender tried to intervene: "Sir, excuse me, you're going to have quiet down or else I'll have to call security."

Without taking his eyes off Vicente, David stopped barking and said, "I'll quiet down when this piece of shit wipes the smile off his face."

Only at that moment did the others finally turn toward Vicente, who stood with his arms crossed, his smile unwavering.

God, he's so handsome, Marcela thought despite herself and the circumstances. But how could she ignore his perfect white teeth, his dimples, that confidence?

Vicente looked around and shrugged.

Satisfied, everyone now turned back to David, except for Marcela, who kept staring at Vicente, waiting for him to look at her. But he was fixed on David. There was a certain twinkle in his eye, and again he mouthed something, less perceptible than before, but Marcela was ready for it.

Bow-wow, she thought. That's what he's mouthing. *Bow-wow,* like a little dog. *Bow-wow,* like the poet Francisco Alarcón's dog. Earlier that day, a colleague in session had described her appreciation for the Chicano poet's verse about his bilingual dog. How when he came home, the dog greeted him, Bow-wow—and in case he didn't understand, the dog then barked, "Güau-güau."

Vicente had made a strange comment. He interrupted to ask what kind of dog it was.

"What?" the speaker didn't get it.

"I haven't read the poem. So I'm curious, does it say what kind of dog it is?"

"It's a bilingual dog."

"No, I mean, is it a bulldog or something, or is it nothing but a *mutt?*"

People were quiet for a moment, but then Vicente smiled

and everyone realized it was a joke and a few people chuckled to be polite.

Marcela shook her head and tried to alleviate the tension. "Ay, you tell the worst jokes, Vicente." He laughed good-naturedly and leaned back in his chair. Not a minute later, David abruptly rose from his seat and walked out of the conference room. No one gave it a second thought, and not until now did Marcela think that the two were connected: Vicente's stupid joke and David's exit.

Vicente did it again. Speaking softly now: "Bow-wow."

David barked in response and lunged toward Vicente. Two other men tried to restrain him but their efforts were pointless. David pushed them aside like the featherweight academics they were.

A glass fell off a table, hitting the floor with a dull thud; someone cried, "Oh my God!" In three bounds, David was on top of Vicente. Vicente didn't attempt to move. He didn't even flinch. David tackled him to the floor, where he straddled him and began punching Vicente's face in a left-right combo.

Marcela kept thinking it would stop, that David had to stop, but he'd lost all control. No one dared step forward. Vicente's head was limp and soft, like a rag doll.

Hotel security pushed through the crowd and grabbed David from behind, cutting short one last punch. They dragged him backward. He gave little resistance, and his wide-eyed expression made him seem as shocked as everyone else. Vicente lay prostrate on the ground, blood streaming from his nose and mouth, his face already swollen. One of the security guards said into his walkie-talkie, "Call the police. Get an ambulance too!"

The Avanza conference attendees, so accustomed to doling out advice to desperate young people, were at a loss. They stared at Vicente's limp body, fearing the worst. Marcela overcame her shock and rushed to his side, collapsing. "Vicente!"

As if beckoned from the dead, he turned his head to her. The last thing she expected was for Vicente to smile and reveal a mouthful of bloody teeth.

"An ambulance is coming!"

"No, I'm fine." He coughed. "Tell them I don't need one."

"Are you crazy?"

"Really, I'm fine," he said. "Just give me a sec." Vicente rose onto his elbows, turned, and pushed himself to his knees. He grabbed a table and with a little hop, hoisted himself up onto his feet. He looked around at everyone. "I'm all good," he said. "Don't worry about me."

Frederico, a counselor at Davis, said, "Vicente, bro, you should go to the hospital, man, it doesn't look good."

Vicente waved him off. "I'll just ice up, get some rest." He turned to Marcela. "Help me to the room, will you?"

Marcela held his arm and together they walked slowly toward the elevator. She turned back to look at their colleagues, wanting someone to stop them. But no one said a thing.

They stepped onto the elevator and a few seconds later the doors slid closed. After a long silence, she realized she'd forgotten to press the floor number. She pressed *3* and stood back, staring at the tile floor, trembling. Mirrors surrounded them. She didn't want to look up. She couldn't bear to look at Vicente's face.

"Baby," Vicente said.

"Yeah?"

"Look at me."

She slowly looked at Vicente's reflection in the mirror. One eye had shut completely. He stared at her through the slit of his other. He started to laugh, revealing his blood-smeared teeth.

"What the *fuck* is wrong with you?" she said. She felt tears streaming down her cheeks.

He let out a long satisfied sigh. "I needed that," he said.

"You—what?"

The elevator dinged and the doors slid open. An elderly white couple was waiting outside. They were dressed for dinner, bubbling with excitement. When they saw Vicente their eyes bulged in unison. The woman gasped, "Oh my God! What happened?"

Marcela was too upset to respond.

Vicente had no problem finding words: "You know, just a little scrap with a bitch-ass nigga."

Vicente slept for an hour with ice-wrapped towels covering his face. Marcela watched over him from a rolling desk chair. Her heart steadied. She knew David was capable of violence. She'd seen it firsthand. She knew what the barking was all about too. After the liquor store incident, she'd confided to a friend from her writing group. Like David, he had grown up in Fresno. "He must be a Bulldog," the friend said.

"What does that have to do with anything?"

"It's a Fresno gang. That's what they do. They bark to show how crazy they are. I swear, look it up on YouTube."

"It's psycho, that's what it is," Marcela said. "A grown man barking. And what the hell, wasn't he supposed to have left that life behind?"

"Vatos locos *forever*," the friend said, doing his best Miklo impression from *Blood In Blood Out* before bursting into giggles.

But as enigmatic as Vicente could be, violence hardly seemed in his nature. In addition to his physical beauty, he was polite, almost debonair, as if he'd been raised at an English boarding school, at least how Marcela imagined one. He rarely cussed. He never raised his voice. He didn't even fumble when he spoke, rarely letting slip an "uh" or an "um." He used words that were odd coming out of a first-generation Mexican kid, such as "preferably" and "perhaps." Vicente adhered to the rules of chivalry as though he'd come across a guidebook, holding doors open for others regardless of gender, the first to give up his seat, always insisting on clearing the table and washing the dishes.

His colleagues loved him, his students worshipped him. And yet to date him, Marcela had learned, was like eating in a dream. The feast might be all hers but she still couldn't taste a goddamn thing.

What did she know about him? He'd grown up nearby in Watsonville. At her insistence, he once brought her there. She had taken him to meet her parents in Woodland, and he remarked that the place reminded him of where he grew up, a small California city surrounded by fields and full of Mexicans. She wanted him to return the favor, show her "his" Watsonville.

She pestered him until one Sunday morning they drove out to the coast, stopping at the first market they passed to buy pan dulce and hot chocolate. The clouds hadn't burned off and it started to drizzle, so they stayed in the car and just drove around. He said he was going to take her down "memory lane." He pointed out where he went to school, where he used to play soccer, the playground where he got his first kiss, yet these were all the things she had shown him in Woodland, as if he were simply repeating her memories and pointing.

But then he would throw in stuff such as, "That's the alley where we jumped my cousin Rafa," and laugh. "In high school, I used to deal from that apartment right there."

"Stop playing," she said.

Then he drove to the outskirts of the city and his tone become more somber: "We used to live in a trailer out here on the farm where my parents worked, and my dad, he would walk home from the bar every night. And one night he didn't come home, so my mom went looking for him. She found him dead on the side of the road. A hit-and-run. Can you believe that?"

"I'm so sorry!" she said. "I didn't know."

But then Vicente began laughing and she thought he was teasing her again.

"Don't do that!" And she slapped him on the arm. "That's not even remotely funny."

She assumed that after driving around they were going to end up at his house and she was going to meet his family. But after circling around a picturesque central plaza with a kiosk, he took the main road out of town and got back on the 101 heading north.

"Aren't we going to visit your family?"

"My family?" He chuckled. "You don't want to do that."

"Do what? Meet them? Of course I do. If it's your family." Then she stopped herself. They had only been dating a few months. Maybe he wasn't ready for that step. "All right," she finally said. "No pressure."

Before getting too far, they pulled over at a roadside fruit stand and she picked up a basket of strawberries. "I know these are your favorite," she said. She took a strawberry out of the basket and went to put it in his mouth.

"What makes you say that?" he asked, backing away.

"Uh, if it's not your favorite fruit, why do you have a tattoo of one on your back?"

The first time they had hooked up, she noticed a tattoo of

a strawberry near the base of his neck. It was so delicate that she almost laughed. It was sweet, and so like him too, like a stamp on his taut skin.

He chuckled. "Oh, yeah, that's right. I forgot."

She laughed too, and attempted again to place the strawberry in his mouth. "Open up," she said.

"Perhaps it'd be wise to wash those first," he said.

She had already eaten half the basket. "Whatever, live a little."

A few weeks later, out with her girlfriends, they got on the topic of things they found odd or gross about their lovers. When it was Marcela's turn, her friends joked that they should just skip her because Vicente was clearly a gift from God. She wanted to share something so she told them about his strawberry tattoo. "Isn't that weird?" she said.

Her friends laughed politely and said it was "adorable," but one of them asked, "Isn't he from Watsonville?"

"Yeah, why?"

"I mean, I think that's a gang thing. In Watsonville it's the strawberry, in Salinas it's a freaking lettuce head. Somewhere else it's an artichoke. My students, I swear, they teach me the randomest shit."

Marcela tried to laugh it off. The idea that Vicente's tattoo was gang-affiliated seemed so ridiculous that she didn't intend to give it any further thought. But later that same night, she went home, poured herself another drink, and googled variations of "beautiful thugs" and "hot gangsters." She found the results entertaining if nothing else.

It was her own romantic history that caused her worry. It was lined with two kinds of men: *machistas* who infuriated her, and one harmless white guy whom she eventually grew bored of. She had married the latter, but had suffered the torture of plenty of the former. Vicente, she thought, was a departure for her. Finally she had learned from her mistakes. She wasn't doomed to repeat herself. Didn't she deserve someone beautiful and kind with an air of mystery?

Marcela heard a loud pounding at the hotel door followed by, "Police department, open up!" She looked over at Vicente, who hadn't stirred in an hour. The towels of ice remained covering his face. The pounding on the door resumed and she rushed to answer. Two officers filled the doorway.

"We're looking for Vicente Cuellar."

"Yes, he's here," she said. "But he's sleeping."

"I'm Officer Fernandez. This is Officer Halston. If you don't mind, we'd like to ask him a few questions about the incident in the downstairs bar. If we can just wake him up, we won't be long."

Marcela hesitated in the doorway. The officers couldn't see the bed from where they were standing. Were they really asking her permission?

"Let them in. I'm up," Vicente called from inside the room.

Marcela stood aside and the officers walked in. As soon as they saw Vicente's face, they looked at each other, then pulled out their pocket notepads and began writing.

"Well, he sure got you good," Officer Fernandez said.

"You should've seen the other guy," Vicente quipped.

The officer looked up from his notepad. "Uh, we did. He's in handcuffs right now. And he's fine."

Vicente chuckled. "It was a joke. Look, officers, let the guy go. It was just a misunderstanding. We were drinking. Tempers flared. I said some things I shouldn't have—"

"And what did you say, exactly?" Officer Fernandez cut in. "The other guy just said, 'Stuff.'"

"It doesn't really matter. All I can say is that I'm over it. We got it out of our systems. I'm sober, he's sober. No need to make it a bigger deal than it is."

"Well, you see, we're staring at your face and it looks like a pretty big deal. If a man is capable of doing what he did to you, then he might be capable of doing that to someone else. It makes us feel like we're not doing our jobs."

"I appreciate what you're saying, sir, but see, the issue is—" Vicente stopped. "I thought I recognized you, Fernandez."

The officer looked up from his notepad. "What was that?"

"It's me, Cuellar. You used to be a guard in juvie, right?"

The officer looked closer. His face brightened. "Holy shit. It's you! I thought that name sounded familiar! What the hell, man! It's been years."

"I know, I know," Vicente said. "You gave up on the little homies or what? After the real bad guys now?"

"That was just my first job. Jesus, I was barely a kid in there myself."

Fernandez's demeanor had relaxed completely. He shook his head in amazement and turned to his partner. "This kid ruled the hall. You would've thought he was Tony Montana." He turned back to Vicente. "So you teach college now? That's what they were saying downstairs in the lobby. I couldn't believe the other guy was a teacher. Looked like a thug to me. And now you, I can't believe it—they letting every banger go to college now? But that's good, Cuellar. I'm proud of you."

Vicente nodded his head. "Look, that guy downstairs. Me and him are cool. We both got pasts, and today they caught up with us. We both spent too many years working to get where we are right now. I wouldn't want to mess that up for him over a little skirmish."

Officer Fernandez smiled. "*Skirmish*. Listen to you. Same old Cuellar. You could always talk your way out of everything. Nothing stuck to you." He looked over at Marcela. "Ain't this guy about the smoothest talker you ever heard?"

Marcela was too stunned to answer. She had leaned against the wall and was digging her fingernails into the textured ridges of the wallpaper, afraid she was going to lose her grip.

The officers left. After a long silence, Vicente turned to Marcela. "You okay?" he asked.

She still hadn't moved from the wall.

"Come here," he said. "Let's sleep this off."

She couldn't even look at him. "I don't know who you are," she said. "We've been together six months and I feel like I don't know you any better than when we first met. That cop called you Tony Montana. All this time, I think you're a sensitive, thoughtful teacher and now suddenly you're Scarface?"

Vicente sighed. "What do you want to know?" His voice was tender, apologetic.

"Why'd you do that down there?"

"I don't know. I just wanted to fight."

"But that's the thing. I saw you. You didn't fight at all. You didn't even try to defend yourself."

Vicente shrugged his shoulders. "Sometimes it feels good to get hit."

"That's not an answer that makes any sense. You know that, right?"

"Marcela, I've been through some shit."

"You need serious help."

He leaned his head back down on the pillow. "Perhaps," he said.

* * *

Next morning Vicente woke her up, gently shaking her shoulder. There was a coffee maker in the bathroom and he had made a pot. He served her some in a Styrofoam cup and placed it on her nightstand. The coffee was weak, but it helped her headache. She pulled aside the curtain and saw it was dawn.

"Why'd you wake me up so early?"

"I wanted to walk with you on the beach. I don't want to scare anyone with my face like this. It'll be empty for a little while. Let's go."

They bundled up and strolled along the wet sand in silence. Neither made any attempt to talk and it was soothing just to listen to the crashing of the waves.

"In all my life living in Watsonville, I'd never been to Santa Cruz except when I was in juvie up the road. I didn't realize it was like twenty miles away. The first time I came over here was when I started going to Cabrillo after I got my GED in County."

"County jail?"

"Yeah," he said. "First juvie. Then I got transferred to County."

"For what?"

"A whole bunch of things. Liked it better inside than I did out."

"Is that why you didn't want me to meet your family?"

He grunted. "What family?"

They passed a man in a baseball cap walking his golden retriever. The man nodded to them, doing a double take when he noticed Vicente's face.

"How bad is it?" he asked

"You didn't look in the mirror?"

"I was afraid to."

"I'm surprised you're alive, let alone walking on the beach."

"I always could take a punch."

Marcela wanted to bring the conversation back. "What do you mean *what family*?"

"After my dad died, my mom, she struggled. I was in and out of foster homes."

"Is that why you joined a gang?" she asked.

He scrunched up his face. "What do you mean?"

"You *know*: didn't have a family so you found one."

"I wasn't in a gang," he said.

She looked up at him. Through his swollen face, she couldn't tell if he was being serious or not.

"Then what about your strawberry tattoo? Don't tell me that's just Watsonville pride."

"Naw, that's my favorite fruit."

She burst out laughing. "You think you're funny, Vicente." She felt his arm around her waist. He turned her toward him.

"Look at me," he said.

She was cold and she pushed herself closer to his warmth, though she couldn't look up. She didn't want to.

"Look at me," he said again.

She allowed herself to stare at his disfigured face. The ice had helped. His eyes were no longer as swollen, yet his face was still covered in welts, cuts, and bruises. She reached up and gently touched his busted bottom lip, then the cuts on his nose. She moved a little higher and ran her fingers over the veins of his swollen eyelids. His eyes were closed. She could hear his breathing and feel his breath on her forehead. He was shivering slightly. She touched his swollen, bruised cheek. He winced, but she kept her hand there anyway.

With the tips of her fingers she dug into his skin and expected him to back away, but he didn't. She pressed harder and harder until she realized that he was resisting, pushing back hard against her fingers—and then he grabbed her wrists. "Hit me."

"No," she whimpered as she tried to wrest her hands away. "Let me go, you're scaring me."

"Hit me," he said again.

"Hit your fucking self."

"I can't!" he screamed—and then softer, "I can't hit anyone."

She stopped struggling. "I'm not going to hit you, Vicente."

He let go of her wrists and her arms fell to her side. She turned and walked quickly back toward the beachfront. She didn't want to look back, but she couldn't help herself. Vicente was still where she'd left him, staring after her through swollen eyes.

CRAB DINNERS

BY LOU MATHEWS
Seacliff

I was in my apartment, above The Mediterranean, Seacliff's favorite dive bar, on Center. If you don't drink and you don't dive, you'll still know the joint, or at least the location, because it's next door to Manuel's, the best Mexican restaurant in Santa Cruz County. My apartment is spitting distance from my office, a realtor's shack on blocks on unused state park land. Estelle Richardson, the realtor who rents me a desk, figures we'll be here for life.

I poked my head out the window to scan the weather and see what the day would bring. There was a girl sitting on the steps of the office, a redhead, reading a book with a finger in her curls. It was nine, an hour at least before Estelle would show, and I didn't think the kid was looking for real estate.

I have access to the Mediterranean's espresso machine, a reliable Gaggia that fires up and delivers in three minutes. In five, I was walking up to my office, coffee in one hand, key in the other to indicate my intent. Red looked up, showing an unspoiled face, freckled, quizzical. I looked at her book. It was Carter Wilson's classic, *Crazy February*. She closed it on her finger and stood up.

"Are you looking for an apartment?" I said.

"I'm looking for a detective," she replied. "I'm looking for Ms. Sukenick."

"It's Sukie," I said, and put the key in the lock. "Come on in."

She sat down across from me. I studied her face. I couldn't figure out where she was from. I mean, from her speech I knew she was a California kid. She had that accent that Californians don't think they have, compressed words, raised inflection, like they're asking a question. But I couldn't place her face. The freckles and coppery curls could have been County Cork, but there was something different in the eyes, which were a shifting green-gray. Then the cheekbones. If I had to make a guess, I would have said some Irish missionary once made a convert in Beijing.

"So, " I said, "what does an anthropology major from UC Berkeley want with me?"

She gave a little gasp. "Wow, you really are a detective. How did you know that?"

She probably thought she hadn't given me any clues, but the blue-and-gold knit cap stuffed in her backpack was definitely Cal and the essential clue was her reading material. *Crazy February* is a classic in Mesoamerican anthropology, about a murder in the Maya highlands of Chiapas, and I knew Lars Guthrie, the Berkeley professor who assigned the book to his upper-division anthro students every quarter.

What I said was, "If you hang around long enough, you learn some things. What can I do for you?"

She gathered herself. "My name is Kelly Wong. I'm looking for my father, Leonard Wong. Do you know him?"

I didn't know the man personally, but I'd eaten in his restaurants and any reader of *Good Times* in the seventies and eighties knew him from his chatty weekly advertisements. "Chef Wong," in his towering toque, had introduced Szechuan peppers and triple-X chile oil to Santa Cruz County.

Something didn't scan. I had to ask. "Were you adopted, Kelly?"

She laughed. "I get that a lot. No, Leonard was my father as far as I know. I know the Mayan *dicho* about you only *really* know who your mother is, but she said Leonard was her one and only. My mom was Uyghur from Xinjiang. There's a lot of red-haired kids there."

"Okay," I said, and took up my pad and pen. "So when did you last communicate with your dad?"

"That's the thing," Kelly said. "Usually, we would talk on the phone every week. He'd call from the restaurant. Sometimes I could tell he'd been drinking, but he always called. Two weeks ago, he didn't. I wasn't too worried because I knew there was a big cockfighting tournament in Watsonville. He usually stayed up all night for those."

She'd mentioned the drinking and I'd seen that at Wong's restaurant. "XO sauce" was a craze developed in Hong Kong and Chef Wong was determined to improve on the recipe. The "XO" symbolized rarity, like XO cognacs, but there wasn't actually cognac in the Hong Kong recipe, just Shaoxing wine and pricey dried seafood.

In Wong's version, there was cognac. When he flambéed scallops, table-side, he would pour a glug of Rémy Martin onto the shellfish, swallow a glug himself, then tip the wok toward the burner. Blue flames would erupt, then applause. Every other table would order the dish. By the second or third order, a lot more of the cognac sauced Chef Wong than the scallops.

"Then," Kelly said, "this came yesterday, registered mail." She handed me a nine-by-twelve envelope. The return address was an impressive San Francisco law firm. The sheaf of papers inside explained that a trust had been established in the name of Kelly Wong. On the last page was the full dollar amount, a little over a quarter-mil.

Kelly had teared up. I pushed the tissues across. She wiped

her eyes and blew her nose. "I'd been calling him since Sunday and he wasn't home and he wasn't at the restaurant. Nobody knew where he was."

"Your mom?" I ventured.

She teared up again. "I lost my mom two years ago. There were too many problems for her." I let that one slide. "My dad has a lot of enemies," she continued, "because of the restaurants, the investors. He likes to gamble. So, I'm worried. Can you please look for him?"

I was still mulling. "How did you hear about me?"

"That was kind of weird. I have finals starting Monday, so I went to my advisor to see if I could do a makeup. I told her the whole story. I didn't want to go to the cops in case it turned out to be a ransom situation. She thought I needed legal advice and called a friend at the law school. He recommended you."

"What's his name?"

"Brad Turner. You know him?"

"We have some history. Do you have someplace to stay here? I don't want you staying at your dad's."

"I can stay with my dad's cooks. They won't say anything."

"Do that." I told her what I'd need to get started. She didn't blink. The only thing she asked was if she could pay the thousand-dollar retainer in two checks. Sure. She wrote two checks for $499 each and handed me two dollar bills. She explained that it was a condition of the trust. Any checks above $500 had to be approved by the trustee. "My dad told the lawyers he didn't want me paying off his debts."

"Go get some rest," I said. "Call me here tomorrow morning and I'll give you an update."

"Don't you want my phone number, or the address where I'm staying?"

"I don't want to be able to answer that question until I figure out what's going on. As you said, your dad has enemies. You want me to call you a cab?"

"No," Kelly said, "I want to walk down the railroad tracks. I can catch the bus on Park. My dad's first restaurant was in Capitola. It was just my mom and dad cooking and working the front. I helped out from the time I was five or six. A lot of customers couldn't figure out who I was. I was my dad's favorite joke. He'd say, 'This is my daughter Kelly. She's living proof that two Wongs can make a white!'"

"He's got a lot to answer for."

"Yeah, not many customers laughed, even back then." She put on her pack and jammed the stocking cap over her curls. I watched her walk up Center.

At Manuel's, Leobardo, the head waiter, was lounging on the bench in front, reading the *Santa Cruz Sentinel.* Leobardo didn't even look up as Kelly passed, which surprised me. Usually he checked out anything with a bounce and a pulse.

Kelly crossed to State Park Drive, walked up to Moulton's Union '76, and headed north on the railroad tracks.

So Kelly Wong had said Brad Turner recommended me. A blast from the past. I knew Brad for the same reason I knew Lars Guthrie and Carter Wilson: my shady academic past. I was a failed professor. I did my four-year stretch in Rubber City. When I was denied tenure at UCSC, I did what my role model Annie Steinhardt did when she was denied. I went over the hill and started dancing at Jolly's, a topless bar in the pits of San Jose. Annie wrote a book about it, *Thunder La Boom.* There wasn't a novel in my future, I wrote poetry—but I liked the idea and the money was good and immediate.

About my third month at Jolly's, I encountered a former student, Brad Turner. Or, should I say, Brad Turner looked me up, and looked me down. It's a little hard, peering over your own bouncing breasts, to acknowledge a former student, but I nodded and we met in the parking lot.

"Dr. Sukenick," Brad said.

I had to smile. "Call me Sukie." It was my stage name, but it fit. "Did you graduate?"

"Yeah," Brad said with a grin, "my stepdad just about stroked out." Brad was one of my salvage jobs.

"I'm here to return the favor," he said. "I'm working for the public defender's office. They want smart people and I thought you might fit." Brad came from a family of lawyers and he'd avoided that fate as long as he could, but the PD's office had sniffed him out, and hired him as an investigator. He was off to Boalt and he thought I might be the ideal replacement.

It worked out. More than worked out. Turned out that intuitive instinct I thought would lead to chapbooks and tenure was ideally suited to listening to liars. I spent six years learning the trade and, more valuably, getting to know every judge, prosecutor, public defender, and most of the cops in Santa Cruz County. My three-month stint, topless, had more cachet with them than my four years at the university.

I made the obligatory calls on Chef Wong. Leonard didn't turn up much on the criminal front: two DUIs and an arrest without charge in a mass bust in Prunedale—one of a crowd of two hundred–plus at an alleged cockfight.

Civil was a different matter. Leonard Wong had been, and was currently being, sued by investors, landlords, suppliers, contractors, and even a live seafood supplier from Korea who he'd stiffed. The investors came in clumps. It appeared that he had sold the restaurants at least four times to five groups of overseas investors. He hadn't done the bankruptcy out, which was interesting. That meant he hoped for new investors. I checked with my sources in the DA's office and learned there were more lawsuits pending. Then I checked my darker sources and learned that in addition to his drinking and money problems, Leonard also had a cocaine problem, and that was overtaking the rest. The profile was shaping.

Estelle blew in around eleven thirty a.m., looking, as she was wont to say, *rid hard and put away wet.*

"If you look in the dictionary under *blowsy* . . ." I said.

"Stuff it." Estelle reached for the Visine, tilted back, and shuddered as the drops hit her tender eyeballs. "Made the sale. At least I damn well better have made that sale. His wife would not like to see what my security camera saw."

"Leonard Wong?"

Estelle sat up. "Interesting story, but I only know the parameters. He used to own the land his restaurants sit on. Three refi's in three years. New case?"

"Time for lunch."

"Gotcha." Estelle turned on her desk lamp, put on her dark glasses, and spun her Rolodex.

I walked over to Manny's. It was pleasantly dark, as always, and quieter than usual. You could actually hear Manny's favorite soundtrack, delicate *jarocho* harp music from Veracruz. Manuel Santana was an interesting man, successful restaurateur, and failed artist, according to him—and Chicano Centrál if you were involved in Democratic Party politics. He kept the lights low and stocked chardonnay, which kept the gringas of a certain age coming back.

The head waiter's wife, Socorro, was behind the cash register, comparing the tale of the tape to the handwritten bills, then stapling them together. I touched her on the shoulder as I went by. She lifted her head and smiled at me. Leobardo approached; he nodded and it was almost a genuflection—then, full smile. He leaned in attentively with his pad and we went through our ritual.

"*Para mi, poquito ensalada de Manuel*," I said. "*Chile relleño combinacion, menos frijoles, solo arroz*."

Leobardo didn't write it down until I finished my recitation, and then he began his own: "One small Manny's salad, one stuffed chile, no beans, only rice. And to drink?"

"*Una* Bohemia, *por favor*."

Leobardo winked. "It's December. We just got our shipment of Noche Buena. "

The Christmas beer, a joy, a dark beer with some sweetness but more body and a great aftertaste. The German braumeisters who came to Monterrey in the nineteenth century lived on in this great beer, available once a year. "Noche Buena," I agreed.

Leobardo bowed and smiled again. At the cash register, Socorro cackled. As always, Leobardo ignored his wife and maintained his chivalrous flirtation. "*Esta bién, señorita*. Your accent is really improving."

As he set down the beer, I said, "Leobardo. A question, and this is professional."

"For your work?"

"Yes. Do you know anyone who knows about cockfighting in South County?"

He sat down across from me. "You need this?"

"Yeah, it matters."

"Then you should talk to my uncle Mike. Miguel to me, but he'll want you to call him Mike. Did you know about my family?"

"No. Just a shot. Cockfighting's been big in Watsonville since the sixties and I know your family has been here longer than that."

"My family is from Michoacán, and that's the center of cockfighting in Mexico. We've bred champion roosters for more than a century."

At the cash register, Socorro spiked a sheaf of bills, rolled the tape around the spike, and punched the empty cash drawer closed. She stood with the bank bag and peered at us with some humor. "If I had a peso for every macho from Michoacán who claimed he raised the best cock in the country, I'd be a happier woman than I am today."

Leobardo rolled his eyes and blew a kiss in Socorro's direction, "*Besos y pesos, mi amor*." He tore off a page from his order pad, wrote furiously, and then handed it to me like a check. "That's the address and phone number. I'll go make the call."

The address was in Corralitos. Back at the office, Estelle looked up the parcel. It was a good-sized ranch for the area, 180 acres off Eureka Canyon Road. Miguel Sandoval was the owner.

Estelle spotted something interesting, the parcel opposite Miguel's, which fronted on Amesti Road. It was owned by another Sandoval, Benjamin. Corralitos Creek separated the properties.

Estelle pointed out the window, "There's your flag boy."

I looked out. Leobardo had stepped out the front door of Manny's and was waving a red napkin. When he saw he had my attention, he jabbed a forefinger south. It was time to go.

The day was too nice for the freeway. I took my Karmann Ghia through the apple orchards and Victorian farmhouses, then rolled down my window as I passed the Corralitos meat market to enjoy the scent of burning applewood and smoking linguiça.

I found the address, an impressive stone gate with a bronze sign affixed, *Rancho Sandoval.* Uncle Mike was behind the gate, an older, sturdier version of Leobardo, on horseback, a beautiful roan that must have stood seventeen hands high. I waved, and he walked the gate open and then walked it closed behind me, a nice bit of horsemanship.

I leaned out and looked up at him, "Don Miguel, *cómo estás?*"

He laughed, "Yeah, Leobardo said you would try out your Spanish. He said not to encourage you. It's Mike. Follow me."

He set out at a canter and then got up to speed, cutting through short grass and vetch that fronted the rows of apple trees. I followed on the concrete, which became well-graded dirt out of sight of the frontage road. It was almost three minutes to the house and outbuildings, clustered on a wide meadow, backed onto Corralitos Creek. It was as close to a hacienda as anything I'd seen on this side of the border.

Off to one side was what looked like a full-sized rodeo arena, with metal stands. In back, a parking lot. Mike went inside and came out bearing two sweating bottles of Noche Buena. He handed one over. "Let's walk and talk. Leobardo told me two things. He said you wanted to know about cockfighting and he said you were to be trusted."

I pointed to the arena. "Is that where they're held? The cockfights?"

He laughed. "No, we actually do hold rodeos here, once a month at least, both *vaquero* and American."

He took my elbow and guided me around an oak to a smaller path, which led to a pristine metal building with tiers of canted rows of windows, tilted to let in sunlight, but at an angle that made it impossible to see in from outside.

Inside, I understood I was in the Taj Mahal of henhouses—climate-controlled with filtered air, sunlit apartments filled with happy chickens, if the slow contented clucking was any indicator. Chickens of all colors walked and scratched and sat asleep on fresh straw, in tiers stretching to the roof.

"These are the hens," Mike explained. "We sell some eggs at our roadside stand. About half of them are breeders, from long lines of fierce ancestors. Rockefeller couldn't afford these eggs for breakfast." Beyond the hens was a metal wall that had a metal door with a coded entry lock. Mike punched some numbers.

Beyond was Fort Rooster. The walls resounded with roosters in full cry, roosters pacing back and forth on their sawdust runways, roosters pecking at whole corncobs and their reflections in small mirrors. Combs engorged, metallic feathers flashing, mindless bright eyes reflecting us. These birds, with their herky-jerky movements, seemed more reptilian than avian.

I noticed metal bowls in a lot of the cages that seemed to have what looked like steak tartar, diced cubes of dark flesh. I pointed. "You feed them meat?"

"Horse meat," Mike said, "low fat, lots of protein."

"Chickens eat meat?"

"In the wild," Mike said, "chickens eat anything: bugs, lizards, snakes, rats, other chickens—people too, if they find a body."

At the end of the room was a deep pit; two young men were standing in it, holding what looked like younger roosters, one black, one red. They were thrusting the birds forward to excite them. They dropped the birds and there was a flurry of kicks, squawks, slashing beaks, kicking heels, and loose feathers flying. Until one bird, the red, turned away.

The men stepped in and gathered the frantic birds up, turned in different directions, and calmed them, stroking and soothing.

I looked at the confined space. "Is this where it all happens?"

"No, no, no," Mike said. "This is the practice *palenque*. Come on, I'll show you the real deal." As we went through the back door, he turned back and spoke to the men. One nodded, and wrung the neck of the red bird.

We walked to a section of Corralitos Creek that was different from the small stream I knew. Here it was wider and deeper, twenty feet across at least. Mike pointed downstream and up: "Two check dams. We close the gates when we want to stop waders. Now, come round the corner." There was a tall, dense eugenia hedge; on the other side was what looked like a boat landing. "I'm not actually going to show you the real *palenque*. It's a quarter-mile walk on the other side."

"On your brother's land?"

Mike's eyes gleamed with amusement. "I am going to show you how we get there." He lifted the top of one of the pilings. Inside was a panel with four buttons. He pushed the top one. From beneath the deck, a metal rectangle emerged and kept emerging, like the ladder on a fire truck extending up the side of a building. The smoothness suggested hydraulics. The metal span crossed twenty feet of creek and locked into a slot on the other side. Mike pressed a second button, railings unfolded from the bed and swayed upright to lock into place. I was looking at a perfect bridge. The whole process had taken about a minute. Mike pressed the third button, the rails collapsed, and then the fourth. The return trip was less than thirty seconds.

The big ranch had parking, public events, all legal and family friendly. Across the creek at the secluded arena, there was no traffic, no cars, and enough security precautions that if anyone came snooping, the high rollers would fade back across an uncrossable creek to join innocent crowds at the rodeo.

"Ridiculous, no?" Mike tugged on his mustache. "A rope bridge would have worked as well and cost nothing. This bridge is designed to impress. I showed it to you to give you an idea how much money is involved in these events."

"I'm guessing a lot."

"This ain't Prunedale. Cops bust some flaky Filipinos and they think they've wrapped it up. Santa Cruz County has been the center of cockfighting in the US since the 1950s. The prize for our last tournament was fifty grand. More than a million dollars changes hands on side bets . . . So, now that I've told you this, do you want to ask me about Leonard Wong?"

"How did you know?"

"Leobardo saw Kelly on your stoop this morning. He's known her since she was a little girl. She used to come to the cockfights with her dad. If you hadn't asked, he would have told you to come see me."

"Do you know where Leonard is?"

"I think I know who's behind this, but I want you to finish your investigation. I have some prejudices, I don't like the family. I want to have an independent eye on this."

"What's your interest?"

"Leonard Wong was my friend—and he taught me—me, *un hombre de Michoacán*—most of what I know about chickens. People forget, cockfighting started in China, before Jesús. We Mexicans have only been doing this a couple hundred years.

"Leonard was a genius with birds. He used to say, 'I know how to cook them and I know how to pick 'em,' and he was right. He never lost money betting on cockfighting. Just last week he made three hundred large, and he made *me* a lot of money. He helped me build my line of birds to where they are today, champions, just using his eye to pick mates. He taught me how to train, correct their faults."

"So why is he in money trouble?"

"He was as bad at poker as he was good at cockfighting. He thought he could read *gabachos* the same way he read chickens."

Mike closed the cover on the bridge button and went businessman on me: "I gotta go, I have a meeting. Do your digging. If you find out what happened, there's a bonus in it for you. I don't want to make a serious move without being sure. You have my number."

I drove back to the office, a little dazed. There was one little red flag that flew up during that drive. Mike had said that Leobardo had *seen* Kelly Wong on my stoop. That he had known her since she was a little girl.

I'd watched Kelly walk down Center, past Manuel's where Leobardo was sitting on the bench in front. He didn't look at her, not even to study her schoolgirl ass. I thought at the time it was odd, but then I thought, well, maybe Socorro was over his shoulder, watching.

But how do you explain childhood friends not even looking at each other? That was a red flag that might stay up.

It took about three calls for me to connect the dots. What I said was, "Big-time, big-money poker games. Cross-category: cocaine access. Santa Cruz County." The answer was the same each time: Joe Morielli.

It was a name I knew but a profile so low he'd never showed up on my screen. Joe Morielli was a black sheep, and perhaps the most successful member of the Watsonville apple cider vinegar clan.

I'd first heard about him at the public defender's office, but even then he was a rumor. Joe, unlike the rest of the Moriellis, hated apples. He'd gone to work at local nightclubs, first as a busboy, then tending bar, then tending bar as a hobby while dealing cocaine. It was a fairly common progression. But Joe was smart and made a smart move. He started giving discounts to local law enforcement and from there moved up the food chain to the legal community: DAs, prosecutors, eventually judges. By then, he was midlevel and no longer had any contact with the buyers, but he knew who they were. They knew he knew.

Joe had never been busted, not even when some competitors disappeared and he took over the longest-running poker game in town. Then the man seemed to vanish. No one I knew could put me in touch with Joe. He was a ghost. No presence. More than that, he was an absence, which spoke to his layers of legal protection. The best intel I could manage was that his regular players were only informed the day of the card game where the game would be held.

I called it a night and trudged home—Campbell's chicken noodle, sprawled on the couch, soothed by Perry Mason and the gentle happy din from downstairs.

Friday, I hired a temp to cover for me with Kelly and anyone else. The temp loved the script I gave her: "I get to say that? You're tracking leads? That is so cool!"

I'd decided the only way to smoke Joe out was to tap into the ground from which he was raised. I hit every bar, lounge, and tavern in Santa Cruz County. I was depending on the loose confederacy of bartenders and cocktail waitresses to pass the word along. I pressed my card and the promise of cash.

By late afternoon I'd covered the county. The temp said no one except Kelly had called. I paid her to stay and monitor the phones, in case of a tipster. At seven I gave up, sent the temp home, and went downstairs to join the cheerful roar.

The Friday-night Mediterranean was packed and in full fling. I found an empty two-top in the back corner and waited for a waitress to find me.

Sacha Howells found me first, and he bore my signature drink, a Red Bomb: Carpano Antica, twist of lemon, rocks.

Sacha spun a napkin onto my table and set the drink down. I was surprised to see him. Sacha is on the day shift. He leaned in. "I was told to give you this." He handed over another Mediterranean napkin. I could see the ink bleeding through from the middle.

I heard you're looking for me.
Why don't you join me on a voyage.
Aboard the SS Palo Alto.
I'm there now.
Joe

A little frost descended my spine. I swallowed my vermouth and headed for the door. I went upstairs for my peacoat. It was going to be cold out there on the boat. The SS *Palo Alto* was one of two cement ships built in 1919 at the US Navy shipyards in Oakland. The war ended before the ship went into service, so they mothballed her for a decade until the Seacliff Amusement Corporation bought her and towed her to Seacliff Beach, where they tethered her to a pier, built a dance hall, a swimming pool, and a café on board—and sank her. Probably a great entertainment idea, but not in 1929. They closed in '31, stripped her, and left her as a fishing pier, the focal point of the new state park.

I spent a lot of time there fishing and watching the bay. The boat had split apart in '58 and become a paradise for fishermen, an ideal reef, full of fish, mussels, crabs, and the birds that fed on them.

I was looking down on the pier and the ship from the cliffs. I put my watch cap on and started down the endless Seacliff stairs. With the wind chill, it was close to freezing.

I walked out onto the pier. It was a long way out. It was a clear, beautiful night, with a moon over the bay beating a silvery path toward me. There was a constant crash of waves on the broken bow of the ship, then the sough and sigh of the tide working back from the beach.

On the ship there was a solitary fisherman looking down into the dark water. A big bucket beside him. He grabbed a braided yellow nylon rope that was tied to the railing. As soon as I saw him start hauling on the rope, I knew exactly what he was doing: fishing for the rock crabs that congregated around the cement ship.

My first husband, my only husband, Elron, taught me how to fish for crabs. He grew up in Brooklyn and haunted the piers of Jamaica Bay. The only Jew-boy there, he said, and he learned from old Italians. Later, he would learn from the young heiresses he taught at Vassar another way to catch crabs, but I fucking digress.

The guy was really hauling on the line now, end over end, slack rope looping behind him. When you pull the trap up, a small hoop drops down, trapping the crabs, but you have to haul fast before the crabs scramble to the rim and drop back in the water.

As the trap came up into the moonlight, I could see that it was swarming with crabs, seven or eight in there, more than I ever caught in one pull. The guy yanked the hoop net over the rail and let it slap down on the deck. He moved fast, plucking them out of the netting and tossing them into his bucket. A few got out and scuttled toward the water. I ran and grabbed one, put my sneaker on the other, and then picked him up too. I dropped them in the bucket and glanced up to see the man peering at me.

He was decent-looking guy, wavy black hair, olive complexion, but there was something wrong in the eyes. There was nothing there—like looking into that rooster's eyes.

"Sukenick," he said.

"Yeah, Morielli?"

"Allegedly."

"I have to ask," I said. "What the hell are you using for bait?" There must've been thirty crabs in the bucket.

"Tonight? Liver." He pulled a flashlight from his jacket and shined it on the hoop net. I was looking at liver, but not calf's liver. What I saw, wired to the netting, looked like a slice of bad Spam hit with a blowtorch. The unmistakable cirrhotic liver of a drinking man.

He switched the light off. "I hear you're looking for Leonard Wong." I didn't want to know how he knew that. "Well, you found him."

Morielli tossed the hoop net over the side. I flinched at the splash.

"Yeah, Leonard's paying his debt off in installments. Well, he's just paying the vig. These crab dinners have been a big feature at my poker nights. And there's kind of a neat side effect since I started serving the crab. A whole bunch of slow payers have sped up."

I started to back away.

"When you talk to Kelly tomorrow, tell her I'll be in touch. You could really help this whole process along for me."

I threw up my hands, "Come on, man. That's not on her."

He seemed to swell, like his hackles had raised up. He said, very quietly, "People die. Debts don't die."

I walked away. About the time I cleared the ship, he called after me, "You tell Kelly, checks are just fine, and $499 a week sounds about right. We'll be in touch."

I picked up my pace. I figured I'd check into a no-tell motel for a few days. I would stop at home first, time for one phone call, to Corralitos. Mike Sandoval wanted to know the deal, and if I knew my man, he'd be ready and he would move fast.

The red flag was flapping. Now I understood why Kelly and Leobardo had ignored each other. Kelly knew who killed her father. She knew the scumbag would come after her inheritance, and she knew the only man, Don Miguel, who could stop him.

Kelly had played me, but she'd played it right. I would absolutely confirm to Mike Sandoval what he wanted to be true.

Joe Morielli might have time for a few more crab parties. But I expected Joe would be attending a lot more chicken dinners in his future.

PINBALLS

BY BETH LISICK

Corralitos

Living by the ocean had always been my plan—a third-act strategy. What a cool way to get old and wrinkled: go for long swims, walk in the sand, eat tacos every day, drink beer. When Dave freaked out on me again, I figured there was no time like the present. I ditched the mountains for lower ground. Under the cover of night, like you see in the movies.

Sure, I washed up on the beach a little earlier than I thought I would—only halfway old and halfway wrinkled—but what a relief to be on to my next chapter.

Now I'd be pedaling toward the white light at the end of the tunnel on one of those sparkly beach cruisers with the fat seats: sunburned and pleasantly buzzed. It was going to be a good few years.

The rent wasn't cheap, even back then—especially if you wanted to live solo, like I did. But you know what worked? Driving south on Highway 1 and parking underneath a eucalyptus grove.

You get off the freeway on Riverside Drive, right where you see that abandoned Queen Anne. Go past the strawberry fields, the artichokes and brussels sprouts, and that's where my spot was. You're not going the wrong way, even when you start seeing signs for the condo development. Keep curving around. You can practically smell your way there, there's so much eucalyptus. Chances are, the lot will be empty. It's in between two private beaches, so it seems like you don't belong there, but there's no trick. Pull up, hike over the little path, and thar she blows: a mile of beach almost all to yourself.

In one day, my life went from flat zero to watching pelicans dive-bomb for their breakfast. Walking along the beach for hours. After what I'd been through, being all alone in my sleeping bag in the back of the square-back was a pleasure: a promising turnaround.

Marta knew all about beaches because her family had been in Watsonville before all those condos were a gleam in the developer's eye.

The morning I met her, she showed up in her station wagon with a whole brood. I peeked out of the checked curtains I had sewn for some privacy, and there were all these kids, piling out, clown-car style. I knew they couldn't be hers because there were at least ten of them. Little ones. They were bouncing around like pinballs! This was before they passed the seat belt laws, so it's not like she was doing anything wrong. It was just how you did it back then. She wanted to take ten kids to the beach, so she squeezed them all together in the Olds.

It was cold out, and early, so the kids had their colorful little jackets and hats on, and they were yelling and goofing off. A couple were crying. Marta was the only one wrangling them and they all started heading up over the dunes. I wanted to see how this was going to pan out, so I followed. One little guy, he started lagging behind, and pretty soon he was running off the path.

There used to be real tall grass in the dunes; it was like a maze in there. You could easily lose a kid that way.

They were small. None of them over five. So I chased after the little guy and scooped him up and got him back on track. I brought him over to the group and Marta smiled at me, but she didn't seem worried at all. She hadn't even noticed he was missing. She had the kids all plopped in the sand and playing with their toys and I sat down. She spoke plenty of English and I spoke Spanish pretty well from my *abuela*, so we chitchatted the way you do: a mishmash. I didn't tell her my whole situation, but I got the feeling she knew. She could tell I'd been places and seen some things. She told me my eyes reminded her of a turtle, which might not sound like the nicest thing to say, but I could tell she meant something good by it. She said it in Spanish, *tortuga*. I think she was telling me I was smart, or serious, or something.

I stayed and played with the kids all morning. We dug holes and got sand in everything and she offered me some food from her big paper grocery sack. She had these corn tortillas, wrapped in a cloth and still warm, that she'd roll around hunks of white cheese. A big jug of pineapple juice with Dixie cups. I never wanted kids of my own, but I loved the way these guys were climbing all over me from the get-go. It made me feel purposeful, like I was an animal assisting other animals.

When I helped her pile everyone back into the car, she asked me what I was doing the next morning—if I wanted to help her again, maybe at her house. She showed me on my map and I wrote down her address in the margin and all of a sudden I had a job! Just for the mornings, but it was a start. I didn't need to have a degree, or a resume, or fill out any paperwork. I could go ahead and call myself a teacher if I wanted.

It's funny because working at a day care turned out to be a lot closer to sex work than you'd think. You have to be present in your body and not overthink things. You have to trust that your body is being used for good. Also, it helped that my immune system was bulletproof from all those years dancing. I had developed a lot of patience too.

By the end of the week, Marta and I already had this mother/daughter thing going on. Nothing like what I had with my own mom, thank god. The house was warm and comfy, and with all the kids and cousins around, it felt like family real quick. I thought it was a blessing to find her so soon after moving, to be welcomed in like that. It was special. I tried not to talk about my past or that I was still sleeping in my car, but she worried. She packed me meals to bring back and gave me a whistle. When I made a crack about who would hear a whistle all the way out there—she opened her purse and tried to give me her knife.

One day, we were back at the beach with the kids and she said that Ricky might have a lead on a place for me. I think she called Ricky her brother or brother-in-law; but maybe Ricky was another cousin?

Hoo-boy, Ricky was hot. I'm going to be blunt about it because one thing that makes me nuts is when people can't just call it for what it is. Ricky was a stone fox and no sane person would refute it. He wore these tight black jeans and boots all caked with mud, Western shirts with snaps. Mustache. You get the picture. He fixed stuff around Marta's house, like the garbage disposal and the toilet, and he had a formality about him that turned me on. He passed me a tub of margarine one time at dinner and my hand touched his, and I thought I was gonna die.

Now this whole time I was assuming Ricky made his money as a fix-it guy and a fisherman. He had poles in his truck, and he was always unloading coolers into the backyard, hosing them out, filling them with fresh ice. There were a lot of fishermen around, selling cod or rockfish out of their coolers by the gas station or near St. Patrick's.

If you pressed me, I guess I'd say it was illegal. Maybe you had to have a license? People sold a lot of stuff around Watsonville. Tortillas, tamales, churros, blankets, flags. And I'm sure there were drugs, like all places, but I didn't see them. I was around a different crowd back then, mostly older Catholic people who worked hard and had one eye on *la Migra*.

Ricky came twice a week—sometimes with kids, sometimes not. He had an "office" that was a converted bathroom where he took the little ones. Marta said he was checking for lice, signs of chicken pox. The kids' parents were too scared to take them to the public clinic. God, I remember hating my nits getting picked too; I would cry my head off, just like they did.

One morning I got to work—I usually showed up around six thirty and we'd eat and get everything set for the kids to arrive—and Marta hugged me so tight. She told me Ricky had a place I could live for cheap. A place just for me. It was out in Corralitos, where there wasn't much except for a meat market and a lot of apple orchards. But it was sitting there empty. There had been a huge flood the winter before, the famous one that triggered all the landslides, thousands of them, and the cabin had gotten pretty well dumped on and waterlogged. It was going to be moldy, but it wasn't anything we couldn't fix. Spring was coming, and we could open everything up and let it dry out.

We laid out the snacks for the kids and then Ricky showed up. He arrived with two little ones I hadn't seen before, though I don't think they were his. The number of kids fluctuated daily, I think, because most of the parents worked in the fields, and not all the moms worked every day.

Marta never turned away anyone, even when kids were swinging from the curtain rods and diapers were running low. It was chaos, but it worked somehow. Some of them practically lived there. One set of twins, a boy and girl (named Albino and Blanca—*White* and *White,* if you can believe it), had been staying overnight every weekday for months. Their mom was deported after being pulled over for some traffic nonsense and it was impossible for their dad to take care of them and work at the same time. Marta was keeping them until they could fly down to Mexico with another relative to be reunited with their mom.

I thought those kids were lucky. In rich neighborhoods, you couldn't have a group of more than three children in a home without the California Department of Social Services breathing down your neck, and here were all these babies getting loving care practically for free.

I should've taken my own car to see the cabin instead of riding with Ricky. I knew that the minute I started talking to him, my mouth would be leaking honey. I hated that about myself—used to be if there was an attractive man around, my whole everything changed. My voice got softer, I held my body differently, I said the stupidest shit. I had just learned to get ahold of myself and I didn't want to ruin things.

Then Ricky opened the car door for me and Marta put a jade plant on my lap and I started to fall apart, ever so slightly.

The cab of his Chevy was tidy. I remember the carpet on the floor was freshly vacuumed in those long professional-detailer strokes, first one direction and then the next. He had a cup holder attached to a sandbag laid across the hump below the stick shift and an air freshener with *la Virgen* on it. He kept his eyes on the road, even when I couldn't stop thanking him. I was so grateful to be given this fresh start, yet I was probably giving off a vibe of wild desperation.

We wound back onto the country roads, past orchards, getting farther and farther from the ocean. It was only about twenty minutes away, but it was rural, and I didn't have a sense where I was at first. He pulled off the road and we dropped down into a driveway. The cabin was a bitty thing, surrounded by brush and fallen branches, but it had two windows in the front with window boxes underneath them. I imagined I would fill them with flowers, maybe herbs—buy a bright yellow watering can and even learn to cook. I didn't have any furniture, but I did have a welcome mat. For some reason I'll never know, I had grabbed it from me and my old man's place when I stormed out the door. I think it was my way of saying, *Now you gotta wipe your feet somewhere else, asshole*. Dave probably hadn't even noticed it was gone.

Ricky walked around to the back and I followed him. He climbed up on a pile of wood, hoisted open a small window, and went through it, headfirst. I'll never forget the look on his face when he popped up from the other side of the window, like, *Ta-da!* It was the first genuine smile I'd seen from him, and I laughed.

I started to climb in myself and he was saying, "No, no," and motioning toward the front door, but I dove in right after him. He helped pull me all the way through by my armpits and the minute my feet hit the floor, it was on. We were going at it. We were kissing and pawing each other, we wrestled ourselves into the main room, and then we were peeling our pants off and rolling around on that filthy, disgusting floor. God, it felt good.

It wasn't until after that I could see what a real mess the place was, and boy did it smell bad too. Garbage and animal turds and big holes in the walls. It looked like whomever had been squatting had vacated awhile ago.

I tried to make a joke and said, "I'll take it!" and grabbed at his crotch, but Ricky didn't seem to like that.

He put his arm around my shoulder when we walked back out to the truck, though he had turned quiet again. I took a swig out of the bottle he offered from under his seat. We stole looks at each other. Or maybe he was checking to see if I was still staring at him? Honestly, I tried to be cool, yet it wasn't my nature.

When he said he had to make a quick stop, I knew I should get back to Marta, but I didn't say anything.

"It's fine," he said, "I'm fast." And it was. We drove to this residential neighborhood in Freedom, boring but nice, and left one of his coolers on the doorstep and brought what I assumed to be an empty one back. And that was it. I didn't think anything of it.

He dropped me back off at work and Marta was really weird to me right away. I apologized for taking so long, but it was like she could tell I'd just bagged Ricky in the landslide cabin.

I slept one more night in my car out at the beach, and then Saturday I bought some cleaning supplies and went up there to see what I could do. Ricky came by just before nightfall and we screwed again. At least this time I had made a bed of sorts out of my sleeping bag and some blankets. The candlelight softened the dankness. I tried to make some small talk with him afterward, but he wasn't having it.

Instead of seeming hot and mysterious, it just seemed rude. *Do I feel used?* I asked myself. And then a few minutes after he left, I remembered that I had wanted and enjoyed the sex, and I now had my own place to live for the first time in my life. *Be that way*, I thought. I'd be fine.

* * *

When I came to work on Monday, Marta was standing on the porch waiting for me. She said that she didn't need me anymore. "Go," she said. "You're finished." I hated how cold she was. I tried to talk to her, but she walked in her house and shut the door and I knew that was it. The kids would start showing up any minute and I couldn't make a scene. There'd been enough of that in my life anyway. Marta had so much dignity that it made me want to leave with some of my own. But what was it? Had she been in love with Ricky? Weren't they related?

Marta wasn't returning my calls. Ricky wasn't stopping by. I needed a new job quick if I was going to stay at the cabin for another month. I started working at a "private entertainment" company, promising myself it would be temporary. Twice while I was driving around I thought I saw Ricky's truck, once taking the on ramp toward Monterey, and once in the bakery parking lot.

That second time, I circled around and parked on the opposite end. I got out with no plan. As I drew closer, I saw the old coolers in the back. My hands were shaking when I reached for them. I could hear Ricky yelling from the bakery. I lifted the Styrofoam lid and pushed back the bag of ice, and there were shiny vials full of dark liquid. *The fuck were these things?* Ricky was walking right at me. "You whore!" he shouted. "Get away from my life, you whore!"

I turned and ran back to my car while he stood there, arms folded across his chest, watching me. I should have let it go, but I rolled past him on the way out, slow enough to look him in the face. I kept my voice calm, the way I did when I was working. "I wish I had a dollar for every man who's called me a whore," I said.

I drove off and grabbed everything I needed from the cabin

in three minutes flat. I found a new spot at a new beach. That look in Ricky's eyes? I never wanted to see him again.

Almost a year later, the story came out. I was working in a real day care by then, a licensed place, living in a nice house near Struve Slough with one of my coworkers and her girlfriend.

It was in all the papers. Marta and Ricky had been arrested for trafficking.

They'd been extracting the kids' plasma and blood and urine, and selling it to a research start-up. Some tech crew over the hill had formed their own biotech company and needed raw materials. How they found Ricky and Marta, I'll never know.

The case didn't end up going to trial. The children didn't matter. That company is listed on the NYSE today.

I had to quit my job after that, stop working with kids. Marta had been the only contact on my resume and my employers couldn't risk it. Oh well, there's always "private entertainment." I don't live by the ocean anymore—but I always go to sleep where I can hear it.

THE SHOOTER

BY LEE QUARNSTROM

Watsonville

I'd picked out the shooter's car by the time I hopped out of my Plymouth and crossed the dusty parking lot toward the front of the two-story building. It was the rust-speckled Studebaker, backed in against the head lettuce field dotted with thousands, maybe millions, of tiny, shiny green shoots sprouting from the chunky black soil of the fertile fields just outside Watsonville.

Out here, row crops planted since the war had pushed the valley's once-ubiquitous apple orchards back to rolling acres and narrow *barrancas* where the steep slopes of the redwood foothills began to flatten into furrowed farmland, better-suited for irrigation ditches that watered endless rows where leafy greens were bringing in more bucks per acre than Bellflowers and Newton Pippins and Granny Smiths ever would!

For one thing, the Studebaker was clean, if a bit rusty around the chrome, with no telltale smears of the region's rich topsoil spattered across its fenders. For another, like all gunmen, this shooter had parked facing out; he could make a speedy getaway from here or from anywhere else he'd ever parked his automobile. If he had business to attend to here at the bar below Hildegard's whorehouse, or in one of the rooms upstairs, it wouldn't take him half a minute to run to his car and hit the road.

He'd missed the weekend carloads of soldier boys getting

trained how to shoot North Koreans—they'd all headed back toward Fort Ord: loud youngsters, always drunk, pimply, stopping for a quickie if they'd failed to find any gash. They'd all leave Watsonville to weave down the dark and narrow Coast Highway toward the army base built on massive dunes just northeast of the Monterey Peninsula.

I spotted the shooter as soon as I walked into the joint, even before I took a seat at the end of the bar near the front door. He was a Mexican, of course, like almost everyone else in the room, but he was wearing neither the dungarees nor the overhauls of the *campesino,* nor the dusty white outfit sewn from flour sacks sported by *los viejos,* old men, single old-timers too bent and broken to chop lettuce anymore or work at any of the other stoop labor that the growers depended on.

Much of the *campesinos'* meager haul, of course, eventually crossed this polished slab in front of me where the stocky gal pouring drinks—Hildegard herself—slapped down a shot of Four Roses and a glass of whatever was on tap before she grabbed a few quarters from those I'd dug out of my pocket before I'd parked my butt on the stool.

Take it easy, Nelson, she mouthed at me.

I wouldn't say the guy I'd tagged as the shooter was dressed like a *pachuco*—for one thing, he wasn't flashy; he wore a suit that didn't make him look any sharper than the fieldworkers standing or sitting along the bar. But the tan gabardine outfit with draped trousers pegged at his ankles did cover a smooth leather holster. I could tell it sat against his white shirt where the fabric was bunching beneath the lapel of his jacket.

Also, his two-tone Western boots, shiny brown-and-white leather, were luxuries none of the farmworkers in the place would have wasted money on. Cash like that could buy some necessary relaxation down here in the barroom or some relief upstairs with the *chamacas* whom Hildegard's customers kept busy from sundown to almost midnight—and even later on weekends.

The main reason I picked the shooter out was that he, at least the guy I'd made as the shooter, didn't look at me even for an instant when I came in through the front door. All the other drinkers had at least given me a side-eyed peek as I walked in; some glances had been bored, some had been hostile in a macho sort of way. The *pistolero,* however, didn't turn his head, didn't glance at me in the mirror, or didn't, in any other way that I could discern, check me out.

I knew immediately that he'd instantly sensed everything he needed to know about me—and about every other man doling out quarters to Hildegard as she patrolled her beat behind the stick. He focused on no one. Hildie pocketed some cash from pitiful little stashes on the bar and nodded the other customers toward a beaded curtain that led to the toilet and to the rickety stairway to the rooms upstairs.

As I was on my second Four Roses, Blue Ribbon back, Hildegard came up to me for a good hard stare. Like every barkeep, she was polishing a smudged glass—one of those squat cocktail glasses that you can't tip over because they're wide and weighted at the bottom even when they're empty—with a rag so soiled that no customer in his right mind would have noticed on purpose unless he was eyeing it to use as a fly swatter.

"Hey, *amigo*," Hildegard whispered loudly enough that the guy to my right had to act like he couldn't hear, "Maruca's workin' tonight!"

"Why you telling me?"

"'Cause you and Maruca could be making some sweet music upstairs instead of you and the gunsel down the bar making a lot of racket down here."

I nodded; I understood.

A minute or two later, a beefy fieldworker, still tucking a short-sleeved cowboy shirt into his Roebuck jeans, six-inch cuffs rolled tightly up over the tops of his work boots, came out through the beaded curtain and headed for the front door. Maruca followed him, sidling into the barroom, where she saw me and smiled. She then strode to the jukebox and slipped in a couple of nickels. She played "Bell Bottom Trousers," the Moe Jaffe version, but no one made a move. Then, with her second nickel, she played Lalo Guerrero and his band harmonizing on "Los Chucos Suaves." Maruca was a Filipina close to my age who thought she still looked like a teenage *señorita.* She sashayed—and that's the right word; that's exactly what she did, shaking her skinny hips like a hoochie-coochie girl—right up to where I was sitting.

"Hey, mister," Maruca said. She knew my name all too well. "Hey, mister," as she waited for me to light her Lucky Strike, "you wanna screw?"

I put my Zippo flame to her Lucky. I did want to screw, but not right now. I wanted to keep an eye on the shooter sitting a few feet down the bar. Killing this *vato* was what I needed to do as well as wanted to do. Maruca could wait for another time.

"Maybe later," I said loud enough that Hildegard flashed her tired-looking eyes at me, then at the gunman.

"Maybe now!" Hildie demanded.

Maruca grabbed my arm and started to pull toward the string of beads hanging beneath the hand-painted sign that read *Baños*. "He still be here when we come back, bud," Maruca said.

Hildegard nodded in agreement. "Más *tarde*!"

Maruca, having figured out the whole scene, gritted her teeth, nodded, and walked away, not sashaying the slightest bit. She walked along the bar until she reached the *pistolero* who was so obviously paying no attention at all to me or her or Hildegard. She whispered in the guy's ear and he whispered something back and slowly, slowly he stood and followed the woman across the room and through the strands of beads. I could hear their footsteps starting up the stairs. Goddamn him all to hell.

After the Lalo Guerrero tune ended, I crossed to the Seaburg jukebox and popped in a coin of my own. Following a quick look at the selections, I pushed a couple of buttons and put on another Lalo special, "Marihuana Boogie." I went back to my drinks, made sure my shoulder holster was sitting comfortably beneath my armpit, and sipped my beer.

I waited.

A few minutes later I heard Maruca's footsteps coming back down the stairs. She passed through the doorway, looked at me, and nodded at someone behind her on the steps. Then she walked to the other end of the bar. Ordered three fingers of aguardiente. Our drink.

Hildegard gave her a glance, then gave me the evil eye. "I told you, Nelson. Take it easy."

The shooter walked back into the room. No one had taken his place at the bar so he returned to his stool and nodded at Hildegard for another *cerveza.* As the bartender turned to grab a cleaner glass, the shooter looked at me for the first and only time.

In an instant he stood, reached under his jacket, jerked his automatic from its holster, and fired two quick shots in my general direction. But I'd known it was coming and I had my Smith & Wesson in my hand before the shooter even got to his feet.

He pumped one long spurt of blood right through the hole I'd shot in his forehead, then slumped to the barroom floor.

"Ah, Jesus, Nelson," Hildegard spat at me. "Jesus Christ, why'd you have to do that?"

"You saw him," I shouted, "you saw him grab his gun! What the fuck was I supposed to do?"

I watched as Maruca ran back through the beads, no doubt to vanish upstairs so she could tell the coppers that she'd missed the whole thing.

In a few seconds the bar was empty. I could hear car engines turning over and tires screeching as a half-dozen drunks and their passengers tried to back out of the dusty parking area without turning on their headlights before heading back into town, or out toward the shacks where they rented beds by the week. Hildegard was on the phone and two or three minutes later I could hear sirens coming from the direction of town.

I sat back on my barstool and finished my drink. I slapped down a few bills to cover the costs and then stood and headed toward the door.

The sirens got closer.

"*Buenas noches*, Hildegard," I called out. "Say goodnight for me to Maruca."

The dead man's Studebaker was still parked in the dusty lot. I thought about shooting out a couple of the tires for practice, but on second thought left it.

I got in the Plymouth, turned the key, and stomped on the gas till the motor caught. As I headed down Riverside, I looked in the rearview mirror. A squad car, siren loud and red lights flashing, turned into the parking lot. I lit a Chesterfield and tuned the radio to a Mex station out of Salinas. Some Trio Los Panchos tune was playing.

IT FOLLOWS UNTIL IT LEADS

BY DILLON KAISER

San Juan Road

My papa died when I was a baby, shot in the crossfire between the cartel and the police.

This, I only heard from my mama, later. What a way to die, I always thought—innocent and found by a bullet not meant for you.

Mama worked the streets, but she had tried to raise me better, tried to keep me in school. It did not work. The wary respect I was given, with a gun in my hand, was intoxicating.

The police found Mama blindfolded in the trunk of a car, tied up, her throat cut. I was seventeen, and hadn't seen her in years when this happened. By then, I had already risen from a *charoliar*, a wannabe, to a *halcón*, a lookout runner. I was twenty when I became a *narco soldado*, a soldier of the *cartel de Arellano Felix* and the right hand of *pez gordo*, a big boss. Arellano Felix was all I knew, all any of us knew in Tijuana. If you were ruthless, if you were smart, if you were loyal—Arellano provided.

I was ruthless, and I was smart. The loyalty? Love changes a man.

The gun on the kitchen table is not mine. Yet there it lies, insisting upon its own *fealdad*, its ugliness. Infecting my home. Sunlight streams through the window above the sink where Martha has set a vase of flowers and glints upon the gun. It breeds disease. And there, on the table next to my daughter Lupe's doll, the disease spreads.

The gun is not mine. Worse, it is my son's.

Se sigue.

"Get it away from the doll, *eso infecta*," I say. Martha raises her eyebrow. Perhaps I have said a crazy thing, but I cannot think with the gun so close to Lupe's doll. "*Por favor*."

I look away. Out the window, green berry fields stretch to the hills beyond. The cultivated rows are identical to the ones I hunched over sweating and picking just hours ago. My hands still ache, the fingers throbbing and slow to uncurl unless I will them. Martha purses her lips. She lays the gun on a dishtowel, checks the safety, wraps it, and carefully sets it on the chair beside her. She glances at me, her mouth so small I fear it will not open again.

"Luis," Martha says.

I gaze into her eyes, wide and watering. A kitchen chair creaks in protest, resisting my heavy body. I heave myself into it. This life—I'm soft now, no longer the *jefe's* right hand. I'm simply Papa, and I am happy. *Was* happy, until this moment. I wonder how my son caught the sickness.

"Luis," Martha says again, and sits herself beside me. My hands tremble, and I thrust them beneath the table. She sees, but I pretend she does not.

"Where did you find it?" My voice coarse and hushed.

"Out back. In the shed. I knocked over a box on the shelf. It was in the box, Luis. Loaded. I checked. You said you'd never have one again, ever."

"I know." I tell myself to look down. To be ashamed. *Bien*. Maybe I can fool her after all. Just to buy time. All I need is time to think.

"Talk to me," she says. "Just tell me. Why?"

The sunlight washes over me, and dust floats in the empty space, at peace. In the stillness, the refrigerator rattles to life. Beneath letter-shaped magnets our pictures cover the outside: Juan on his first day of school. Me and Martha after she got her license. (The test, all in English, was a mountain we climbed together.) Juan holding Lupita after she was born (so tiny she was, and Juan, so proud to hold her).

"After that day. We needed protection, just in case."

She shakes her head. "But loaded, Luis? It's not like you."

I bang my hand on the table. "So I made a mistake! I cannot make mistakes? I was a *tarado*, I left it loaded!"

Her eyes widen again. They have seen something terrible. They have seen the truth. My theatrics pushed too far. A gasp escapes her, and her hand flies to cover her mouth. She presses her hand tight over her lips, as if the knowledge is airborne, and if only she does not breathe she will not know. She pushes herself backward, chair scraping the floor, and she is on her feet. Not saying a word, her eyes pleading, *No, no*. Tears spill down her cheeks.

"Talk to him. Now," she says.

I stand and turn from her, my boots heavy on the floor, softer on the carpet down the hall toward Juan's room. The music from one of his video games thumps through the wall. He told us he bought the speakers, the TV, the clothes, all from the money he made stocking shelves at the grocery store after school. I wonder when he became a better liar than me.

In front of his room my hand floats above the doorknob. If I open it, I do not know what will follow me inside. But too late for that. Time now to speak to my son of death.

Se sigue.

A policeman shot Arellano at a traffic stop, of all things. Arellano drew on the officer first, and in seconds both men lay dead on the road. The cartel fell into chaos after that, the narcos like chickens running around with their heads lopped off, or roosters fighting to dominate. Allegiances formed. Killing. Choosing a side was important. And I did not choose.

When Martha told me she was pregnant with Juan, I told her to pack her things. She looked at me in shock, in doubt. We had never thought the idea possible. But her face soon hardened into stone. She would go. For us, for her family.

We went north to Watsonville, a town with a community and work for *Mexicanos*. Hard work, picking the fields or cleaning. But we found friends. Lived with them, worked with them. I had some money left from my old life. Not much, but enough to help us create a new life.

Juan was five when they found me. That day, I drove home after work, my rusted Toyota pickup grinding through the field roads at the bottom of the Royal Oaks Hills. When I pulled into our driveway and saw the shiny black SUV, I knew. The wicked thing had come breathing hot on my back.

I stopped the truck, my sweatshirt damp and roasting in the cab's stale heat. My throat suddenly dry. I squinted at the SUV, the tinted windows. No movement. Only sunlight glinting on the black paint. *Please let Martha and Juan be okay, oh God, please let them—*

No. Worry would not help me. I was not a hero. I was a man who had done bad things, and my family was in danger.

I got out of the truck and bit the inside of my cheek, to keep me sharp. Blood welled up, copper pain like an angry spark. I crouched down, crawled to the back of the SUV. Raised my fist and rapped on the back window. Waited. Pressed my ear to the car. Silence. I hunched over, back aching, and ran to the driver's-side door. Tried the handle. The door opened and

I squatted by the tire. Nothing from the SUV. I opened the door wider, pressed up on the leather driver's seat, and peered inside.

No one in the car. They were inside the house.

I swayed through the front door, already open. Waiting for me. Laughter, loud and familiar, drifted from the kitchen. I followed.

"Señor Cruz! Good of you to join us! Good to see you, *mi amigo!*"

I had not heard that voice in many years, save perhaps in nightmares, but I could never forget it. My eyes flicked quickly, seeing without looking. Registering. Preparing.

Martha sat hunched at the table, eye swollen shut, puffed black, blood running down her chin. Still breathing, thank God. At the sight of her, I wanted to scream. But screaming would not save her. And where was Juan?

A man leaned back over the counter. Thin, corded with muscle, a mustache drooping down his face like a frown. Hair slicked back with grease. A gold plated AK-47 dangled in his hands. Too much for me, *mano a mano*, even if I somehow wrestled the rifle from him.

The other man, the one who had spoken, sat next to my wife—grinning at me through misshapen teeth stained the color of old urine. Clean shaven. Sharp eyes. *Eyes that see beyond,* we used to say in Mexico, cursed eyes. Wearing crocodile cowboy boots and a bolo tie. His rolled-up shirt sleeves, tattoos of skulls and M-16s creeping out like a rash on his skin. Waving around a diamond-encrusted Browning 9 millimeter, with a custom grip. A good gun. The type of gun I used once.

I nodded. "*Hola*, Rojelio."

"He remembers!" Rojelio said. "How good to be remembered. Especially by the great Señor Cruz, and after so much time. Your wife, she has not been hospitable; she did not offer us coffee. You know how I enjoy my coffee, Luis." He tapped his piss-colored teeth with the barrel of his gun and laughed.

Perhaps they did not know I had a son. If they had killed him, Rojelio would tell me soon enough. Just to see my face. *M'ijo,* if you are hiding, stay hidden.

"I've missed you," Rojelio said, still smiling, always smiling. We used to say he would smile even when *la bala lo encuentra,* the bullet finds him. "Sit down, sit down!" He pointed to a seat by Martha.

"I cannot say the same."

He laughed again. A strange, wet sound. No humor. Only amusement. Martha's head rolled on her shoulders toward me, and she blinked her good eye. I tried not to see her swelling, bruised face. A lump rose to my throat. Heat rushed through me, prickled my skin, and balled in my aching hands. Anger. Good. I had tried to forget that feeling, that *candencia.* Time I remembered.

Martha blinked at me again. A movement so subtle as to mean nothing. But her clenched jaw, her gaze locked onto mine, showed me different. She had every reason to be scared, but she was not.

"Not many remembered you left, Luis." Rojelio studied me as if I was a simple curiosity. "But I did. I remembered. You know too much. I had business, you know, after Arellano was killed." He crossed himself—in earnest or mockery I could not tell. "But Luis. I remembered to come for you. Aye. Arellano thought much of you. But this place? Your work?" He waved the Browning into space, his head nodding to accommodate the gesture. "This is beneath you. Truthfully, it disgusts me.

You disgust me. Do you see it? Smell it on your body, when you come home after working for them, doing something so low they would never sink to it?" He wiped his mouth. Flicked his tongue across his dry lips. A lizard in the clothes of a man.

"You would not understand," I told him. His *compañero*, unhappy with my words, shifted his frame from the kitchen sink. He lifted the rifle. Rojelio glanced back, cocked his head, and the *compañero* faded into the kitchen once more.

"Luis." Rojelio stared at me, beady eyes narrowed, as if in disappointment. Then he laughed again. "What makes you think I want to understand?" He sighed, shrugged his shoulders. "This life. Our life. You cannot leave it behind. It follows. It follows, until it leads you where you've been going all along, kicking and screaming *con espuma en la boca!*"

Se sigue.

Martha blinked, moved her lips, and moved her lips again. I finally understood the words Martha mouthed to me: *Ven aquí.* Come closer.

"No! Please!" I begged, and leaned forward. Under the table, Martha slid the cold steel of a kitchen knife into my sweating palm. I clenched it tight. Blinked at her. I had to be faster, not only than Rojelio, but his *compañero.* I did not know if I was so fast, not anymore.

"Do you wish me to shoot her?" Rojelio said. Holding the gun to Martha's head. She whimpered.

I ground my teeth. Patience. Wait for the moment.

Rojelio slid his free hand onto the table. There. Now. Or my family died.

I arced the knife from beneath, sliced the air, and it landed with a soft *thunk*! In the back of Rojelio's palm, pinning it to the surface. He screamed and dropped the Browning. I dove for it, smacking the floor hard enough the air left my lungs.

The *compañero* had already raised his AK-47, eyes burning. I pointed the gun at him and squeezed the trigger.

His knee exploded in red-and-white pulp, like the splatter of a rotten apple. Warm, wet, red, and hard flecks of white sprayed my face. I fired again. This time I found my mark, and the *compañero* clawed at his chest, as if to dig the hole deeper.

Screaming overcame the fading thunder. Rojelio. I whipped the gun back, saw the color drained from his cheeks, yet he clutched at the knife handle, nearly had it free. I put a bullet in his head. He did not smile when it found him.

Martha fell into my arms, shaking, sobbing into my shoulder. I held her as tight as I could. Tasted wet salt on my lips. I let the gun drop, jerked my hand. As if it had bitten me.

"Papa?" A voice so soft. A voice so scared.

I looked down the hall, and there stood Juan. My eyes closed tight, tighter. But no matter how much I shut out the nauseating light, I could not undo what my son had seen.

Juan stands next to me in our backyard, and I hold his gun in my hand, still wrapped in the dishtowel. Sunlight burns orange across the fields and streaks the clouds with red as it lays itself to rest beyond the horizon. There is Lupe's playhouse, bought at Kmart last Christmas. Juan's old soccer ball still sits on the grass, untouched by anyone except time. My son has gained weight, like his father. Wears a goatee. It does not make him look more of a man, only like a boy playing pretend. I think to tell him this—this and how ridiculous he looks in his sagging jeans and shirt so large it hangs nearly to his knees.

"What is it, Pops? What's up?" he says. "You and Mama need help with English on the bills again? It's cool; I got time."

I shake my head no. "Juan."

"Come on, Pops. Call me Johnny, remember? Johnny Cruz!" He laughs.

"I'll call you the name you were given."

The laugh stops. He kicks his feet. Useless to start this fight with him. We watch the sun sink lower beyond the valley, setting the sky on fire.

"I found this," I say, unwrapping the dishtowel.

Juan stares at the gun. His mouth opens, he stiffens. Then he relaxes, cool all over. "Whose is it?"

This game. I am so tired. "Juan."

"*Qué*? You mean? Oh shit. Ha. You mean you think it's mine?"

I will not hit him. I never have and I never will. I have seen men hit their sons, their wives, their daughters. It is only part of the sickness, not a cure.

A different strategy, then. I put my hand on his back. His body rigid beneath my touch, brittle. I have caught him. He knows I have caught him. "Juan. Listen. You are a good boy. I know this, in my heart. *Por favor,* tell me. Why?"

His shoulders slump. He crumbles beneath my hand. My soft, aching hand. "Pops . . ."

"Your mama found it. Not me. Think, Juan, if it had been Lupe."

"Lupe would never go in the shed!" His voice cracks.

I sigh, and sit myself on the porch step, knees buckling, back sore.

"Juan! Juan! Play with me!" my daughter yells, her tiny footsteps rushing through the house, to us. I wrap the gun and cradle it in my lap before she bursts from the back door.

"Lupe, hey, *hermanita*. Go back inside, yeah? I'll play with you in a little bit," Juan says.

"But I heard you and Papa talking! Are you in trouble?"

"Lupe, *escucha a tu hermano*. He will play later," I tell her, and offer a smile, the best one I can manage.

"Lupe! Lupe! Come in the house!" Martha shouts after her.

"I'm coming!" Lupe responds. She looks up at her brother. "Promise to play with me! You gotta promise."

"I promise," Juan says, and chuckles.

Lupe nods, and runs inside, banging the door behind her. It slams in the frame, *BLAM, BLAM*, until it rests.

Juan whistles, a dry, nervous sound, and rubs his eyes.

"You see?" I tell him.

"Yes," he says, and sits beside me.

"Now. Answer my question."

He cocks his head, eyebrows raised. "I thought you'd know, Pops. If anyone did, I thought you'd know."

My turn to raise an eyebrow.

"Because of that," he nods at the gun in my lap, "you get respect. I get it, with that. It's like power, you know? You have one, your name rings out. Like *your* name used to."

I shake my head, grit my teeth. "No. Respect from fear, Juan, is not the same. Your sister respects you. And not from fear. Your mama respects you, because you care for your sister, and you help us, and go to school. I respect you, because you are smart, and you have a good heart. The gun? It disappoints me. It is low. It is not for you, *m'ijo*. Your name should mean more."

He cries, and looks away from me. It is okay for him to cry. If he cries, and knows he does not need the gun, he can cry.

"You will stop? For this family? For the ones that love you?"

"Yes, Pops, yeah."

I smile at him. "Me and your mama, we left Mexico because of bad men. Because I did not want to be a bad man. I do not want my son to be a bad man. You can be better, Juan. Here, in this town. If you go to school. If you work hard. You can be better than me."

I embrace him. He stiffens again, then becomes limp, and slowly he wraps his arms around me.

"Swear to me," I say.

"I swear, Pops."

Tonight, I will bury the gun at the edge of the yard after I dismantle it piece by piece. I will bury it next to the bodies of two dead men who once came to my home. I think perhaps Rojelio was wrong, perhaps the sickness won't follow this time.

Me and Martha are cleaning the house on my day off. Her *telenovela* plays on TV, something to laugh at while we mop and sweep. Lupe is in her room playing dolls. Juan is still at school. Because he's been good this week, I let him take the Toyota.

The phone rings from the kitchen, and I go to answer. When Juan's voice crackles high and frantic into my ear, part of me wishes I had let it ring. I remember, then. He is a better liar than me.

"Pops!" he says. "Pops, I did something. It's bad, and they won't stop now, so I'm coming, I'm coming—"

"Juan. Slowly. Where are you?"

"Fuck fuck fuck. Aw man. Aw maaan."

"Juan." I keep my voice low, but Martha hears anyway. She hurries into the kitchen, her face creased in worry.

"Is it him?" she says. I nod. "He's in trouble?" I squeeze my eyes shut, nod again.

"Where are you?" I say to him.

"Driving, Pops. They're following me. They keep following me!"

Sirens sing, far away through the phone. A song for Juan. If he listens, if he stops—yes, prison maybe, but he will have a life still.

"Stop for them, Juan. Do it." The kitchen darkens, and I lean against the refrigerator. Martha grasps my arm, steadies me.

"They're following me! They won't stop! I'm coming home. Okay? I don't know where to go. I'm coming home."

"Be calm, *m'ijo*. What did you do?" My ear burns against the plastic of the phone.

"A cop pulled me over and . . . Fuck. I had weed, okay? A lot. And I just drove away. All I did was drive! But now there's more cops, and I'm scared, I'm scared, I'm—"

The sirens scream. Loud in the phone, too loud. They are not only coming from the phone. My eyes meet Martha's. I see my terror mirrored in them. She shakes her head, mouths one word: *No*.

"What's that noise?" My daughter runs into the sitting room. Her hair held back by a plastic tiara, her face scrunched in wonder, cradling her doll.

"Stay with her. Stay inside," I tell Martha. Nausea wrestles with me. I push it down. Bury it deep. My wobbling legs carry me to the front door. I open it, and peer down the road into the late afternoon.

The screech of tires, the roar of an engine. There. My truck. A blur down the pavement, but filling my sight faster than I can believe. It slides across the road, leaving black marks like streaks of blood in front of the driveway. The smell of burning rubber, and I cough. Smoke fills the air. Juan stumbles from the car drenched in thick sweat, his eyes rolling wildly, panting. The police follow.

"Listen to them! Juan, whatever they say! LISTEN!" I scream at him, descending the front steps to our walk, running past the old oak and the swing I built for him long ago.

He stares beyond, at something I cannot see. Police cars screech to a stop, fencing him in. A young officer, crazed with adrenaline, yells into a bullhorn: "*Put your hands in the air! Drop to your knees and put your hands in the air!*"

"Do it, Juan! Do what they say!" I scream. Can he hear me over the damn noise? He jerks his head again. Okay, okay. He will stop.

Instead, he runs toward our home.

"*Stop! Stop or we will fire!*" the officer shrieks. His hand crawling toward his gun belt.

No.

The sirens scream into my ears.

"Stop! Juan, *por favor,* stop!" My voice straining over the noise.

"Pops?" he says. For a wonder, he listens, and stops near our fence. He sees me for the first time.

"*Turn around slowly, with your hands on your head!*" the cop commands.

"Juan. Turn around. Show them you do not have a gun," I say.

He opens his mouth, as if to tell me something.

"Listen to them *m'ijo*. Do it!"

He breathes out a short laugh, and turns.

I catch the glint of metal tucked into his jeans.

"I'm taking it out now, it's okay, I'm taking it out," says my son, as his hand dips down.

They shoot him. His body whirls in mad circles, while the police fire again and again. A bullet whines by my side, almost finds me. The guns roar until smoke chokes the air. Juan rests, finally, in a twisted heap by our fence, one hand curled around a post. He almost made it home.

I cannot swallow. Cannot breathe. The stench burns my nose. I slump forward until my knees settle on the ground.

"Back away, sir! Back away!" the police yell.

I hold up my hands and crawl to my boy on my knees. They let me do this until I am close.

An officer walks toward me, the calm one. He kicks Juan's gun away. "That's close enough."

Still I cannot swallow. "But he's my son."

"Papa! Papa!"

Shivers nearly knock me over. My teeth rattling in my skull, I twist my neck around. My daughter. Why is she covered in red? Blood? Not her blood, please God.

"Papa! Mama won't get up!"

I frown. My eyes wander to the front of our home. I see Martha crumpled in the doorframe, dark red blooming across her blouse, spilling down the step. Her body still, as if she is sleeping. In that moment, I understand.

I understand everything.

Se sigue hasta que se conduce.

ABOUT THE CONTRIBUTORS

Wallace Baine is a critic, columnist, and editor in Santa Cruz, and the author of *A Light in the Midst of Darkness,* a history of Bookshop Santa Cruz. His work is nationally syndicated and his fiction appears in the *Catamaran Literary Reader* and the *Chicago Quarterly Review.* He is the author of *Rhymes with Vain: Belabored humor and attempted profundity* and *The Last Temptation of Lincoln,* from which his play *Oscar's Wallpaper* was adapted.

Laurie Sirois

Jon Bailiff is a retired lifeguard EMT, union shop steward, and marine rescue guard. He's been a blacksmith, carpenter, artist, painter, weaver, and art teacher with Creativity Unlimited, William James Association, County Office of Probation, and Hope Services. He has lived in Santa Cruz for thirty years—not a local.

Jessica Breheny's work has been published in *Avery: An Anthology of New Fiction*, *Electric Velocipede*, *Eleven Eleven*, *elimae*, *Fugue*, *LIT*, *Otoliths*, *Other Voices*, and *Santa Monica Review*. She is the author of the chapbooks *Some Mythology* and *Ephemeride*. She lives in Santa Cruz.

Honey Lee Cottrell

Susie Bright is a best-selling author, journalist, audio producer, and editor. Her past works include *The Best American Erotica*, *Herotica*, and *Full Exposure*, as well as the memoir *Big Sex Little Death*. Bright was a screenwriter and/or consultant for *Bound*, *Erotique*, *The Celluloid Closet*, *Transparent*, and Criterion Collection's reissue of *Belle de Jour*. She is Editor-at-Large for Audible Studios, and the host of Audible's longest-running podcast, *In Bed with Susie Bright*. She is a lifelong Californian.

Margaret Elysia Garcia is the author of the short story collections *Sad Girls & Other Stories* and *Mary of the Chance Encounters*. She is cofounder of the microtheater company Pachuca Productions. She is also completing her first nonfiction manuscript, *Throwing the Curve*, about the world of plus-size alternative models.

Ariel Gore is an award-winning editor and the author of ten books, including *Atlas of the Human Heart*, *The End of Eve*, and *We Were Witches*. She teaches online at Ariel Gore's School for Wayward Writers.

Julie Graham

Seana Graham's short stories have appeared in the journals *Eleven Eleven* and *Salamander Magazine*, and the anthology *The Very Best of Lady Churchill's Rosebud Wristlet*. She is the book review editor at *Escape Into Life*.

Vinnie Hansen, a Claymore Award finalist, fled the howling winds of the South Dakota prairie and headed for the California coast the day after high school graduation. She is the author of numerous short stories and the Carol Sabala mystery series. Still sane after twenty-seven years of teaching high school English, Hansen has retired and lives in Santa Cruz with her husband and the requisite cat.

Naomi Hirahara is the Edgar Award–winning author of two mystery series set in Southern California. Her Mas Arai series, which features a Hiroshima survivor and gardener, ends with the publication of *Hiroshima Boy* in 2018. The first in her Officer Ellie Rush, Bicycle Cop mystery series received the T. Jefferson Parker Mystery Award. Her father was a native of Watsonville, California.

Dillon Kaiser has lived in Santa Cruz County most of his life. He now lives in Sacramento with his wife and daughter, but part of him will always think of Watsonville as home. He holds a BA in comparative literature from UC Davis.

Beth Lisick is a writer and actor. She is the author of five books, including the *New York Times* best seller *Everybody into the Pool.* She cofounded San Francisco's Porchlight Storytelling Series, traveled the country with the Sister Spit performance tours, and received a Creative Work Fund grant for a chapbook series with Creativity Explored, a studio for artists with developmental disabilities. Lisick grew up in San Jose and attended UC Santa Cruz.

Miguel Sandoval

Lou Mathews is a journalist, fiction writer, playwright, and fourth-generation Angeleno. Married at nineteen, he worked his way through UC Santa Cruz as a gas station attendant and mechanic. His first novel, *LA Breakdown*, was a *Los Angeles Times* best book of the year. He has received an NEA fellowship in fiction, a Pushcart Prize, and a Katherine Anne Porter Prize. He has taught in the UCLA Extension Writers' Program since 1989.

Elizabeth McKenzie's novel *The Portable Veblen* was long-listed for the 2016 National Book Award for fiction. She is the author of the novel *MacGregor Tells the World* and the story collection *Stop That Girl.* Her work has appeared in the *New Yorker*, the *Atlantic*, and *The Best American Nonrequired Reading.* McKenzie is senior editor of the *Chicago Quarterly Review* and the managing editor of *Catamaran Literary Reader.*

Calvin McMillin is a writer, teacher, and scholar. Born in Singapore and raised in rural Oklahoma, he went on to earn a PhD in literature from UC Santa Cruz. He is the author of the short story collection *The Sushi Bar at the Edge of Forever*, and the editor of Frank Chin's novel *The Confessions of a Number One Son.* McMillin is currently a lecturer at the University of Michigan, Dearborn, where he teaches literature and creative writing.

Liza Monroy is the author of the novel *Mexican High*, the memoir *The Marriage Act: The Risk I Took to Keep My Best Friend in America and What It Taught Us About Love*, and *Seeing As Your Shoes Are Soon to Be on Fire.* She has written for the *New York Times, O, Marie Claire,* and the *Los Angeles Times.* Monroy currently teaches in the writing program at UC Santa Cruz.

Maceo Montoya has published three works of fiction—*The Scoundrel and the Optimist*, *The Deportation of Wopper Barraza*, *You Must Fight Them*—and *Letters to the Poet from His Brother*. His most recent publication is *Chicano Movement for Beginners*, a work of graphic nonfiction. Montoya is an associate professor in Chicana/o Studies at UC Davis. He is also an affiliated faculty member of Taller Arte del Nuevo Amanecer, a community-based art center in Woodland, California.

Tommy Moore graduated from UC Santa Cruz working in film and video production. In 2013, he was one of six writers selected for a PEN Emerging Voices Fellowship. He and his wife Amie recently welcomed their first child, Charles Joseph. They live in Malibu and Moore is currently writing a collection of short stories. "Buck Low" is his first published story.

Micah Perks is the author of *We Are Gathered Here*, *What Becomes Us*, *Pagan Time*, and *Alone in the Woods: Cheryl Strayed, My Daughter, and Me*. The *Guardian* rated *What Becomes Us* one of the top ten apocalyptic novels. Her short story collection *True Love and Other Dreams of Miraculous Escape* will be published in October 2018. She has lived in Santa Cruz for twenty years.

Lee Quarnstrom, author of *When I Was a Dynamiter! Or, How a Nice Catholic Boy Became a Merry Prankster, a Pornographer, and a Bridegroom Seven Times*, lives with his wife, poet Christine Quarnstrom, in Southern California. He was a legendary newspaper reporter in Santa Cruz for more than thirty years.

Peggy Townsend is an award-winning journalist who has written on everything from serial killers to county fairs. She divides her time between Santa Cruz and Lake Tahoe. Her new mystery novel is *See Her Run*.

Wendy McGarry

Jill Wolfson is the author of four young adult novels. Her story in this collection stems from her decades as a writing teacher for incarcerated teens and from her son's stint working for a local donut shop. She is a Santa Cruz–based writer whose work has appeared in many publications, including the *Sun* magazine and on the radio show *This American Life*.

Acknowledgments

In addition to the talent and camaraderie of the *Santa Cruz Noir* writers, I have critical friends and artists to acknowledge. First, the out-of-town pros: fellow noir author and editor extraordinaire Ariel Gore and Akashic Books publisher Johnny Temple.

My appreciation and thanks to: Kat Bailey, Joe Mancino, Tristan Miley-Medina, Jennifer Taillac Gustafson, Shmuel Thaler, Carter Wilson, Don Wallace, the UCSC Creative Writing Program, Bookshop Santa Cruz—let's do a sequel. Thank you to my family, Jon and Aretha, who know every crevice of Santa Cruz better than I do. And, always by my side, my late father Bill Bright and his poet friends William Everson and Gary Snyder, for my earliest Santa Cruz memories and precontact inspirations.

—S.B.

Also available in the Akashic Noir Series

SAN FRANCISCO NOIR

edited by Peter Maravelis

312 pages, trade paperback original, $15.95

BRAND-NEW STORIES BY: Barry Gifford, Robert Mailer Anderson, Michelle Tea, Peter Plate, Kate Braverman, Domenic Stansberry, David Corbett, Eddie Muller, Alejandro Murguía, Sin Soracco, Alvin Lu, John Longhi, Will Christopher Baer, Jim Nisbet, and David Henry Sterry.

"An entertaining anthology of overheated short stories by local writers . . . Here the city becomes the central character, the strongest on the page." —*San Francisco Chronicle*

"Reflecting changing conditions, multicultural authors are well represented here, and female writers definitely make their mark . . . There's enough here to cause us to want more." —*Library Journal*

LOS ANGELES NOIR

edited by Denise Hamilton

320 pages, trade paperback original, $15.95

*A *Los Angeles Times* best seller and winner of an Edgar Award.

BRAND-NEW STORIES BY: Michael Connelly, Janet Fitch, Susan Straight, Héctor Tobar, Patt Morrison, Emory Holmes II, Robert Ferrigno, Gary Phillips, Christopher Rice, Naomi Hirahara, Jim Pascoe, Neal Pollack, Scott Phillips, Diana Wagman, Lienna Silver, Brian Ascalon Roley, and Denise Hamilton.

"Akashic is making an argument about the universality of noir; it's sort of flattering, really, and *Los Angeles Noir*, arriving at last, is a kaleidoscopic collection filled with the ethos of noir pioneers Raymond Chandler and James M. Cain." —*Los Angeles Times Book Review*

ORANGE COUNTY NOIR

edited by Gary Phillips

312 pages, trade paperback original, $15.95

BRAND-NEW STORIES BY: Susan Straight, Robert S. Levinson, Rob Roberge, Nathan Walpow, Barbara DeMarco-Barrett, Dan Duling, Mary Castillo, Lawrence Maddox, Dick Lochte, Robert Ward, Gary Phillips, Gordon McAlpine, Martin J. Smith, and Patricia McFall, with a forward by T. Jefferson Parker.

"'There's a dark side to most places,' even California's sunny Orange County, Edgar-winner T. Jefferson Parker observes in his foreword to this outstanding entry in Akashic's noir series . . . The crisp, often seductive prose of the 14 contributors, most of them relatively unknown, is a tribute to the critical judgment of the editor." —*Publishers Weekly* (starred review)

OAKLAND NOIR

edited by Jerry Thompson & Eddie Muller
272 pages, trade paperback original, $15.95

BRAND-NEW STORIES BY: Nick Petrulakis, Kim Addonizio, Keenan Norris, Keri Miki-Lani Schroeder, Katie Gilmartin, Dorothy Lazard, Harry Louis Williams II, Carolyn Alexander, Phil Canalin, Judy Juanita, Jamie DeWolf, Nayomi Munaweera, Mahmud Rahman, Tom McElravey, Joe Loya, and Eddie Muller.

"Wonderfully, in Akashic's *Oakland Noir,* the stereotypes about the city suffer the fate of your average noir character—they die brutally. Kudos to the editors, Jerry Thompson and Eddie Muller, for getting Oakland right." —*San Francisco Chronicle*

SAN DIEGO NOIR

edited by Maryelizabeth Hart
280 pages, trade paperback original, $15.95

BRAND-NEW STORIES BY: T. Jefferson Parker, Don Winslow, Luis Alberto Urrea, Gar Anthony Haywood, Gabriel R. Barillas, Maria Lima, Debra Ginsberg, Diane Clark & Astrid Bear, Ken Kuhlken, Lisa Brackmann, Cameron Pierce Hughes, Morgan Hunt, Jeffrey J. Mariotte, Martha C. Lawrence, and Taffy Cannon.

"When it's done right, noir is a darkly delicious thrill: smart, sharp-tongued, surprising. The knife goes in at the end with a twist. *San Diego Noir* has all that going for it, and the steady supply of hometown references makes it even more fun." —*San Diego Union-Tribune.*

USA NOIR

edited by Johnny Temple
544 pages, trade paperback original, $16.95

The best USA-based stories in the Akashic Noir Series, compiled into one volume and edited by Johnny Temple!

STORIES BY: Dennis Lehane, Don Winslow, Michael Connelly, George Pelecanos, Susan Straight, Jonathan Safran Foer, Laura Lippman, Pete Hamill, Joyce Carol Oates, Lee Child, T. Jefferson Parker, Lawrence Block, Terrance Hayes, Jerome Charyn, Jeffery Deaver, Maggie Estep, Bayo Ojikutu, Tim McLoughlin, Barbara DeMarco-Barrett, Reed Farrel Coleman, Megan Abbott, Elyssa East, James W. Hall, J. Malcolm Garcia, Julie Smith, Joseph Bruchac, Pir Rothenberg, Luis Alberto Urrea, Domenic Stansberry, John O'Brien, S.J. Rozan, Asali Solomon, William Kent Krueger, Tim Broderick, Bharti Kirchner, Karen Karbo, and Lisa Sandlin.